8 SECONDS TO LOVE

MONICA WALTERS

D1367924

Edited by
NATALYA MUNCUFF

B. LOVE PUBLICATIONS

B. LOVE PUBLICATIONS

Visit bit.ly/BLovePub or click here to join our mailing list!

B. Love Publications - where Authors celebrate black men, black women, and black love.

To submit a manuscript for consideration, email your first three chapters to blovepublications@gmail.com with SUBMISSION as the subject.

Let's connect on social media!

Facebook - B. Love Publications

Twitter - @blovepub

Instagram - @blovepublications

arper

"THESE HOES STAY in your inbox, and this bitch..." I said, pointing to her name on my computer screen. "She a repeat offender. That's prolly 'cause she got a response the first time. I'm getting sick of this bullshit, Zaire."

"Come here, baby."

He pulled me from the chair where I was sitting.. "I can't control who inboxes me. I love you, and only you. Don't let bullshit make your crown slip. You my queen. Okay?"

I gave him the side-eye. Zaire was always a smooth talker. Smooth-talked me right outta my panties a year ago. He was so fine; tall, light brown skin, curly hair, and thick, pink lips, that made magic. The moment I saw him in the mall, I knew that I had to have him. Little did I know, he thought the same thing when he saw me.

Zaire had followed me into Victoria's Secret and said he couldn't keep his eyes off me. And here we were a year later, in another countless argument, or rather, questioning about females hitting him up.

He wrapped his arms around me and kissed my forehead. "Harper, I've told you countless times, that you are my forever. I knew it the first time I saw you, but you have to trust me, baby."

"It's hard to trust you when I constantly see hoes posting on your wall about how fine you are and inboxing you pictures of their naked asses."

"Baby... I don't care about all those other women. It's you that I desire... that I want... that I need. Look at me."

Hesitantly, I looked in those dark brown eyes, wanting to get lost in them all over again. I had my argument all planned out, but yet he managed to make me forget everything I wanted to say. Staring into his eyes, I put my hand to his cheek and rubbed it with my thumb. "What do you see in my eyes, baby?"

"Love," I said softly. "I'm sorry, Zaire. These hoes just make me crazy. I love you so much."

"Why would I go anywhere, Harper? You take care of my heart, my soul, and my mind. You're the total package. Not to mention, you're fine as hell. This beautiful milk chocolate skin, these thick ass lips."

I blushed as he ran his thumb across my bottom lip, then lowered his lips to mine, placing a tender kiss on them. His hands went to my cheeks, sliding down to my neck and shoulders, then rested at my hips. Zaire pulled me closer to him as a moan involuntarily left my lips. Lips like soft pillows and sweet like honey continued to kiss mine, then lowered to my neck. "Harp, I have to go, baby," he said softly, near my ear.

"Do you have to?"

"Yeah. I'm only on my lunch break. I'll be back when I get off."

"Okay, Zaire."

He kissed me on the lips again, entangling his tongue with mine and left me speechless. Watching him leave, I felt grateful to have a man that loved me and knew how to calm me down. I looked at my computer and exited his account. Why would I think he's entertaining those stupid hoes? If he had something to hide, he wouldn't have given me access to his Facebook account and email. He was just so damned fine.

Working at a car dealership as a finance manager, I knew Zaire met women all the time. He made really good money because he was charming and knew how to sweet talk people into spending their money on those luxury cars. I witnessed his pitch before and I couldn't do anything but stare at him in amazement. He was so cultured and refined. He spent most of his summers in some kind of prep school in England, and his parents were rolling in dough. His dad's family owned a couple of department stores and locally he owned a few dry cleaners and a couple of clothing boutiques.

It was rare that he even uttered slang. Only when I was putting it to his ass. His parents were somewhat disappointed in the career path he'd chosen, but Zaire was so smart, he never worked a job intending that to be the final stop. He had plans of owning his own dealership one day, and I believed that he would get there sooner rather than later, with or without their help.

As I left my desk to get the cake from the oven, my phone rang. My loud, country-ass cousin was calling. "Hey, Shana."

"Hey, girl! Ugh, why you sound so blah?"

"I'm not blah, bitch. I'm calm."

"Zaire ass must've just left. That nigga fine."

"Uh, Shana. Really?"

"Really what? I can't say he fine? Bitch, I ain't blind."

I laughed loudly with her. I swear, this chick ain't had the sense

God gave her. I took the cake layers from the oven. "What's up, Shana?"

She rarely called to just shoot the shit. Running my own specialty cake business kept me busy, so if she just wanted to clown around, she'd come over instead of calling. "I wanted to see if you wanted to come to the Livestock Show in Houston with me. It's the week after next."

"Why in the hell would I want to go to a livestock show? You know I ain't into all that rodeo shit y'all be going to."

"I'll tell you why you would wanna go. Trey Songz gon' be performing there."

I damn near dropped my cake as I flipped it out of the pan. "You bullshittin'?"

"Nope. Trey Songz performing one night and Tank performing the next night."

"Oh, hell yeah. Buy my ticket, and I'll pay you."

"Yay! Okay. I'm just gon' get tickets for the whole week if you cool with that. I haven't looked to see who performing the other days yet."

"Ooh, I don't know if I can do a whole week, Shana. I can do that weekend though. I'll check my calendar and make sure I don't have anything booked."

"Okay. I'm just excited you gon' come that weekend. We gon' turn the fuck up! You know that right?"

"Yeah, I know. I could use it. I been working my ass off."

"I'm proud of you, cuz. Well, I'll let you go. Call me after you check your calendar."

"I will."

I ended the call and started on my fruit filling. This business just sprang from my natural ability to make cute designs and good cakes. It started by just making cakes for my family. One year, my older cousin had a fabulous and forty party and had asked me to make a cake. People were raving over it and killed it. That same night, Delectable Desserts was born, working strictly from word of mouth at first.

After profiting my first grand, I started investing in my business, and now three years later, I had to quit my day job to keep up with the orders. It was a decision that took me a year to make, but after renting my own spot, I knew it was time. Today I was baking from home, though. On days when I had a few orders, I went to my bakery, because it had five commercial-sized ovens. The cake I was working on today, would have three layers and be in the shape of a Hennessy bottle.

As I made the necessary cuts, rounding the edges, I thought about Zaire. A smile broke out on my face, just thinking about how sweet he was. We didn't live together, but we saw one another almost every day. He worked a lot of hours some days and so did I. From the very beginning, he treated me with respect, and my mama adored him. She told me that God had smiled on me when he sent Zaire. I felt the same way until I came across stupid shit like today.

I wasn't a jealous person, but for some reason, I always felt like I needed to protect what was mine. Women came from every direction, trying to get at him. Like, why in the hell they so damned thirsty? When I was single, I wouldn't dare be all up in anybody's inbox or DM's. That was crazy as hell. Some were sending naked pictures, others were leaving their phone numbers and talking nasty to him. I started to respond to some of them, but for what? So, I could get myself all riled up at whatever they said back to me? No thank you. I had enough stress in my life.

Zaire's mother didn't too much care for me, and I still hadn't figured out why. Whenever we visited, she ignored me the entire time. His dad always kept me company. Although his wife was black, me and Mr. Schroeder never really had much to talk about. He was a middle-aged white man, that seemed to be somewhat afraid of his wife. She treated Zaire with more respect than she did him. After questioning Zaire about it, he kind of dismissed her behavior, so I never brought it up again.

After I finished decorating the cake, I boxed it, then shot a text to the customer, letting them know it was done an hour early if they wanted to come to get it now. Pouring myself a glass of wine, I went to my couch and turned on the TV. The news was on, and they'd mentioned the livestock show in Houston. I almost couldn't wait to go. Good R&B music was my weakness. I couldn't listen while I was working, because I got distracted easily if I heard a nice run or chord. The kind of songs Tank and Trey Songz were singing lately, surely would have me all riled up.

Just as I gulped the last of my wine, my customer text back to let me know they were on their way. I was happy about that. Once they left, I could soak in a hot bath with another glass of wine and call it a night early.

egend

"DAMN, LEGEND SHIT!"

"Uh huh. Throw that shit back at me, girl."

Watching that ass twerk, took me over. Baby girl had put it down just like I knew she would. The way that ass sat on that geldedhorse she was riding, I knew I had to get her back to my trailer. Plus, I'd heard about her skills. "Thank you, lil mama. That shit calmed my nerves."

"Well, if you get your eight seconds, you better give me a shout-out."

"What's your name again?"

"Really, Legend?"

"I'm sorry, shit. That pussy made me lose all train of thought."

"Neffie."

"That's right, like Keyshia Cole sister."

She rolled her eyes as she got dressed. We had the living quarters of this horse trailer rockin'. Them fucking horses were probably wondering, *what the fuck*. I chuckled to myself thinking about that shit. I had a couple of hours until my ride. Bull-riding was my fucking life and I made pretty good money at that shit too. Within the past year, there hadn't been a jackpot that I hadn't won. Niggas got pissed when they found out I'd entered the competition.

My mama hated that I'd chosen to make this a professional career. She was always worried that one day I would get bucked off and that bull was gonna kill me. I'd just shake my head and tell her to pray, then point to the tattoo on my arm. She would slap it right on my 'ridin' on faith' tat and walk away after that. My pops loved that I was into it. He rode bulls himself when he was younger, but he'd never made a career out of it.

"I'm about to go, Legend. Good luck."

"Thanks, lil mama. Good luck to you too."

"Thanks."

She left the trailer just as my friend, Red, came in. He watched her leave out and licked his lips. "That's that barrel racing chick, umm... Neffie."

"Yeah, that was her," I said calmly.

"Aww shit. She done got that fucking beast calm and ready to ride. Shit, I'm so fucking amped right now. I'ma be the champ of this bulldogging shit! Mark my words."

I shook my head at Red's stupid ass. Craig Anderson, whom everybody called Red, was a steer wrestler, but we called it bulldogging. He'd already had the best time earlier, but he still had one more ride tomorrow before they crowned the king of this shit. He performed better when he was hype, and I performed better when I was calm. That was some crazy shit since we rode here together.

We rode to most of the rodeos together, even when one of us wasn't competing. This was his horse trailer because as a bull rider, I didn't need all that shit. Just somewhere to sleep. "Damn nigga, air this shit out! I'd rather smell horse shit. Got my three-slant and a large smelling like pussy. I ain't gettin' none, so this odor got to get the fuck outta hea."

I laughed at Red as he opened a couple of windows. His trailer had three slants for his three horses and the large was the living quarters. I turned my fitted to the back, then pulled the blunt from my pocket. After this, I'd be ready. "Nigga shut up. All that fucking talking, that's why you ain't getting no pussy. I never say shit, they come to the Legend."

He rolled his eyes. "Nigga, you done let these announcers fuck yo' head up. You ain't no got damned legend. Only thang legend about you is yo' name."

"Gon' tell yourself that if you want to. Hatin' ass."

"Whatever. I can't wait until the livestock show next week."

"Shit, me either. Houston always on."

I sparked up and laid my head back. Red came and got a hit, then left me to it. On the first inhale, I allowed it to clear my mind of everything but riding the fuck outta that bull. Visualizing my technique and how I would spur the shit out of it, calmed my spirit. After taking my last pull, I stood and changed shirts. To the outside world when I wasn't riding, I just looked like an ordinary nigga. However, the minute it was go time, the cowboy was front and center. My spurs were already on my boots, so I slid them on just as Red came out of the bedroom.

He still had on his shit too, because he would be on the back of the chute when I slid down onto the bull. While everybody was amped around me, Red knew me well enough to know how to keep me calm. It was funny how he could do that shit because he would be about to burst at the seams the whole time. I grabbed my bull bag that held all my gear, then kissed the cross around my neck and closed my eyes. *God, protect me. Help me have a good ride, teaching that bull who the boss is. Amen.*

I said the same prayer before exiting the trailer to ride. Looking back at Red, I saw his eyes were still closed. He prayed for me all the time. Although we liked to clown around, we kept each other lifted in prayer. This rodeo shit could kill you, but you couldn't think of it like that. You'd die fa sho' if you did. The second his eyes opened, I said, "Let's do this."

"I hope y'all readaaayyyy to see a legend in the makin'!"

People were screaming, and I could hear them chanting my name as I bowed my head for a second, taking deep, steady breaths. "The Lord is my light, and my salvation; whom shall I fear? The Lord is the strength of my life; of whom shall I be afraid?"

That was how Red kept me calm. He always recited scriptures that kept me calm but also encouraged me as well. While the crowd and the announcers were trying to amp me up, he kept me on the ground. "When the wicked, even mine enemies and my foes, came upon me to eat up my flesh, they stumbled and fell."

Putting on my vest, chaps, and headgear, then adjusting it to where it was comfortable, Red continued, "Put on the whole armour of God, that ye may be able to stand against the wiles of the devil."

The bull was the devil, and the devil was defeated. He taped my right wrist, then I put on my glove and he taped it to my wrist as well. Red did a quick massage on my neck, then I climbed up the shoot. That bull was raging, and I was ready to put my mark on him. As I slid down on the bull, he bucked against the gate. He was gon' be a son of a bitch, but I was ready for the challenge. I slid my right hand into the rigging of the rope and took a deep breath as the announcer yelled excitedly. ***"Legeeeend Semieeeen!!!!!!"***

The crowd roared, but in my ears, everything began to go silent, blocking out the unnecessary. "Ready?" Red asked me as he tightened my rope.

I gave him a head nod and lifted my left arm, then the gate opened. That bull turned right back into the gate, but I was clamped on his ass like a vice. In my mind, I was counting the seconds and spurring the shit out of him, while I held on for dear life. Eight seconds didn't seem long to be able to stay on until you were riding. That shit felt like eight hours. Felt like this mutha-fucka had done a damned backflip as high as he was bucking.

The minute I heard that buzzer, I let go and dismounted. The clowns immediately distracted him, so he wouldn't attack me, and I ran to the gate. The noise was deafening, as I climbed the railing and did my signature salute to the crowd. The announcer was losing his damned mind. After they'd gotten the bull out of the arena, I waited to see my score. The best score I could get would be a perfect fifty. The bull also got a score up to fifty as well. The more difficult the ride, the better the score. So, my total score could get to one hundred, but that rarely happened for anybody. Even on a good day, you barely saw a rider get to ninety.

As I stared at the scoreboard, it lit up to 89.8, and I yelled in excitement along with the crowd. The announcer then said excitedly over the mic, ***"Ladies and gentlemen that's how it's done! Nearly a perfect ride by the legend in the makin'! 89.8, tying his record score! That puts him in the number one spot!"***

I jumped off the gate and headed out of the pin, as Red nearly attacked my ass! "You mutha-fucka! When that bull turned back into the gate, I was like 'aww shit', but yo' ass rode the shit outta that bull. He was running from yo' ass outta that pin."

I laughed at his stupid ass. "Where my shout out, Legend?"

I turned to see Neffie's fine ass. Giving her a smirk, I walked over to her as people congratulated me by shaking my hand and patting me on the back. I licked my lips, then put my hand at her waist. "Thank you, Neffie."

I kissed her on the lips and gently bit her bottom one, then pulled away and winked at her as she shifted her weight. I chuckled inwardly while watching her. Looked like she'd creamed in her panties. The whole time we were fucking earlier, I hadn't even tried to kiss her. My only concern was getting a nut so I could relax. She was fine, but I wasn't trying to pursue anything with somebody who'd fucked the whole rodeo circuit.

Walking away as Red waited on me, I could feel her still staring at me. "Keep on. Yo' ass gon' catch something."

"Says the hater that ain't getting no pussy."

He side-eyed me as I turned my fitted to the front. I went to the concession to get a coke, then hung around the arena to watch the rest of the competition. I was the third rider, so there were seven more after me. Red had gone to talk with some other bulldoggers that were there but not in the competition. The next couple of riders were bucked off before the eight seconds, so they would be nowhere in the running.

So far, I was still leading the scores. One had come close with an 81.6, but I was still holding on with one rider left. This dude was my competition for real. I hated riding last though. Some people liked being last, so they knew what score they had to beat. I didn't need that kind of pressure. Just giving my best ride every time was my focus. As he got ready, I closed my eyes and took a deep breath. I'd beaten him the last few times, but it was always close.

The gate opened, and I watched every turn the bull made, every spur the rider made. Just when he looked like he was about to fall off, he regained his balance. As the buzzer sounded and he ran to the gate, I watched the scoreboard. When that shit lit up 88.9, I exhaled and held my hands in the air. Our margin wasn't even a whole point. That didn't matter right now, though. I was still the champion.

I went down and accepted my buckle and my winnings, took pictures, and headed to the trailer. Red was waiting on my ass too. "I guess you think you big shit." We both laughed. He said the same shit every time I won. "Congratulations, bruh."

"Thanks, Red."

As soon as we got back to his trailer, I called my mama. I swore, Rose got all worked up when she knew I had to ride. We'd talked this morning, and I told her I would call back after everything was over. "Hello?"

"Hey, Ma. First place by point nine points."

"I'm happy for you, Legend. Congratulations!"

"Thank you, Ma. Now you can calm down until next week."

"Shut up, boy. Yo' daddy wanna talk."

"Aight."

"Champ!"

I laughed. My dad lived his bull-riding days vicariously through me. He was always more excited than I was. "What's up, Pops?"

"Man, I wish I coulda been there to see that ride. You get a ninety, and you'll break your record ride."

"I know. Hopefully, that'll happen next week at the Livestock show. You gon' make it right?"

"That's the plan, son."

"Okay. Well, I gotta go take a shower. I'll come see y'all tomorrow."

"Okay, Legend."

"Love y'all."

"Love you too," they said in unison, putting a smile on my face.

I ended the call, then started the shower. After getting undressed, I could still smell Neffie's scent on me. Red didn't have to worry about me catching anything. I always strapped up. Ain't none of these hoes was gon' burn my ass.

arper

THE PAST TWO weeks had been so fucking draining. I was just ready for the rush to be over. Zaire had taken me out this past weekend to an upscale restaurant in Houston when he'd gotten off Saturday. We stayed overnight, then headed back. It was so romantic, but most of the time we spent together was. Zaire was always affectionate and loving, even when I was pissed about something. I'd managed to refrain from logging into his Facebook account, so I wouldn't get all riled up. Now, if he gave me a reason to be suspicious, that would be a whole 'notha story.

I was at my bakery, getting cakes done so I could go get ready for the weekend. Shana and I would be leaving out tonight. I had a few orders for tomorrow that had to be picked up this evening. We'd spend tomorrow and Saturday having a great time and head back

Sunday. Boxing up my third cake for the day, I received a picture message from Shana. Before I could open the picture, I saw the wide-eyed emojis.

When that fucking picture loaded, I almost fell to pieces. Zaire was standing outside somewhere, kissing a woman on her lips. Before I could respond, Shana was calling. I answered, nearly in tears and seething with anger. "Hello?"

"I took more pictures. I'm in shock right now, Harp. I'm so sorry."

"Where are you?"

"The lil convenience store in Cheek. Cheek Grocery."

"I can't believe Zaire would do this to me. I'm so hurt, Shana. All the bullshit he's been feeding me about these lil bitches in his inbox. Are you still there?"

"Yeah. So is he."

"Clearly he hasn't seen you, otherwise he would've left by now."

"I'm sitting in my car, looking at him and taking pictures, boo. No good ass."

I allowed the tear to roll down my cheek. "I swear if I didn't have cakes in the oven, I'd be on my way over there."

"Don't worry. We gon' enjoy our time in Houston, and you can handle this shit when we get back."

"Yeah. I think I'm gon' hire a PI for his ass. He gon' get bold this weekend since I won't be here. I can feel that shit in my bones."

"That's a good idea. I'm picking you up from the bakery or your place?"

"I'll be at home. I have two orders in the oven right now. Once I finish them up and get them boxed, I'm outta here. Whitney will be here tomorrow when they come to pick up."

"Okay, cuz. I really am sorry."

"Thank you, Shana. Thank you for not leaving me in the dark. I still feel like a stupid bitch, though."

"Nah, don't do that. That's your man. You supposed to be able to trust him. This bullshit is on him."

"I'll see you in about three hours, okay?"

"Okay. Yeah, I'll be there at six."

I wanted to just crawl in bed now and cry myself to sleep. The man that I held at such high esteem, was fucking around on me. My mama used to say all the time that a woman's intuition couldn't be fucked with, and for months I'd been feeling a certain type of way. Every time I tried to address it, Zaire would sweet talk me to the point where I'd forget what I was saying. That lying, bitch-ass nigga. I couldn't wait to get to his ass when I got back. I grabbed my phone and queued up Trina's first album to get me in that frame of mind. The frame of mind that said, niggas ain't shit.

As I left the bakery, I called my friend Phoenix, whom I'd taken a business class with. He'd become a private investigator after graduating. We tried to date in college but after a couple of dates, we came to the conclusion that we were better off as friends. We got along great but trying to be romantically involved just felt weird. "Phoenix Lane. How can I help you?"

"Hey, Phoenix."

"Harper?"

"Yeah."

"What's up, girl? Where you been? Get a lil nigga in yo' life, you forget all about lil ol'me."

"I'm sorry, Phoenix, for real. I need you, though."

My voice quivered. As much as I tried to stay angry about the situation, I was still hurt. I was angry at myself for being something I'd never been. Gullible. "What's going on, Harp?"

"Zaire is cheating on me. I need proof."

"Damn, baby girl. How do you know?"

"My cousin sent me a picture of him earlier today at a convenience store with some stank-looking bitch. Why don't they ever upgrade, Nix?"

The tears were falling as the bitch's image came to the forefront of my mind. She had on some damned tight-ass cut off shorts and a tight halter. Her weave was horrible. I could tell where her hair stopped, and it started. There was acne in her face from what I could see in the picture and on her upper arms. "Harp, please don't cry. Tell me where I can find him."

"He works at Classic Acura, and he lives at 4215 N Major Drive at West End Lodge, apartment 306."

"Okay. Where will you be?"

"I'm going to Houston this weekend with Shana."

"Okay. How is her crazy ass doing?"

"She's good. Still crazy. She's the one that sent me the picture."

"Okay. Send me a picture of him, and I'll start tailing his ass tomorrow."

"Thank you, Phoenix."

"Anytime. You know you still my boo. I got'chu, Harp."

"Talk to you soon."

I ended the call and wiped my face, then walked inside my place. My whole wardrobe for this weekend was about to change. I wasn't trying to get laid or anything, but attention from another nigga would keep my mind off the fuck boy I would be leaving behind. I put a few sexy pieces in there along with what I had already packed. I usually only wore those when Zaire and I were together in a club atmosphere.

An hour later, there was a knock at the door. I was sure it was Shana, although she was an hour early. My phone was ringing at the same time. Checking the peephole, I saw Shana standing there, so I opened the door for her. Afterward, I ran to my phone to see it was Zaire. "Hello?"

"Hey, baby. I just wanted to let you know that I won't be able to see you off. We still have five customers waiting and there's only two of us here today. I love you and have a great time."

"Okay. I love you too."

I ended the call and almost threw up. It took everything within me to get those words out and not go the fuck off on his ass. Throwing my phone to the bed, I continued packing, making sure I had the shoes packed to wear with those scandalous outfits. "That's what the fuck I'm talkin' 'bout, Harp!"

Shana was looking through the outfits I'd put on top. I rolled my eyes and got my shoes and makeup from the vanity. After zipping up my luggage, I looked around to make sure I had everything, then took a deep breath. "Let's go turn the fuck up, Shana."

"Yes! I got my nigga back! That bougie bitch done took a backseat."

All I could do was laugh at her ass. Since I'd been dating Zaire, I'd toned down significantly. It had nothing to do with him personally, but if I had a boyfriend, there was no need for me to be in the clubs, hanging out with Shana all the time. Grabbing the handle to my luggage, I rolled it out to Shana's BMW. Although she was ratchet sometimes, the heifer had a good ass job at the federal prison. She was making at least seventy thousand a year.

Once we got in, I sent the picture of Zaire to Phoenix. "Oh, Phoenix asked about you."

"Yeah? What his ass been up to?"

"Not too much. He's gonna watch Zaire's ass while we're gone."

"I figured that was who you were gonna call. I wish y'all had more of a romantic connection. He so cool."

"Yeah, I know, but we tried."

"I know. At least y'all did explore the possibility. Did y'all have sex?"

"No. We kissed, but there was nothing there. It didn't even feel right."

We continued the rest of the drive to Houston, jamming to Trina and Cardi B all the way there. If anyone could help me keep my mind off Zaire, it was Shana. We'd laughed about some of the shit that happened at her job and some of the crazy-ass orders I'd gotten. "One dude was like, no disrespect, lil mama, but do you think you can make it look like a pussy? I nearly choked, when his ass asked that. Talkin' 'bout it was a bachelor party and it was a personal cake for the groom."

"Are you serious? Did you make that shit?"

"I sure in the hell did! Had some cream cummin' out that shit too."

We laughed hysterically as we talked about how that nigga prolly ate the fuck outta that cake. After getting settled in our room, Shana was ready to hit up a club already. No fucking rest for the weary. I put on a short romper that dipped extremely low in the front and had to use double-stick tape to keep it in place. I accented it with some four-inched heels and my diamond studs and bracelet that Zaire bought me last year. We headed to 5th Amendment, a hip-hop club where we were sure to have a great time.

Shana walked in ahead of me, in her all in one. It was pants, but a halter at the top. Niggas were checking for us left and right. Before we could order a drink, somebody had already bought us one. The minute the DJ spun Cardi, we went to the dance floor. The club was so hype, you couldn't help but enjoy yourself. As I danced, some dude started dancing behind me. Normally, that kind of shit irritated me, but not tonight. I backed my ass up on him as he rested his hand at my hip.

Hopefully, he didn't think that shit made me easy. I didn't even look at him until the song hand gone off. Shit, he was fine though. I gave him a grin and walked off. He gently grabbed my hand, and I pulled him from the dance floor with me. "What's your name?"

"Harper. Yours?"

"Joe. I like your name. So, can I get your number?"

"Nah, sorry. You seem like a sweet guy though."

"It's cool, baby girl. What'chu drinkin'?"

"I just had Crown Black and coke."

"You want another one?"

"I better not. My girl seem kinda lit. Somebody gotta drive home. Thank you, though."

"You seem cool too. Maybe I'll come back later for another dance."

"That'll be cool, Joe. Thanks."

He winked at me and walked away. I wasn't trying to give anybody my number already. Zaire hadn't even been put on notice yet. He still thought everything was fine. I was trying to have a good time and forget about Zaire, but that shit was gon' be impossible tonight. We'd have to get an Uber tomorrow for sure. Shana sure in the hell wasn't worried about how we would get back to our room. So much for forgetting my troubles tonight.

4

Legend

IT WAS CROWDED like a mutha-fucka at NRG Stadium in Houston. I couldn't wait to get this show on the road. Before the rodeo, Trey Songz would be performing, so women were going to be all over the place. My pops had made it and was already in his seat, waiting for the show. Me and Red walked around the arena, just trying to see who we could see when these two beautiful chocolate sisters caught my attention. I nudged him. "Damn. Look over there."

"Damn. I seen one of them before at a trail ride in Cheek."

"I hope you ain't feeling the one with the long hair, 'cause damn. She fine as hell."

"She look bougie as hell too. Nah, I'm going after the one I done seen before."

They were walking toward us. I just wanted to watch her. The way she was moving was so damned sexy. Red was right though. She wasn't going for no spur of the moment shit, but she might be down to party with us later. As they approached, I stared at her, looking her body over. Those damned curves had a nigga dizzy. She had a full sleeve tat on one arm, slanted eyes, and thick lips. She was thick in all the right places, as I noticed her belly ring. Those jeans looked like they'd been painted on those thick legs. Just like a stallion.

She looked over at me as if she could feel me staring and held my gaze for a moment. I licked my lips and hoped she'd come to me like all the rest, but I was terribly mistaken. They stopped walking and looked around, I suppose trying to find their seats. Then her friend noticed me watching them and her eyes widened slightly. She said something to chocolate thighs, and she looked back at me. "You can stand here and stare at them if you want, but I'm going introduce myself."

I watched him walk over and they both stared at him, then smiled. They shook his hand, so I decided to walk over. The thinner one was smiling really hard in Red's face. When she saw me approach, she said, "Oh shit, the legend finna talk to us?"

They all laughed as I smirked. "What's up, ladies?"

I was mainly watching chocolate thighs. She was bad for real. "We good. How are you?"

"I'm aight. What's y'all names?"

"I'm Shana, this is Harper."

"How you doing, Harper?"

"I'm fine, thank you."

Damn, she was proper as hell. She almost didn't look like she fit in. Ain't nothing about her said rodeo. She was probably just here for the concert. Her friend nudged her a little. "What's your name?" she asked me.

She didn't seem to be interested, like her mind was preoccupied with something else. "Legend."

Her eyes met mine like she was waiting for me to continue. "Legend? That's your real name?"

"Yeah. Legend Semien."

"Hmm. That's unique."

She looked back down at her ticket stub, as her friend and Red was hitting it off. "Where y'all from?"

"Beaumont."

"That's cool. We from out that way too."

She nodded, then nudged her friend. I wasn't much of a small talker. I hated the shit actually, so I said, "Nice to meet you, Harper."

I left them standing there. Ain't no way I was gon' stand there and try to force conversation out of her. I went back to where I was standing and just watched her. She looked like a fish outta water, like she was nervous just being here amongst all the cowboy hats and shit. Red and her friend looked to be exchanging info, then he kissed her hand. When he got back over to me, he smiled. I rolled my eyes. "I told you she was bougie. Shana all that though, and she goes to the trail rides. I knew I'd seen her before. Harper is her cousin."

"Good for you."

"Good for you too. Where ever Shana goes, so will Harper. She said they would hook up with us tonight."

"Whatever. I hate tryna get to know people. Small talk irritates me, and obviously, she ain't feelin' me no how."

"Well, I wanna see Shana. Y'all ain't even gotta hang with each other."

I just nodded at him. Truth was, I was used to females approaching me. I didn't have to have game, be a smooth talker, or none of that shit. Hell, I didn't even have to be friendly. Women usually just gravitated toward me. "You goin' watch Trey Songz?"

"Naw, I'm going see where Shana sat her fine, chocolate ass at."

"You need to be thinking about this competition."

"Nigga, did you see me last night? If you did, then you know I'm ready tonight. Ain't shit changed. I'm gon' take an hour before go time to get ready and get amped up, and I'll be fine."

"Aight, whatever. I'll meet you at the chute."

"Aight."

He walked off, and I went to find my daddy. Red was the socializer, and I was everything but. He could literally talk to anybody and become friends with them that same day. The only reason he and I were even friends was because he wouldn't leave me alone. Before I even decided to become a professional bull rider, bruh was all in my face. Finally, I couldn't help but ease up when he was around. We've been close ever since. That was five years ago. Just as I reached Pops, the show was starting. "You aight, Pops?"

"I'm good. Who is this about to perform?"

"Trey Songz. You don't know him, so don't worry about it."

I chuckled and sat next to him. When I did, I noticed I was right across from Harper. Instead of being engrossed in the show, she was all in her phone and looked to had dropped a tear or two. Yeah, she was preoccupied.

"Watch that barrier. Three niggas done broke it tonight."

"Aight, Legend. I'm watching. Pac antsy too. You see this nigga?"

He was talking about his horse like it was a person. He named it Tupac because he said that it was a thug. Those horses knew when it was go time though, and they got anxious just like the rider did. I think that was why so many had broken the barrier. They couldn't contain their horse. "I see, Red. Just hold on to him. You better wrestle the fuck outta that steer too. We need to sweep this shit up tonight."

"I gotcha, Legend."

He backed the horse up in the box and nodded, then went just as the rope barrier dropped, his hazer was on the other side of the steer. Red had a good lean as he grabbed the horns of the steer. As his body came off the horse, he wrestled that steer to the ground, flipping that bitch over fast as shit. I looked up at the clock to see he'd gotten 3.5 seconds. That was good as hell. That put him in first place for now. There were still three more to go. I looked over toward Pops and saw him standing, cheering for Red.

"That was Craig 'Red' Anderson, ladies and gentlemen. Our new front man, leading with an average of 3.65 seconds!"

The announcer was as excited as we were. I slapped his hand as he made his way back toward the box. "You hammered the fuck outta that steer, Red!"

"I told you, nigga. I'm about my shit tonight."

"That's what's up. Let's see what these other mutha-fuckas gon' do."

We stood around to watch the last three riders. I saw Red searching the crowd, and ol' girl was waving at him. I slightly rolled my eyes as I noticed Harper, sitting there looking confused as shit. Why was I even still checking for her ass? He waved back. "Sensitive nigga."

"Now who's the hater?"

"Whatever."

The next to last wrestler came in close, averaging 4.1 seconds between his two rides. So, there was only one bulldogger to beat. As we stood there, I could feel eyes on me. I looked up to see Neffie, signaling me out of the arena. She needed to get tightened up. Shit, I did too, but I doubted I would tonight. She seemed like the type to catch feelings for a nigga, and I wasn't tryna go there with her. "That mutha-fucka broke the barrier!"

Red was jumping up and down in excitement. This would only be his second time winning first place at a major rodeo. Breaking the barrier didn't disqualify the dogger, but it might as well did. It added ten seconds to his time. So, even if that bulldogger did that shit in three fucking seconds, his time would be thirteen seconds. "Congratulations, Red!" He was so happy, he hugged me. "Hard work pay off! You been putting in the work, now it's time to get paid!"

"Yeah, nigga!"

I looked up to see us on the big screen as Red walked out to the pin with his hands up. The applause was loud, and Red couldn't be any happier. He was gon' cry when we got to the trailer. I laughed out loud at my own thoughts of the movie Friday. What made it even funnier was that his name was Red too.

When we got back to the trailer, and I tried to unwind, there was a knock. Red went to it, and I heard him say, "Thank you."

In walked Neffie. I slightly rolled my eyes, because my dick was standing at attention. So, there was no way I was gon' let her leave without me nutting. Red winked, then walked out, leaving me and her alone. "What's up, Legend?"

"My dick. You ready to bring it down fa me?"

She licked her lips, then locked the door. I watched her fine ass walk over to me and get on her knees in between my legs. Unbuckling my belt, she asked, "You always this forward?"

"Yep."

After she freed my dick, she immediately pulled him in her mouth as I laid my head back. I grabbed the blunt from my pocket and lit up while she was sucking me off. That shit was so good. I looked down and blew the smoke on her as she looked up at me. She was slobbing my shit to death, and he was about to die for the moment. There was no point in trying to make the shit last. I released in the back of her throat and almost choked on the smoke I'd inhaled. I had to push her off it. "Damn girl. It's sensitive."

"I'm just tryna give you my best work. You gon' give me yours?"

"Naw. I'm good now, lil mama."

I adjusted my clothes and zipped my pants up. "Really Legend? You not gon' fuck me?"

"What for? I done got what I needed."

"Fuck, nigga."

I shrugged as she grabbed her shit and left the trailer. She was mad as hell too. I chuckled as Red came in. "What the hell wrong with her?"

"She sucked me off. I didn't need her anymore after that."

His eyebrows went up as he tried to hold in his laughter. "That's cold, nigga."

"I didn't ask her to come here. I was just fine without her. Now let me get my peace."

"Whatever, dude."

~

"GET ready to see a legend in the makin'! Legeeeend Semien!"

"Ready?"

I gave the head nod and rode till the wheels fell off. I was spurring that bull so hard, we could have had sliced beef tonight. After hearing the buzzer indicating that I'd ridden for eight seconds, I dismounted. I could see my daddy standing, anxiously waiting for my score along with everyone else. Unfortunately, I was the last rider this time. So, if I beat an 89.1, I would have the win. As I climbed the railing, and the bull cleared the arena, the scoreboard lit up, showing an 89.5! Shit!

The crowd erupted, and my daddy ran down the stairs to me and hugged me tightly. He even kissed me on the cheek. I laughed as I made my way down. Red came running to the pin and hugged me, then pushed me in the chest. I pushed him back, and we hugged again. After saluting the crowd, I took pictures with my buckle and winnings as they did the same with Red. Then we had to get in a few pictures together and some with my daddy.

I was excited as hell. We done turned out the livestock rodeo. As we were leaving the arena, somebody yelled, "Red! Legend!"

We both turned around to see Shana and her cousin Harper approach. "Wow! That was a show, y'all! Congratulations! This turn up finna be real tonight!"

We both laughed at Shana, and said in unison, "Thanks."

My eyes slid over to Harper. She smiled and said, "Congratulations. That was more exciting than I thought it would be. I almost couldn't watch."

I smiled back. "Thanks."

Red had put his arm around Shana's shoulders. Could have sworn they'd been knowing each other forever. I continued to stare at Harper, and I could tell I was making her uncomfortable. I was about to walk off until she broke the silence. "You been riding bulls a long time?"

"About ten years, since I was a teenager. Professionally about three years."

"That's cool. Do you work a regular job too?"

"Naw. I travel most of the year. This year I hope to make it to Vegas."

"What's in Vegas?"

Damn her voice was driving me crazy, along with those thick

thighs and ass. I could see that shit from the front. "The National Finals Rodeo."

"Oh wow. That's cool."

"Yeah. So, what do you do?"

"I own my own business, making specialty cakes and pastries."

"Oh okay. You in high demand?"

"Usually."

She giggled. That shit made me smile, feeling all sensitive. I had to get away from her. "Well, we'll see y'all at the Sky Bar," Red said to Shana.

I turned to see him walking closer to us, so I nodded my head at Harper. "See you later."

She nodded, then walked off with her cousin. "Yo! She talked to you? That ride got her fucking attention."

I laughed. "I guess so, but I ain't tryna be all chummy with her now. She didn't want no parts of me earlier."

"Aww nigga, it ain't like that. I think she was just excited about what she saw. This her first time at a rodeo."

"Oh well, whatever."

He rolled his eyes as we went back to the trailer to take showers and get ready to hit the town.

5

arper

"THAT SHIT WAS EXCITING, SHANA!"

"I told yo' ass the rodeos be lit! Legend rode the fuck outta that bull! Red coming into his own too. His ass gon' be mine. Watch."

I laughed at Shana's theatrics, then looked back at my phone. I couldn't even enjoy the fucking Trey Songz concert. Something told me not to check my fucking email, but I did anyway. Phoenix had decided to go to Classic Acura and saw Zaire leaving. He followed him to a restaurant where he met that same bitch Shana had seen him with earlier. The pain that pierced my soul when I saw pictures of them kissing, him holding her face in his hands, was almost unbearable. Before I could stop the tears, they'd fallen down my face, and I was in my head most of the night until the steer wrestling.

The excitement of the events had temporarily made me forget

about Zaire, but he was back on my mind. So, I decided to focus on that dark chocolate I saw earlier. Legend Semien. When I first saw him staring at me, my first thought was, *who in the fuck is that dark chocolate?* I never really was into dark-skinned men, but something about him drew me in, and it scared the fuck outta me. I didn't feel that much pull when I first saw Zaire. It was crazy as hell. He wasn't even really my type. He had tats all over his arms, and he was muscular. Everything from the diamond studs in his ears to those tinted, thick lips, turned me on. I usually went for the clean-cut, educated, well dressed, light-skinned dude, with a traditional job.

I knew I was judging him strictly by his appearance, but I was willing to bet that he didn't have a degree. He wore a fitted baseball cap, t-shirt, and jeans. It seemed when he tried talking to me before the rodeo, he was as uncomfortable as I was. Then he just gave up altogether. He wasn't what I was used to dealing with, so I didn't have a clue about what to say.

"So what'chu think about Legend?"

"He seems cool. You know he ain't really my type."

"Uh huh. That's what yo' mouth saying. Those hard ass nipples wasn't saying that when we left."

"Shut up, Shana! My nipples were not hard!"

"Oh yes, the fuck they were. I wish I would've taken a picture of them shits. He probably noticed too."

"Fuck. I hope not. Now I'm gon' be uncomfortable all over again."

"So, you are feeling him."

"Yeah, but it's too soon. I got shit to tie up at home."

"Speaking of, I saw you crying, Harp. What's up?"

"Phoenix emailed me pictures. I'm sure there will be more."

"I'm so sorry."

"Me too."

"Well, look at the bright side. Legend will be a welcomed distraction. And if not him, then some other nigga at the Sky Bar."

I rolled my eyes. I didn't want a distraction, I wanted Zaire to be everything I thought he was. Swallowing hard to keep the tears at bay, I turned up the radio just to hear *Be Careful* by Cardi B. That only made the tears spring from my eyes. Dropping my head to my hands, I let out a cry that I hadn't heard since I was a teenager, heartbroken for the first time. "Harp, please don't cry."

"This shit hurts. He wasted over a year of my life. I can't get that shit back. He looked me in my fucking eyes and lied to me. I trusted him, Shana!"

"Oh, baby girl."

I lifted my head and saw that she was crying too. "I'm sorry, Shana. I think I should probably stay at the hotel."

"Hell naw. You gon' put on that sexy-ass Band-Aid looking dress you got in your luggage, and we gon' get fucked up. You hear me?"

I nodded and wiped my face as my phone alerted me of another email. This shit had to stop. Grabbing the phone from the console, I opened my email to see another picture of them walking inside of his apartment, hot and heavy. Fucking bastard! I wanted to throw my fucking phone out the window. "Turn it off, Harper. You ain't gon' ever get it off your mind if you keep looking at Phoenix's emails. You already know he fucking around. That's just proof so you can show his ass when we get back. Turn that shit off."

I did as she said, then put the phone back in my bag.

We got out of the Uber, and I tugged at my dress. I shouldn't have worn this shit. The word uncomfortable wasn't even touching the surface of how I felt. My entire chest was practically out, displaying my amazing cleavage. I knew my body was fire, so that wasn't the problem. I just wasn't used to showing it to the world anymore. The dress was super short, so if I didn't adjust it when I stood, it would practically show my ass. "You wore boy shorts, right?"

"Yeah."

"So, relax. If they see it, so the fuck what? Let your hair down tonight and tomorrow night. You can be a bougie prude when we get back to Beaumont."

"Ugh!"

She grabbed her phone and called someone. "We're here... okay. I'll wave when I see you."

She'd called Red. "They're already here?"

"Yeah."

I really iced up with nervousness when I saw Red at the door with the bouncer. He waved us up there as people eye-balled us for walking to the front of the line. Red and Legend must have been VIP. He removed the rope and let us in as he licked his lips. "Damn. You look good, Shana," Red said. "Hey, Harper. You look good too. Legend gon' swallow his damned tongue."

Shana giggled as I iced up even more. All that shit she did to convince me to wear this shit, she wore a less revealing dress. It was tight as hell, but it was almost to her knees. Taking a deep breath, I got on the elevator. When we exited, the party was in full swing. Red led us to where they were seated in VIP. There was some chick dancing all over Legend, and I instantly got an attitude.

I sat a little ways down from him and ordered three shots of Patron. I was here to get fucked up. That was it. Why was I trippin'? Before she could come back, ol' girl that was all over Legend left. Just as Red said, when he saw me his eyes widened. I watched him lick his lips and look me over, and I couldn't stop my body from reacting to his gaze. The waitress came back with my shots and I threw them back one after the other. "Three more, please."

"Damn, girl. You look good as fuck," Legend said.

"Thank you."

"You might wanna slow down on them shots. That shit gon' sneak up on you."

"I don't care."

I hadn't even looked back at him while he was talking. That shit was gone get me loose, and I was all for it. Shrugging his shoulders, he went back to his drink. Shana was dancing on Red having a good time, while I was sulking. When she came back with my shots, I threw them back one after the other, then crossed my legs. I was aware that he could probably see my ass, but at the moment I didn't give a fuck. I just wanted those shots to kick in.

"What's up, shawty? You wanna dance?"

"No. Thank you, though."

He walked away as I rolled my eyes. "Why you here if you in a shitty-ass mood?"

I frowned and turned to Legend. "Why the fuck you worried about it?"

He rolled his eyes, then left our section. I watched him sit next to a chick that he seemed to be familiar with, then got up and went to the restroom. Those shots were finally starting to kick in and I was starting to feel a little dizzy. After handling my business, I went back to my seat. I ordered three more, then crossed my legs again. "You okay, Harper?"

"I'm good, Shana. Enjoy yourself."

"I want you to enjoy yourself too."

I rolled my eyes, then wiped the tear that fell. After downing the three shots, Shana pulled me from my seat. "This yo' shit! Let's dance!"

The DJ was playing "After Dark" by Drake. I was practically falling over Shana, trying to roll my hips. Before long, I was laughing, because I knew I was finally fucked up. Feeling hands on my hips, I turned to see Legend holding on to me. I smiled at him, then looped my arms around his neck. "You fucked up, girl."

"That was the plan." Ty Dolla Sign was singing his part in the song and I sang along with him, "Fuck these niggas!" Legend laughed. "Oh, that shit funny?"

He kept laughing as I started working my hips against him. He shut that shit up quick. I watched him bite his bottom lip as I turned back around and put my ass in his crotch. Feeling his hands somewhat grope me felt good as fuck. That hard dick against my ass felt good too. "What'chu tryna do, Harper?"

"I ain't tryna do shit but what I'm doing right now."

"Tease the fuck outta my dick? 'Cause that's what'chu doing."

"Well, you can walk off. You must like that shit."

"I think I like you better drunk."

"Shut up, and dance, nigga."

Just when he started grooving with me, the song went off. Then, they played a throwback from Lil Wayne, "Pussy Monster". I turned back around and faced him. We just stared at one another as I grinded all over him. He ran his finger down my chest, between my breasts. That shit felt so good. I was soaking wet with sweat and so was he. Pressing my body against him, I asked, "You da pussy monster?"

He didn't answer me, just held me tightly to him, then grabbed my ass. Our faces were inches apart. We were so close, I could feel his breath on my face. With the four-inch heels I wore, we were practically the same height. That alcohol had my eyes so fucking low, I could barely see his ass, even though he was right in front of me. "You wanna eat me, Legend?"

"Girl, chill out."

"Or what?"

"I'm gon' have you doin' some shit you gon' regret tomorrow."

"Whatever, nigga."

He brought his hand in front of me and practically grabbed me by the pussy. "Don't get scared now, Harper. This that shit you asking for?"

He was talking right in my ear. Shit. "Play with that pussy, Legend."

Shit, I wasn't scared. I was horny as fuck. He started a rhythm on my pearl through my boy shorts as my knees weakened. I kissed his neck, then bit his earlobe. Lifting my head, I looked in his face, then licked his bottom lip. My legs were trembling like crazy, so I wrapped my arms around his neck once again, to hold myself up as my orgasm ripped through me. He held me steady by wrapping his other arm around me because my ass would've hit that floor. My eyes closed, and I wanted to scream out the pleasure I was feeling.

He moved his hand, then led me to my seat. He ain't say shit. I ordered another shot, then leaned against him. He put his arm around me. "You think you need another drink?"

"Nope, but I sure in the hell want another one."

I laughed, then hiccupped as he shook his head. Adjusting my dress to cover my titties, he grazed my nipple as I bit my bottom lip. My tape was no longer sticking, so it was a good thing I wore pasties just in case. I figured I would sweat, so I came prepared. Coming close to me, he put his lips to mine and kissed me hungrily. Good thing I couldn't get away with fucking him in this club because I sure in the hell would have straddled him by now.

I pulled away from him, as my Patron came back, and downed my last shot. "Let's get the fuck outta here."

He stared at me, trying to see if I was serious, I supposed. "Naw.

You drunk. The first time I fuck you, I want it to be while you sober. That way I'll know for sure you want it."

I attempted to straddle him, but he sat my ass back down beside him. "You'll thank me for not destroying your insides tomorrow."

"Fuck, then I need another drink."

I leaned against him again and waited for the waitress to come back.

6
_____

egend

I COULDN'T BELIEVE her ass went straight to sleep. When the wait-ress came back with at least her thirteenth shot of Patron, Harper was laid against me, knocked the fuck out. I didn't know what the fuck was going on in her personal life, but whatever it was had to have been fucked all the way up. Red and Shana came over from the dance floor and sat next to us. "My poor cousin. She fucked all the way up."

They both laughed as I glanced at Harper. She never even flinched. Shana was drunk too, but not like Harper. "She found out her boyfriend was cheating on her yesterday. I told her we were gon' get fucked up so she can get her mind off the shit, at least for a couple of days anyway."

So that was the problem. She was heartbroken. It made me a little more sympathetic toward her. "How long were they together?" I asked.

"A little over a year. A fucking waste," Harper said.

I looked at her as she tried to sit up. When she did, she pulled me closer to her and kissed me on the lips. The taste of Patron filled my mouth as she slid her tongue inside it. Damn, she was turning me on. The problem was that I knew it was only the alcohol. I pulled away from her and she laid on my arm again. Shana said, "She's really feeling you. I've seen Harper drunk before, and she was never this loose."

"Shut the fuck up, Shana," Harper slurred.

I chuckled. "Well, we need to get y'all back to your room. How did y'all get here?"

"We got an Uber because I knew neither one of us would be able to drive when we left."

Red smiled and he and Shana stood. Leaning over to where I could speak directly in Harper's ear, I lifted her head from my shoulder. "Come on, baby girl. It's time to go."

"Already?" she whined.

"Yep."

I stood, and she slid over in the plush seating. Shana and Red laughed, but her ass was literally out for everyone to see. For some reason, I wasn't too happy about that. I sat her up, then scooped her in my arms. Red took off his button-down, since he had on a full t-shirt underneath and covered her up. She was sexy as fuck. Her ass was eating them damned boy shorts.

When we got to Red's Dodge Dually, he opened the door for me to slide her in the backseat. Just as I was about to walk away, she reached for me. "Legend. Stay with me."

I slightly rolled my eyes, then got in the back seat with her. She had me feeling all sensitive, and I didn't like that shit one bit. Being in a relationship or catching feelings for anybody wasn't on my to-do list. Getting to Vegas for the nationals was all I was concerned about. Of course, I wouldn't turn down a good fuck, but I didn't want anything more than that. Harper was threatening to alter my plans. Maybe when she sobered up, she'd come to her senses. I knew she wasn't ready for what she was offering. After making her cum on the dance floor and seeing her fuck faces, my mind was gone.

Harper laid on my chest and draped her arm across me. "Thank you, Legend."

I gently brushed her hair from her face and kissed her forehead. She looked up at me and kissed my lips softly, and I could feel my erection. Squeezing her thigh, I kissed her back, then pulled her into my lap. Damn, I wanted to fuck her bad. "Legend, you turn me on."

Just the way she whispered in my ear had me wanting to bust in my pants. I ain't never felt no shit like this before. My hands went to her ass and caressed it, then I slid them beneath her boy shorts. The heat coming from her pussy was begging me to slide my fingers inside of her. "Do it," she whispered slowly.

Was she reading my mind now? She lowered her mouth to mine and I sucked her tongue, then her bottom lip. The way she was gyrating her hips on my dick, was killing me. I licked my lips, then slid a finger inside of her. I couldn't help it. That pussy was calling my name. Shit, that pussy was *screaming* my name. She was so hot and fucking wet. Harper moaned in my ear as I slid a second finger inside of her. As I started a rhythm, I felt the truck come to a stop. When I glanced around Harper, I could see Shana looking with a smirk on her face.

I slowly slid my fingers out of her as she said, "Please, don't stop."

Something definitely had to have possessed me, because I brought my fingers to my mouth and tasted her. I closed my eyes as I savored her flavor, searing it to my taste buds. When I opened them, she was staring at me, still straddled across my lap. I slid her to my side and opened the door as she grabbed her clutch from Shana. After getting out, I helped her down and she was still wobbling everywhere, so I scooped her up once again.

Shana and Red stayed in the truck, I assumed to talk. "What's yo' room number, Harper?"

"I don't know. It's on the card in my clutch."

She opened it and gave it to me as I walked in the automatic doors. She was sweating and didn't look so good anymore. I knew I had to get to her room quick. After leaving the elevator, I damn near wanted to run to her room. No sooner than I'd kicked the door closed, she jumped out of my arms and ran to the bathroom. That shit was disgusting. I hoped Shana and Red didn't take too long, because I wasn't trying to clean up no damned throw up. After hearing the water running, I decided to check on her.

When I opened the door, she was at the sink only in her boy shorts. She still had those damned pasties on her nipples, but she was fire. I noticed the complete sleeve tattoo she had on her arm as she gargled. She looked over at me, then spit. Starting the shower, she turned toward me and peeled off her pasties. I licked my lips as she walked toward me, then pulled me in the bathroom by my shirt. There were two things on my mind, and they were both on separate ends of the spectrum. One thing was lifting her up and touching every part of her insides with my dick, and the other was running the hell up out of that room without looking back.

Harper pulled my shirt over my head and rubbed her hands down my chest. She pressed her body against mine, then licked my neck. When I felt her hand squeeze my package, I knew I needed to get out of there. I backed away from her. "What's wrong? You don't wanna fuck me, Legend?"

She turned her back to me, showing me all that ass as she pulled her boy shorts off. Her bending over gave me the perfect view of that clean-shaven pussy. The lips of it was glistening. I walked closer to her and slid my fingers back inside of her. Reaching around her and pinching her nipple, I kept a steady rhythm as she moaned. She slowly pulled away from me and was about to unbutton my pants, when I saw it on her face. She was about to throw up again.

I quickly turned my head as she dove for the toilet. That alcohol was slowly leaving her. I grabbed my shirt and put it on as I stepped out of the bathroom. I called Red. "What's up?"

"Tell Shana she throwing up everywhere. I can't stay here all night."

"Aight."

I knocked on the door, and she screamed, "Get out of here! Go away!"

The bougie bitch was back. "I ain't leaving you in here by yourself. When Shana comes back, I'll gladly leave."

She swung the door open, still butt ass naked. "A minute ago, you were gladly finger-fucking me."

"You wanted that shit. You can't blame me when the pussy being thrown at me. Be glad I ain't fucked you up. I know yo' ass drunk. You gon' be embarrassed as shit tomorrow."

She glared at me, then must've felt a wave of nausea again. After slamming the door, I could hear her coughing and throwing up. Turning my lip up, I walked toward the sink and washed my hands, then headed toward the door. Just as I was about to open it, I heard a key card deactivating the lock. When it opened, Shana walked in and said, "Sorry. She gon' be embarrassed as hell tomorrow."

"Yeah, especially since she in there butt ass naked."

"Did y'all fuck?"

"No. We ain't do no more than what we did in the truck. My pants never came unzipped."

"Aight. We'll see y'all tomorrow. Thanks, Legend, for looking out for her."

I nodded, then left. Walking to the truck, I was almost sure I would never see her again, the way I saw her tonight.

Once I got in, Red stared at me. "What? Let's go, nigga."

"Uh huh. Y'all fucked? You was sure having a good time finger fucking her in my damned truck."

"That's as far as it went."

"You looked pissed. You aight?"

"Yeah. I just wanna get some sleep."

Truth was, she had my head fucked up. And for what? I already knew that she probably wouldn't speak to me tomorrow. I was just glad this happened tonight and not last night. That would have thrown me all off on my ride. At least something good happened today, but at the moment, I could still taste her. I could still feel those pretty lips on mine, her nipples grazing my chest, and her walls wrapped around my fingers. Her whole aura was overwhelming my senses.

When we got back to the trailer, I got out the truck without a word. As soon as Red unlocked the door, I went in to take a shower and tried to wash away the remnants and memories of Harper, whatever the fuck her last name was.

arper

I FELT LIKE SHIT. I dreamed all night about fucking Legend. Although I was drunk as hell, I remembered every detail. From him making me cum on the dancefloor to him finger fucking me in our hotel bathroom. Even with as far as we went, he was respectful as hell. He could have fucked me and left me in my vomit. I couldn't believe I'd thrown it at him the way I did. Letting him see me completely naked, made me look like a hoe, and that was probably what he thought of me as now.

After brushing my teeth, I laid back in the bed and covered up to my neck. Since I was fucking in my damned sleep, it didn't feel like I'd gotten any rest. I noticed my phone was on the charger, so I powered it up and it went crazy. There were emails from potential customers, but the ones that caught my attention were the ones from Phoenix. I refused to open them. Zaire hadn't even texted me since I'd been gone. I couldn't let his bitch-ass enter my mind, though. I only wanted to think about Legend.

Regardless of how drunk I was, I still remembered how he made me feel. Those feelings of wanting had nothing to do with my level of toxicity either. That shit was dangerous. He didn't seem like the settling down type. There was no way I was gonna let him in, in no capacity. The way my body tingled from his touch, it wasn't even safe for us to be friends or even acquaintances. "Uh uh, get'cho ass up, Harp."

Shana had walked in the room. I didn't know where she'd been, but she was fully clothed. "Why?" I whined.

"The rodeo starts at three today. It's already one. You was so fucked up, it was ridiculous. I ain't never seen you that bad. You was throwing that pussy at Legend. I thought y'all was gon' fuck in Red's truck. It was like you didn't give a fuck whether we were watching or not. Red had turned to look at y'all, and he hurriedly turned forward. Watching y'all asses had me all hot and bothered."

I rolled my eyes and threw the covers over my head. "Come on Harper! You gon' need a full face of makeup, so we ain't got time to waste."

I drug myself from the bed and made my way to the mirror. She wasn't lying. I was gon' need some serious contouring to hide the bags under my eyes. Thank God I wasn't hung over.

As we walked through the gated entrance, I put my head down. I immediately saw Legend and Red, and I could feel the heat rush to my face. Of course, Shana walked straight to them. "Hey, baby girl," Red said as she hugged him.

I couldn't bear even looking at either of them. "Hey, Harper."

When I looked up, Legend's eyes were on me and his face was serious as hell. Something was going on between my legs and I couldn't make that shit stop. "Hey, Legend."

He grabbed my hand and pulled me away from Shana and Red. "Look, forget about last night. You feel okay?"

I searched his face for a clue. If he was joking, I was gonna cuss him out, but he seemed to be dead serious. "I feel okay, other than being embarrassed as hell. I'm sorry for my behavior. I remember everything, and I feel so cheap."

He frowned a bit, still holding my hands in his. "You far from cheap. We allowed to have off days. I'm just glad your off day was with me."

There was the smile. The gorgeous smile that displayed beautiful, white teeth. I smirked, then averted my gaze. He grabbed me by the chin. "Hold your head up."

He stepped closer to me, but I backed away. I couldn't go there with him. Instead of letting me be, he grabbed me by the waist and pulled me to him. "I had the feeling that you would be standoffish. Just kick it with me today. Get to know me, then make that decision. I know you got some shit going on but just chill with me today. If you don't wanna see me again after you leave Houston, I'll have to be okay with that."

I could see the sincerity in his eyes and hear it in his tone. Then again, I thought I could see and hear it with Zaire too. However, I could give him today, since he took care of me last night. After today, I'd probably never see him again. "Okay."

He smiled again, then put his arm around my shoulders as this chick glared at us. He kissed my head, then we walked back over to Red and Shana. "You want something to eat?"

"No. I don't think I can handle it. You got a spectator that seems to want your attention, though."

"My bad. Maybe a Sprite later?"

"Yeah. What about..."

"I already seen her. I got whose attention I want, and she has mine."

"Oh yeah? Who's the lucky woman?"

"Oh, the woman is lucky?"

I giggled. He knew how to play along with me. "Well, damn. She laughs."

My face heated up as I smiled brightly at him. Where did this guy come from? "So, are you competing in anything today?"

"No. I was done last night. You think you might come to another rodeo?"

"I don't know. Maybe."

I averted my gaze as he stared at me. He was asking to see me again. We stopped walking and he lifted my chin. "You scared of me?"

"Huh? Why would I be scared of you?"

"You seem to be holding back. I got tough skin. Say what you want. Say how you really feel. This rodeo shit ain't for everybody. I know that."

"I did enjoy the rodeo last night. Is it something I could see myself at all the time? Probably not. Not unless I was there for someone, in particular, to root them on."

"Who you know that compete?"

"Just this bull rider that thinks he's the shit. Got people believing that he's a legend in the making."

"Is that right? I know that nigga too."

I laughed. "I swear, you are really crazy."

"You think so?"

His face was somewhat serious, except for the slight smirk on his lips. "Yes, I do."

He lowered his lips to mine and kissed me softly. Damn. What was I doing? What was I allowing him to do to me? "Come on. Let's get our seats before Tank starts. I know that's who you really here for."

"How did you guess that?"

He laughed, and it felt like it melted my insides. I could see Shana smiling at us in my peripheral like we were young love or some shit. Legend gently pulled me by the hand and I followed him, wishing my hand never had to leave his.

When we were seated, he put my hand between his. "How long you been baking cakes for folks?"

"Professionally, a couple of years. I've been baking since my mama first showed me around the kitchen at eight years old."

"That's cool. So, you have a lot of experience. Maybe you'll bake me a cake one day."

"Maybe."

After Tank's voice came over the mic all conversation had to cease. Legend and Red watched me and Shana the entire time as we got our party on with Tank. When he got to a slower tempo song, I pulled Legend from his seat. When Tank sang, *let that thang take me on a trip, to every private place inside of it...* I rolled my hips against him, my ass in his crotch. The way his body felt against mine wasn't something I'd imagined last night. That shit was as real as it gets.

He rested his hand on my hip. "You sober tonight, Harper. Keep it up, and I won't hold back on your ass."

The goosebumps that appeared on my flesh said just how much my body craved him. I lifted my arm and let my hand caress the back of his head as his fingers ran from my neck down the side of my breast to my hips. Shit. Why did he have to feel so good? Before I got carried away, I brought my arm down. Hell, he'd seen me naked already! All there was left to do was to have sex. I refused to cross that barrier. All the other lines had been crossed, but I was gonna stay in my place tonight, even if it killed me.

"What's the matter?"

He said that shit so low and seductively in my ear, I wanted to turn around and just give all my shit to him. Instead, I turned to him and wrapped my arms around his neck. "I can't have sex with you. No matter how much I want to. I'm not a hoe, Legend, and it would kill me if you thought of me as one."

"Why would I think you a hoe? A hoe is what was looking at me earlier. You wanna have sex with me, Harper?"

He kissed my lips, then grabbed my arm from his neck and spun me back around, pressing his hard dick against me. After placing a soft kiss on my neck, then biting my earlobe, he said, "I wanna fuck the shit out of you. Then be all sensitive and shit afterwards."

The tremble in my breath reverberated through my entire body. Why did he turn me on so much? It was like no matter what he said, however rough, or rude that shit was, I wanted to jump his bones in public and not give a shit what anybody had to say about it. But Zaire? That was a fucking loose end that needed tying up like them cowboys roping those calves. The longer I stood there with Legend, the more Zaire bubbled up in my chest like indigestion.

"You didn't answer me, Harper. You wanna have sex with me?"

"I do, but I can't."

"Why not?"

"I'm too emotional with all the shit I have going on, plus we barely know each other."

He took a deep breath and exhaled against my neck, but he didn't say another word as Tank continued his show.

As we walked to Shana's car, Legend held my hand. I'd enjoyed spending time with him at the rodeo. He explained almost everything that was going on, and we even got to know each other a little more. We were the same age and liked a lot of the same things and foods. "Harper Richardson, it's been a pleasure gettin' to know you, ma'am."

I giggled, listening to him imitate a country accent. "Likewise, Legend Semien."

He laughed louder than I did at me trying to imitate the country twang as well. "Can I have your number?"

I dropped my head, feeling the sting in what I was about to say. "No. I don't think that'll be good for me right now."

"So, this is it, then huh?"

"Yeah. This is it."

He drew me in his arms and laid a passionate kiss on me that made me dizzy with desire. When he pulled away, he leaned his forehead against mine. "You sure, Harper?"

"Yeah," I whispered.

"Well, if you change your mind, you know how to find me."

With that, he walked away and left me standing there watching him leave. My heart was in the pit of my stomach, and I felt like I wanted to throw up. "Harper! You gon' get in the car or not?"

I slid in the front seat quietly as Shana stared at me. It felt like I wanted to cry. I had to deny myself to be sure it was real. Maybe I was just so attracted to him because of what I was going through with Zaire. I was too vulnerable. Even with knowing all that, it felt like both my lungs were about to collapse. "Harp, you okay?"

I only nodded, and we continued our ride back to the hotel, so I could pack my things and get ready to leave in the morning.

8

egend

"Yo! Legend! Wait up!"

I could hear Red yelling for me, but I couldn't stop until I got to the trailer. When I did, I sat on the steps. Everything I said I wasn't gonna do, I did that shit. I opened up to her, let her know how much I wanted her and was publicly affectionate and passionate and shit, only for her to tell me that was it. That crushed a nigga's ego, on some real shit. I had never felt nobody like I was feeling her, and for what?

"What's up? Why you wouldn't wait?"

"I just wanted to get back to the trailer."

"What happened? Looked like y'all were getting along well, but now you look mad as fuck. I was started to see a Legend I ain't ever seen before. You looked beyond happy."

"This is it. She wouldn't give me her number. Said it was best this way."

"Damn. I'm sorry man. You just gone let her go?"

"I told her if she changed her mind, she knew how to find me."

"That she does."

He went inside the trailer and I chose to sit on the steps, thinking about that milk chocolate sauce that I let slip outta my grasp. We had such a good time today, I just knew this was gon' be the start of something special, something a nigga never felt in his life. But whatever.

Just as I stood to go inside, Neffie approached me. "So, you just fuck 'em and move on to the next one, huh?"

"Girl, come on now. Don't come at me with that bullshit. When you came to this trailer last week, I told you what this was. Now don't make me put yo' business in the street. Who you think they gon' cast the negative light on, me or you?"

"Legend. You wouldn't do that shit."

"Quit coming at me sideways then. Miss me with that fuck shit. Who dick you was on before me?" Her eyebrows lifted, but she didn't say a word. "Yeah, I know you was on Zane and Jaxx, the team ropers. Doing both of their asses at the same damn time. Yeah, I know about that shit, and everybody round this bitch know that shit too. You probably been on every mutha-fucka 'round this shit. If you concentrate on your technique like you concentrated on dick hopping, maybe you could win yo' event. Now get the fuck away from me."

I left her standing there in tears and went in the trailer and slammed the fucking door. My nerves were already on edge, so she got all that shit. "Why the fuck you slamming my door?"

I sat on the sofa, not answering Red. He came out of his room and stared at me until I said, "My bad. Neffie almost got fucked up a minute ago."

"If she know like I know, she better move the fuck around. Harper got you all sensitive and shit right now. Anybody can get it."

"Shut the fuck up."

"See what I mean. Sensitive ass, nigga."

He walked off and went back to his room. I grabbed my phone and looked at the picture I'd taken of me and Harper during the Tank concert. What the fuck was I gonna do? I couldn't just sit here and wait on her to contact me. I'd give her week though, cause she needed to handle her business, but after that, I was coming for her, and I wasn't gon' give up until she was mine. Nigga be damned.

"What's up, Rose?"

"Boy, just 'cause you done won a little buckle and some chump change don't give you the right to call me by my name. I can still whoop yo' muscle ass."

"Damn, Ma. You ain't have to cut a nigga down like that."

She laughed as I hugged her and kissed her cheek. "And last time I checked, forty grand was far from being chump change."

"Forty grand? That's all you won this year?"

"That's what I won in Houston. I'm almost at sixty-five grand for the year and we just in March. I'm hitting the circuit hard this summer."

"Let me hold a thousand."

"If I let you hold a thousand, then I should be able to call you, Rose."

She laughed loudly. "If you don't shut that mess up! I'm proud of you, Legend."

"Thanks, Ma. Let me holla at'chu about something."

"Please tell me it's about a woman and not this rodeo mess."

"Hey, this rodeo mess pays the bills, but yeah, it's about a woman."

"'Bout time. I never thought we would have this conversation. Who is she, and why she won't give you the time of day?"

I knew they said women and mothers had an intuition you couldn't fuck with but damn. It was like she cracked my damn head open and looked at my thoughts. "Damn. You work for Dionne Warrick and friends?"

"Oh, hush up, boy. What's going on?"

"I met this woman at the rodeo. When I first saw her, she grabbed all my attention. I mean like no other woman ever has. She's so beautiful. Anyway. We got close, we kissed when we were dancing. She got drunk, so I helped her back to her room. The next day she was embarrassed to be around me, but I made her feel comfortable. I could tell, she was feeling me too."

Ain't no way in hell I was finna give Rose *all* the details. "So, what's the problem?"

"Her friend told me she has a boyfriend that she found out was cheating on her right before they left to come to Houston. That's why she got drunk, to numb the hurt for a little while. She hadn't talked to him about it yet. When they got ready to leave, she wouldn't give me her number. She said she didn't think it was a good idea. Our chemistry is undeniable, Ma."

"The only thing I can see is that she isn't sure how things are gonna go with her boyfriend. She may choose to forgive him. How long have they been together?"

"A little over a year."

"She's probably in love, baby. In that case, be glad that she doesn't wanna string you along. Respect her for that."

"I don't wanna let go. I don't give a damn about her boyfriend. What I felt wasn't one-sided. I know it wasn't."

I grabbed my phone and showed her the picture of us. "She's beautiful, baby, and y'all look amazing together."

"But?"

"Give her time to decide what she's gonna do."

"I am. She lives in Beaumont, and they went home Sunday. So, I figured I would give her until the end of this week before I tried to reach out."

"How will you reach out if you don't have her number?"

"Her cousin that she was with at the rodeo is talking to Red. So, I can get to her that way."

"Just protect your heart, Legend. I've never seen you this excited about anybody, so I'm not gonna tell you to leave it alone. I don't wanna see you hurt either, though."

"I'm a grown man, Ma. I can handle it."

"A twenty-six-year-old man who's never been in love. In loves eyes, you're a virgin, so be careful."

"Thanks, Ma," I said while standing to my feet.

"Where you going?"

"See what you cooking in these pots. I'm starving."

"You need to learn how to cook. I'm cooking some turkey necks and black-eyed peas for your daddy."

"And for your son. I'll be back. I need to run to get some hay for the horses."

"Okay. Spoiled ass."

I laughed at her. "It's your fault for not having more kids."

"Uh huh. I only wanted one. After I saw you, my lil chocolate drop, I didn't wanna share my love with another baby."

"I love you, Ma."

"Love you too."

I left the house, then got in my King Ranch and called Red. "What's up?"

"You busy?"

"Just talking to Shana before she go to work."

"Perfect. I need Harper's address and when she'll be there. I'm sending her some flowers."

"Well, I'll be damned. Legend Semien wants to send flowers to a woman. Where in the fuck is my best friend?"

"Just ask her nigga."

"Hold on."

I grabbed my scratch pad from my console with an ink pen as I waited for him to come back to the line. "You there?"

"Yeah."

"Her address is 4040 Crow Road. She lives at The Harbour. Apartment 138. The zip is 77706. Shana said that Harper loves stargaze lilies of any color."

"Okay. Perfect. Thanks, dude. How is she?"

"I don't know. I asked, but Shana won't tell me what's going on, because she doesn't want me to tell you. So, I'm assuming she might have taken him back."

"Fuck, I hope not. Alright."

"Oh, and Harper is usually home on Thursday's, all day."

"Okay. Well, let me call the florist before it gets too late."

"Aight."

I called the florist immediately and ordered a bouquet to be delivered to her tomorrow, then headed out to get my hay. I was hoping like hell that she hadn't given him another chance. Where would that leave me? I went home to my five-bedroom, four thousand square foot home in Liberty, TX to get my trailer. It was a small town almost an hour west of Beaumont. All this house just for me. I had to get my trailer because I planned to get at least ten rolls of hay. Red and I took turns buying hay. Although I was a bull rider, I did own four horses. Whenever I decided I'd had enough of bull riding, I could bulldog or team rope with somebody. I would need a horse for those events.

After hooking up to my trailer, I headed to Dayton to get my hay, then went back to Nome. Red had all the horses out there on his land. Once he unloaded the hay with his tractor, I'd leave the trailer there and head back to Liberty. All this driving. That was the only downside to living in rural areas. It took a minute to get places.

When I got back to my parents' house, I'd been gone for almost three hours and for an hour and a half of it, I was driving. I went into the house to see that Mama had fixed my plate and wrapped it up. They ate dinner at six and it was almost seven. I grabbed my plate, then went to the den to find my daddy in his recliner, watching a basketball game. "Aight old man. I came to get my plate, and I'm about to head home. Tell Mama thank you."

"Okay. I saw that lil woman you were talking to before you came sat with me. She was pretty."

"Yeah."

"She involved with somebody?"

"Yes, sir."

"Oh. Too bad."

I didn't feel like talking about Harper all over again. I'd rather see her. If I had to, I'd talk Shana into having us coincidentally meet somewhere. Hopefully, after she got the flowers, she would reach out. Walking to my truck, I couldn't help but wish I had some shit to do. I had two weeks of downtime until the Easter Rodeo. Spoiling Harper was all I could think about, so hopefully, she'd contact me sooner than later.

arper

"I CAN'T BELIEVE you still denying this fuck-shit with the evidence right in your fucking face! Zaire, what the fuck I look like to you? I been stupid long enough. According to this shit, you been fucking around on me since the beginning of our relationship!"

"Baby, please. Just hear me out."

"Zaire! Ain't shit to explain! What is it that you don't understand about this shit? I have pictures, phone records, and your second Face-book account. All these email addresses. You a fucking professional! That bitch you were with all weekend is the same bitch that was sending the nudes! I have mountains of information, Zaire!"

"What do you want me to say?"

"What'chu mean what I want you to say? I want you to say, I'm sorry, Harper for fucking wasting your time! You a fucking con artist!

You had so much fun while I was gone, you didn't even try to text me once to say you missed me. I can't believe I fell for your lies, Zaire. Then you lied even after I knew and told me you had to go out of town for work when in actuality, you went to meet a bitch in Austin. I can't deal with you anymore. Trust is such an important factor in a relationship, and it's nonexistent now."

"Fine, Harper. You're going to regret the day you let me go. It was because of me that your clientele is what it is. Most of your customers know my family. You're gonna see just how much I was doing for you."

"Are you threatening me, mutha-fucka? Don't make this hood come out of me. I feel like choking yo' ass. Get the fuck outta here, Zaire."

"Okay. I'm leaving, but don't call me, needing me for anything. Understood?"

"The only thing about to be understood in this bitch is my foot in yo' ass. Get the fuck out!"

I was screaming mad. It felt like I could literally spit nails. Here it was Wednesday, and I'd had to stew in the shit even longer than I planned, an extra three nights. Slamming the door after he left, I collapsed on my couch and cried my eyes out. To see him stand there and deny a fucking picture was blowin' me. How could I have been so naïve to what he was doing? I felt like such a fool. Just as I was about to go to bed, my phone rang. It was Shana. "Hello?"

"I take it you finally talked to him. I hear it in your voice."

"He just left about thirty minutes ago."

"I'm coming over."

"No. I just need to be alone right now."

"You sure, Harp? I don't like the way you sound right now."

"Yeah."

"Legend asked about you."

I took a deep breath and exhaled slowly. Legend Semien. I'd been trying my best not to think about him. Too much shit was on my mind, and I didn't need to drag thoughts of him in the mess. After I didn't respond to what she'd said, she continued in a soft voice, "Do you want me to tell him anything?"

"No. Talk to you later."

I ended the call, then laid in my bed, sinking under the covers. My mind went to the last thing Zaire said before he left. Did he really control my clientele the way he said he did? What if I lost my business? Zaire's family had a lot of influence and little ol' me would get trampled by their clout. Before I could close my eyes to attempt to go to sleep, my phone started ringing again. "What Shana?"

"I'm at your door."

"Why?"

"Because I didn't like the way you sounded. Come take the chain off, Harper."

"I told you I needed to be alone."

"I won't bother you, but when you need me, I'll be here."

I ended the call, then got up to open the door for her. It felt like I was gonna pass out at any moment, I was so weak. I hadn't eaten all day. When the door opened, she stared at me for a moment, then walked in. After closing it, she pulled me in her embrace. Before I could stop them, the sobs escaped me. Breaking up with Zaire, threatened everything that meant anything to me. If I lost my business, I would lose everything.

Slowly pulling away from her, while she watched me sympathetically, I walked back to my room and fell in bed, succumbing to the heartbreak I was still feeling.

When I woke up, I smelled food and it was making me nauseated. At the same time, my stomach was still growling, begging me to end this standoff between me and food. It was already 10:00 a.m., and I needed to stop wallowing in heartbreak and move on with my life. While handling my hygiene, I heard the doorbell ring. I never had visitors, and Shana was already here. My mama lived in Lake Charles, so she wouldn't just pop up without calling.

After finishing my hygiene, I put on my housecoat and went to the front. There was a beautiful bouquet of lilies waiting for me. I quickly rolled my eyes. If this was Zaire's way of trying to make up with me, then he could that squash that effort now. "Throw that shit away."

"Why? These flowers are beautiful."

"I don't want shit from Zaire."

"They aren't from Zaire, Harp."

I frowned. Who could be sending me flowers? Walking toward them, I took the card from the stem. The envelope had 'from Legend' scribbled on the outside of it. My heart felt like it skipped a beat at the sight of it. Pulling the card from the envelope, it read, *I miss you. Heard through the grapevine that you liked lilies. I hope these will do. ~Legend*

He sent me flowers. I would have never expected flowers from a guy like him. Romance seemed to be a big step for him. Then I thought about how he held on to me at the concert, kissing me softly and being affectionate. Maybe it wasn't such a big step. "Harper!"

"What?"

"Girl, that man got control of you, honey. I been trying to get your attention since you looked at that damn card. What did it say?"

I handed the card to her as I sniffed my flowers. The arrangement was huge. Shana smiled as she was reading. "Girl, he really feeling you. Red said that Legend don't usually do stuff like this."

"You gave him my address, huh? What if he shows up here?"

"You act like that would be a bad thing."

"I'm not ready."

"Girl, you ain't gotta marry his ass, but what's wrong with spending some time with him?"

I couldn't answer her. There was no way I could spend time with Legend without fucking him. It was bad enough that he already knew that I wanted to. I did need to thank him, though. It was a sweet gesture, that deserved my attention and gratitude. "What's his phone number, Shana?"

"Aye! Let me text Red."

I shook my head slowly and rolled my eyes at her while still playing with my flowers. A soft smile made its way to my lips as I thought about how much I enjoyed Legend last weekend. Her phone chimed, breaking me away from my thoughts. "656-2852."

"Text it to me."

I walked away to my room to get my phone. As I picked it up, I could feel my hand tremble. Why was I nervous? Should I just text him instead? I sat on my bed and my stomach was turning flips. Finally, I decided I would just call. "Hello?"

Oh, God. I should've texted. The sound of his voice had my clit pulsating. For a moment, I couldn't find my voice, and I believed he knew it was me. Legend was just as quiet as I was. My heart was beating out of my chest and I'd begun to sweat. I ended the call without saying a word. What was wrong with me? Why did he make me feel this way? It almost made me wonder if I ever loved Zaire because it never felt this way.

Maybe I was just infatuated with what I thought I wanted and confused it with love. The ringing phone scared me out of my thoughts, and I stared at the number. He was calling back. *Be a woman and not a childish little girl, Harper.* "Hello?"

"Why did you hang up?"

"I'm nervous. I just wanted to say thank you for the flowers. They're beautiful."

"Why are you nervous?"

"Legend, I can't have this conversation right now," I said, trying to control my quivering voice.

"Okay. Do I have permission to call you sometimes?"

"Legend..."

"Harper. I miss you. So, I was just trying to be nice about asking permission. If you don't want me to call, block me."

"I could never block you, Legend. It's just that my emotions are everywhere right now."

"How about you just focus on one emotion."

"Which one is that?"

"The one you're feeling right now."

I allowed the tears to trickle from my eyes, but the sniffle was what I regretted. "I'm coming over."

"No."

"Yeah. What Legend wants, Legend gets. You'll learn that. I'm on my way."

His cocky ass ended the call. I looked like shit, but if his ass wanted to come over here right now, he was gonna see me at my worst. I wasn't about to get all dressed up and put on makeup. What he saw was what he would get, since he couldn't respect my wishes. Calling him was a mistake. Answering his return call was an even bigger mistake. No. They were bad decisions. Shana knocked on my door. "Come in."

"Well..." she said as she opened the door. "What did he say?"

"He's coming over and wouldn't take no for an answer."

"Oh shit. I guess I better get my ass outta here."

"No. Don't leave. I don't want him here, Shana."

"Then don't answer the door. It's your choice, Harper."

"I can't just leave him standing there. He'll hate me."

"Harper just let things be. Quit fighting it. I know it's what you want, otherwise, it wouldn't be this difficult for you. When you would have said no, that would have been final."

I took a deep breath. She was right. Legend was what I wanted. She left me sitting there, then went back to the front. I just wanted to be sure that the reasons why I wanted him so much were authentic and not because of what I was going through with Zaire. Taking a deep breath, I laid back in the bed and pulled the covers over my head.

The knock on the door caused my eyes to pop open. Shana had to be still here, otherwise, she would've awakened me to say she was leaving. Pulling the covers off me, I put my robe on and prepared to head to the front just as there was a knock on my bedroom door. When I opened it, Shana was standing there with Legend. I swallowed hard as he looked me from head to toe. "Hey, Harper."

"Hey."

Shana left us standing there as Legend approached me and drew me in his arms. I wrapped my arms around his neck and hugged him back. "Is it okay if I stay in here with you, or would you rather we went up front?"

I looked at my bed, and although that was where I wanted to be, I knew it was dangerous to be there with him. "We can go up front."

He nodded then backed away from me and headed to the front with me behind him. Shana was gathering her things to leave. She stopped to hug me. "I'll call you later, okay?"

"Okay."

"I also left you a plate of pancakes, bacon, and eggs in the microwave if you want it."

"Thanks, Shana."

I sat next to Legend on the sofa as he stared at me. Letting my head drop somewhat, I averted my gaze to my hands and played with my nails. Gently, he rubbed my cheek with his thumb and pulled my face to his. After kissing my forehead, he held me close. The lump in my throat was driving me crazy. Once Shana left, he asked, "You okay?"

"No, but I will be."

"You loved him?"

"Yeah."

"Did he live here?"

"No. We never lived together. I'm sorry I didn't get dressed. I'm just not feeling the shit, honestly."

"What'chu apologizing for? I'm at the place where you're the most comfortable. No need to change that. You still look beautiful. I just don't like these bags under your eyes. That means you've gotten little sleep and have probably been crying quite a bit."

Just that from him, had the tears falling down my cheeks. I moved away to wipe the tears but he pulled me back to him. Kissing my forehead, he rubbed the back of my head. "I got'chu, baby girl. You gon' get through this."

"Legend, I have too much baggage right now. I'm still hurting from a broken heart. Why would you wanna be here for me?"

He took a deep breath, then laid his head back on my sofa. "I feel things for you that I ain't never felt for nobody. Even though you goin' through a breakup, I can't be complacent and let you slip from my grasp. I have to see where this will go."

I stared at him, in awe of how freely he expressed how he felt about me. It moved me to the point of grabbing his face and putting my lips to his. The way he pulled my hips to him had my body heating up with desire. His hands had slipped inside my robe and was squeezing my bare flesh. Slowly backing away from him, I decided to be truthful. "Someone like you has never been my type."

"Well, damn. I guess letting me down easy was out of the question."

I giggled. "I'm not letting you down. I'm trying to say that regardless of that fact, something inside of me wants you too. I just wanted to be sure that it wasn't because of what I was going through."

"I understand that, but I'm willing to be around while you work through that. Now c'mere."

He pulled me back to him and held me in his arms. Shortly after, I had to pull away from him. I felt like I was about to sweat, I was so hot. "If I take this off, will you behave?"

"Mmm hmm," he said as he looked me over and licked his lips.

"That didn't sound too convincing."

"That's 'cause I ain't convinced my damn self."

His eyes continued to scan my body as I stood and took off my robe. I had on a tank and extremely short pajama shorts. The minute the robe slid from my shoulders, Legend licked his lips again. "Damn girl. How you expect me to behave looking at all that?"

"Okay, well let me go change."

He stood to his feet and pulled me in his arms. "Hell naw, baby girl. Hell naw."

The way he gripped me almost made me cum on myself. I couldn't believe he turned me on the way he did. The shit was crazy, actually. "Legend."

That shit came out with way more passion than I intended. At the sound of me saying his name, his hands traveled to my ass. He cupped my cheeks in his hands, then kissed my neck. "Can all this be mine, Harper?"

Shit, he was driving me crazy. I put my hand at the back of his head, rubbing gently while my panties dampened. "Please, Harper?"

God, what was I supposed to say to that? He was driving me batshit crazy, and he loved every minute of it.

egend

"You not gon' answer me? I think I deserve one the way I got you sweating with barely no clothes on."

She leaned back to look in my eyes with a smirk on her lips. "Legend, can we just chill right now without definitions? I literally just broke up with Zaire yesterday."

"As long as we can spend time together, and I don't have to share you, we don't have to define what we have. Deal?"

She bit her bottom lip and looked at me under-eyed. "Deal."

I picked her up as she squealed. "Wrap them thick legs around me, girl. Quit tripping."

She did as I commanded, and I immediately felt the heat against me. Holding her ass in my hands, I kissed her neck once again, then her shoulder. "Legend, we can't go there. Please."

I let her slide out of my grasp. "I'm sorry. You just so sexy, it's hard to keep my hands and lips to myself.

She blushed. "I look a mess right now."

"You look extremely sexy right now."

"What makes you think so?"

Damn, she was making me hard. Her voice was barely above a whisper, and she was practically naked. On top of that, the way she was looking at me, had me leaking pre-cum. "You have that after sex look right now. Your hair is disheveled. You now have a satisfied look on your face, and your skin is glowing. Damn, you're beautiful."

"Legend, you're dangerously sexy. You make me wanna lose my shit every time I'm in your presence."

She put her hand to my cheek. I closed my eyes for a moment, enjoying her touch. "Please lose that shit then."

"I don't want to completely lose it until I know for sure I've gotten Zaire out of my system. That wouldn't be fair to you."

She was right, but I could fuck him out of her system right now if she'd let me. After she sat back on the sofa, I went to the kitchen and put a little heat to her food. "Come eat this, baby girl. Shana told me you ain't ate shit today."

She slightly rolled her eyes and met me in the kitchen. As she did, her phone chimed. I watched her look at it, then huff loudly, which caused me to assume it was her lil fuck boy. She sat at the bar and I sat her food in front of her as she tapped feverishly on her phone. Once she sat it on the counter, she looked down at the food, then stood. "What you need? I got it."

"It's okay, Legend. I'll get it. Thank you, though." As she got the syrup from the pantry and poured herself a glass of orange juice, she asked, "So, when's your next event?"

"In two weeks. The Easter Rodeo, but that's right in my backyard practically."

"In Beaumont?"

"I don't live in Beaumont. I live in Liberty."

She frowned. "How'd you get here so fast? Isn't that like an hour away?"

"Yeah, just about, but I was in Beaumont when you called. What you got going on this weekend?"

"I have a few orders this weekend, but I plan to get that done tomorrow."

"One of my boys having a crawfish boil out in Nome. You wanna come?"

"Sure, I don't see why not. You wanna meet since you'd have to pass it to come get me?

"Nope. I'm gonna come scoop you up."

"You must like to drive. What time?"

"It won't start until four, so I'll scoop you up about four."

She frowned like she was in thought. "I thought you said it started at four?"

"Have you ever been to a crawfish boil that started on time?" She laughed loudly, her mouth full of pancake. I laughed too. "That's what I thought."

"You have a house out in Liberty or do you stay in an apartment like me?"

"I have a five-bedroom house that I bought dirt cheap."

I'd bought the house from a man that had been trying to sell it but could never get it off his hands. By the time I came along, he was desperate as hell. He sold the house to me for $150 grand. It was appraised for almost twice that. Not to mention, it was on five acres of land. "Five bedrooms? Damn. That's kinda big for just you, huh?"

"It is, which is why I'm hardly ever there. It won't be that way forever though. One day, I'm gon' have a wife and kids."

"Oh yeah? How many kids you want?"

"I don't know. Two or three. As many as you want."

Her eyebrows had risen, then she giggled. "What do you mean as many as I want?"

"Well, I didn't think I was talking in riddles, Harper. I want however many kids you want. If you want five, then shiiid, we'll have five."

She laughed as I smiled at her. "So, you want me to have your legendary babies, Legend Semien? You don't even know me."

"I know enough. Legendary though? You might be on to something, girl."

Her phone chimed again, but she refused to look at it. She continued eating, but her mood had changed drastically. I sat next to her. "Naw, lil mama. I'm spending time with you right now. Ain't no other nigga gon' wipe the smile off your face while you with me. You need me to respond to that fuck boy?"

She looked to have gotten nervous for a split second. "No. I can handle it. If I need help, I'll ask for it."

I nodded my head. She'd gotten a slight attitude. I sat there quietly while she ate. I'd let her have that lil smart-ass remark, 'cause I knew she was in her feelings and shit. That was why she needed me to tap that ass, so she wouldn't be all uptight and shit. Standing from my seat next to her, I went to her fridge and grabbed a bottle of water, leaving her in the kitchen alone. I went to her sofa and waited for her to calm her ass down.

After hearing the emotion in her voice, I knew she needed me, whether she wanted to admit that shit or not. It was true that we didn't know each other. If we did, she would have known that I would've snatched her up for that lil comment and fucked her right there on that bar. I liked my women with a little spice, but don't take your frustrations out on me when they didn't have shit to do with me in the first place. I watched her from my peripheral as she kept turning in her seat to glance at me.

My phone started ringing, and it was this lil girl I'd been training to barrel race. Her dad was paying me to help her out in my free time. We'd gotten some work done the day before yesterday, and she told me she would call when she knew if she would have time to practice again before the week was over. "Hello?"

"Hey, Mr. Semien, this is Lacey."

"What's up, baby girl? You wanna practice?"

"Yes, sir. Can I come to today?"

"What time? I'm in Beaumont."

"Maybe about five? Is that too soon?"

"Naw, five is good. That gives me time to get home."

"Okay, good. See you at five."

"Aight, Lacey."

I ended the call, then finished my water. It was only one-thirty, so I didn't need to leave until four at the latest. I'd probably leave at three though, so I could get something to eat before going home. Before I could take another swig of my water, Red was calling. "What's up?"

"You still in Beaumont?"

"Yeah. You need something?"

"Yeah. Can you go to Tractor Supply and get me another brush and some horse spray? These fucking flies getting out of control around our babies."

He was referring to our horses. As soon as my stables were re-painted, I'd bring them back to my house. "I gotchu. See you about four."

"Aight."

I slid my phone back in my pocket as Harper sat next to me. She had her phone in her hand and was tapping away again. A tear dropped from her eye. Maybe she was right. She was too wrapped up in that nigga right now. Instead of hanging around, I stood from my seat. "Harper, I'm gonna go. Enjoy the rest of your day, okay?"

"Okay," she said, not even looking up from her phone.

I walked toward the door, somewhat in my pitiful feelings. "If you need me, call me."

I saw her head snap up, but before she could respond, I'd walked out. She told me she needed time, but I'd pushed her for more. I'd honor her wishes and quit trying to make her move on my time. I'd kill time with Red and whoever else until it was time for The Easter Rodeo. I was sure I'd find plenty to do. Before I could get to my truck my phone was ringing. Harper. "Yeah?"

"You mad at me?"

"Naw. I figured I'd just give you the time you asked for, instead of trying to force myself on you. Call me when you feel like talking. Aight?"

"Damn. Okay."

She ended the call. Why was she making it seem like I was being a certain way? I rolled my eyes and sat my phone on the console after getting in my truck. I went to Subway and got me a sandwich, then headed to Tractor Supply for Red. My damn feelings were all in my chest as I walked around the store, looking at unnecessary shit. Finally getting what he asked me to get, I grabbed another saddle pad, then headed to the register. "Oh God. You're Legend Semien, right?"

I turned to see a teenaged boy with his mouth open. I smiled slightly. "Yeah, that's me."

"I saw you at the livestock show in Houston. You are amazing!"

"Thanks. I appreciate that."

"Can I have your autograph?"

"Sure."

I signed his bag of horse feed with a permanent marker the clerk gave me, then headed to the truck. My phone chimed, alerting me of a text. It was Harper again. *I'm sorry.*

I responded, *Okay.* Then headed to Nome.

"Did Harper like the flowers?"

"Yeah, she did."

"But?"

"But what?"

"You seem a lil irritated. What happened?"

"Nothing. We sat around and talked for a little bit, then I left."

Red side-eyed me as he brushed one of our horses. "I know you. You too quiet."

"She still trippin' over ol' dude and kinda snapped at me. So, I left. She still needs time and she said that, but you know how I can get when I want something."

"Yeah I do, but I ain't never seen you that way with a woman."

"I know. You going to Trey's crawfish boil Saturday?"

"Yeah, I'm going. Shana coming with me. You bringing Harper?"

"I don't know. She said she would come, but that was before she got a lil snappy. So, I told her if she needed me, to call me. I'm not gonna force myself on her. She'll let me know when she's ready."

"So, what happens if she never calls?"

"Then I guess she wasn't ready for a real nigga like me. I gotta go. I have to meet Lacey at the house."

He shook his head. "Y'all both stubborn. Tell Lacey I said hello."

"Aight."

When I got to the house, I went inside to lay down for a minute. I'd been thinking about Harper so much, I was barely getting enough sleep. I had almost two hours until Lacey was gonna get here, so I set my alarm and took a much-needed nap.

arper

I'D PUSHED LEGEND AWAY. He was pissed, but he refused to say so. I didn't mean to come off so harsh, but Zaire was on my fucking nerves. In his first text, he'd asked if I was done with my temper tantrum. Then the second one, that mutha-fucka had the nerve to say I was going to regret my decision when I stopped behaving like a spoiled child. I was so damned mad, I'd snapped on Legend. That was why I wanted to wait before I tried to move on with him.

I'd texted Legend an apology, and he only responded with okay. I felt bad. Grabbing my phone from the sofa, I called him again, but he didn't answer. I heard him talking about meeting someone, so maybe he was busy. After cleaning the kitchen, I decided to take a shower, then get started on a couple of orders. Before I could get my ingredients to start baking, my phone was ringing. It was an unknown number, so I answered professionally. "Harper Richardson. How can I help you?"

"Hello, Ms. Richardson. This is Chandra Blake. I placed an order with you for next weekend, but it turns out I'm not going to need it. My sister had already ordered and paid for a cake."

"Aww. Okay, Mrs. Blake. I'll refund your deposit right now."

"Thank you."

She ended the call before I could respond. *What the fuck?* That shit hurt me to my lil' heart. That was a $600 order. Her deposit was $100. As I was refunding her money, what Zaire said to me crossed my mind. I hoped this wasn't his doing. Continuing to get my ingredients together to start on a German chocolate cake, my phone started to ring again. It was Shana. "Hello?"

"Girl, what the fuck you did to Legend? Red said he all in his feelings and shit. Legend a no non-sense type of nigga. So, for him to be all sensitive right now, means he feeling the fuck outta you."

"I kinda snapped on him. Zaire texted while he was here, and I got in a funk. He immediately noticed and said I shouldn't be letting another nigga wipe the smile off my face while I was with him."

"That nigga so damned cocky, but shit. He fine as hell, Harp. I can't believe you let that man walk up outta yo' place."

"I can't believe it either. He won't answer my calls now."

"Well, he training a lil' girl to barrel race. In his defense, that may be why he's not answering."

"I think Zaire is gonna try to destroy my business, Shana. I'm scared as hell. I've already had a customer cancel. He said he was helping my business more than I knew."

"Girl quit worrying about his bullshit. Get out there and start networking. You can start by coming to this crawfish boil with some sweets and business cards."

"I'm not going, Shana. Legend is mad at me, and I'm not strong enough to handle him right now."

"Okay, whatever. Well, I'll let you get back to whatever you were doing. I just got to Red's house."

"Okay. Bye."

I ended the call and thought about Legend. He made me feel so good, but my mind and heart weren't ready. My body had jumped in since day two. Why couldn't I just let Zaire go? He fucked over me like it was nothing. *Because you fell in love with him.* I wished I'd never met him. That shit hurt so bad because I'd been somewhat blindsided. Even with all those chicks in his inboxes, I still never really thought he was out there wildin' like that.

I slid the chocolate cake in the oven, then sat on my couch and tried to call Legend again. I needed him to hear me apologize. *He* needed to hear me apologize. Again, he didn't answer. I guess if he wanted to talk to me, he would call me back when he was available. Doing the next best thing when I was bored, I scrolled Facebook, then Instagram, trying to see what I could see. I decided to search Legend Semien and there were tons of pictures of him riding.

I guess I didn't realize just how big a star he was in the rodeo circuit. People were predicting him to win it all if he got the invite to Vegas. Several were pretty sure that he would get that invite. One said he'd recently been invited to the Bill Pickett Rodeo in Memphis right after Easter. That rodeo catered specifically to Black cowboys. Maybe if we were talking by then, he would let me go with him.

Once I'd gotten my cakes from the oven, I flipped them on the tray, then decided to go ahead and do the lemon tarts as well. After I put those in the oven, I began decorating the German chocolate. It was a three-layer, two-tier cake. I couldn't handle that much coconut, but whatever floated their boat. Just as I finished the filling for the layers, my phone was ringing. I ran to it hoping it was

Legend but was extremely annoyed to see it was Zaire. "What do you want?"

"You. I'm sorry, Harper. I was wrong. Please let me come over, so we can talk."

"What is there to talk about, Zaire?"

"About how we can move on from here... together."

"That's not gonna happen."

"Harper, how did you feel when we were together? Isn't that worth giving me another chance?"

I took a deep breath and closed my eyes. My main thoughts were my business. I couldn't lose my business... my independence... my livelihood. Keeping my eyes closed, I said, "Okay."

I felt like I wanted to throw up the minute I said it, and I could see Legend's face in my mind. "I'm on my way, Harper. I'll be there in about thirty minutes."

He ended the call before I could change my mind. I looked at the time to see it was nearly nine. Maybe this was the right decision. Everyone made mistakes, right? *Hell hah. You a dumb-ass broad for agreeing to let him come over.* I blocked out my voice of reason, then went to change into some sweatpants and a T-shirt. There was no way I'd be dressed scantily when Zaire got here. When I got back to the kitchen, I took my lemon tarts from the oven. My phone started ringing, so I looked to see it had only been twenty minutes. When I grabbed it, the butterflies in my stomach took flight. It was Legend. "Hello?"

"You called three times, Harper. What's up?"

"I'm sorry, Legend. I didn't mean to snap at you."

"It's cool. It's my bad for trying to rush you into something you aren't ready for. So, I apologize."

"I feel horrible."

"About what?"

"The way I talked to you when you were only trying to make me feel better."

"Harper, it's okay. I'll back off, so you can properly deal with your emotions without my interference."

"But..."

Before I could continue, there was a knock at the door. Zaire. "But what?"

"Nothing. I have to go."

"Aight. Take care."

That shit sounded like he was done with me. Period. He ended the call before I could even respond. Zaire knocked again, so I went to the door to see him standing there with a bouquet of roses. It caused me to look at the bouquet from Legend. He thought enough about me to find out what my favorite flower was. Zaire had never asked. He just always bought roses. I took a deep breath, then opened the door. A smile spread across his face as I stepped aside to let him in.

He handed the flowers to me and I walked to the kitchen to put them in water. I watched him look over the flowers that were sitting there. "Harper, thank you for allowing me to come over."

I nodded as I sat the flowers next to the bouquet from Legend. My heart sank. This wasn't who was supposed to be here. I sat next to Zaire, and he grabbed my hand. "I'm so sorry. There's no excuse good enough for what I did to you. I love you, and I don't want to be without you, Harper. I promise to do whatever it takes to make you happy and for you to trust me again. Trust is easy to lose and tough as hell to regain, but I'm going to work my hardest to show you how much you mean to me."

As badly as I wanted to believe him, my heart wouldn't allow it. The only thing my heart wanted was to heal itself from the damage he'd caused. It wanted me to move on. The problem was that my brain was working overtime trying to convince me to forgive him, so my business wouldn't be threatened. "I'm not sure that I can move forward in our relationship right now, Zaire. I'm willing to talk this out though and see where it goes."

"So long as I have a chance to make things right, Harper. That's all I ask."

I nodded, then allowed him to embrace me. That only made me want to throw up because I felt like I'd made a deal with the damned devil. "What are you baking?"

"I did a German chocolate cake and some lemon tarts."

"Do you have a lot to do tomorrow?"

"I have four cakes to do. I should be done early."

"You wanna go to dinner?"

"Okay. I'll call you when I get back home."

I snuggled deeper in his embrace and wrapped my arms around him. He kissed my head, then rubbed my back. "Who are the other flowers from?"

"One of Shana's friends."

"Oh. You like him?"

"He's cool."

"Just cool?"

"Yeah."

"I guess I shouldn't be worried then. I love you, Harper, and I promise I'm going to do my best to prove that to you."

"Okay, Zaire."

Did I believe him? Hell naw. But until I could figure out another solution for my business and successfully execute it, I would have to make him think that he had a chance. The problem with that decision was that by allowing that, I was pushing Legend further into the background, and that was eating me alive. A man like him wouldn't stay in the background long, if at all. I was afraid that if he ever found out that I was even entertaining Zaire, he would never answer my calls again. I'd practically lost him already, and he didn't even know that Zaire was here.

"Can I stay here?"

"I don't think that's a good idea right now, Zaire. I don't think I could handle it emotionally right now."

"I understand, baby. Well, I have to go. I have to be to work at eight, but I'm only working half a day. If it's okay, I'll come to meet you at the bakery tomorrow."

"Okay."

He stood from the couch and pulled me to my feet as well. He hugged me tightly, then pulled away slightly and tilted my head up to look in my eyes. Lowering his head, he softly kissed my lips. "I'll see you tomorrow, baby. Sleep well."

"Good night, Zaire."

The minute he left, I allowed the tears to seep from my ducts as well as from my heart. *You're stronger than this, Harper.* Truth was, I didn't feel strong at all at this moment. My phone alerted me of a text. I went to it to see that another customer was canceling an order for next month. Resisting the urge to throw my phone, I walked to the kitchen and covered my baked goods, then went to bed and cried out everything I felt I still had inside of me as I refunded yet another $100 deposit.

 **egend**

It hurt like hell to push Harper away, but I was doing it for my own good. Although that decision was tearing me apart on the inside, I knew I was saving myself from heartache. I'd never been in love, but the way Harper was digging deep on the inside of me without even trying, I knew me falling for her wouldn't take much time or effort. To tell her to take care at the end of that phone call made my heart drop. When someone said, 'take care', usually that meant that they had no intentions of seeing or talking to you anytime soon, if ever again. So, I knew she got the hint.

Today had been uneventful. After training with Lacey a little more this afternoon, I took a shower and hung around the house until Red called. "Hello?"

"What's up?"

"Nothing."

"There's a couple of guys here that are trying to get into promoting rodeos. They've already done concerts, but they wanted to talk to us about being a part of it since we know the ends and outs of it."

"Okay. What time and where?"

"He said to see if you could meet about six this evening at Pappadeaux's."

"That's cool. I'll be there."

"Legend, you aight? You don't sound like yourself."

"I'm good, just tired. See you at six."

I ended the call before he could try to dig any deeper for answers. I was still miserable for pushing away from Harper, and the shit was starting to unnerve me. I needed to find a diversion. Something to take my mind off her. Standing from the sofa, I drug myself to my room to get dressed just as my phone rang. It was my mama. "Hello?"

"Hey, baby. You still coming by?"

"No, sorry. I just got invited to dinner with some guys that want to promote rodeos. I'll come by tomorrow."

"Okay, baby. Legend, I hate to hear you in such a funk."

"It's cool, Ma. I'll be fine."

"I know. Well, enjoy dinner and see you tomorrow."

"Aight, Ma."

She and I had talked this morning when she called to see how yesterday went with Harper. After telling her my decision, she sympathized with me and said she hoped Harper would come to her senses. Unfortunately, I didn't have hope in that situation.

When I got to the restaurant, they were packed as usual. It was a Friday night, so I didn't know how we would be able to discuss anything with the noise. I called Red to see if they were seated and he directed me to where they were. When I reached them, I shook hands with the two gentlemen and Red, then took a seat.

As we were conversing, getting to know one another while waiting on our meals, a couple was being seated at the table right across from us. People were moving about so quickly, I didn't bother to look until I heard her voice. When I turned in her direction, our eyes met. Harper was here and with a date. The hurt and anger that filled my heart surprised the hell outta me. I didn't know if this was her ex or not, but I was about to find out. "Excuse me, gentleman," I said, standing from my seat.

When Red saw where I was going, he kept trying to get my attention, but I ignored him as I walked up to their table. "Hello, Harper. How are you?"

Harper's milk chocolate complexion was fire engine red from embarrassment. "Hello," she said softly.

Her date was sitting there with a confused look on his face. It was only making me angrier that Harper wouldn't even look at me. "I'm sorry. I didn't mean to be rude. I'm Legend."

I extended my hand as a smirk surfaced on his lips. "Nice to meet you. I'm Zaire."

She was back with her ex. This was the shit I was glad I avoided. I nodded my head at him, but before I could leave, he decided to continue talking. "So, you sent her the flowers yesterday."

I looked over at Harper and she kept her head down. Returning my attention to her fuck boy, I smirked. "Yeah, that was me."

He nodded but didn't say anything else. Again, looking back at Harper, I said, "It was nice to see you again."

"Nice to see you again, too."

She still didn't look at me, and everything in me wanted to snatch her up out of her seat. Instead, I walked away to go cool off, with Red not far behind me. Once I got outside, I heard Red yelling at me. "Legend!"

"What?"

"Who was that she was with?"

"Her ex. The same mutha-fucka that fucked around on her."

"Damn. Shana didn't tell me they got back together."

"I'm glad I dodged that bullet."

"I'm really surprised. She didn't seem like the type that would put up with the foolishness."

He squeezed my shoulder, then made his way back inside as I sat at a bench outside for a minute. These emotions running through me were about to drive me crazy. Once I felt like I had my shit under control, I walked back inside to see that my entrée had arrived. I apologized to the promoters and did my best not to look in Harper's direction again.

After the waiter boxed my food, I saw the fuck boy leave their table. When he did, I felt my phone vibrate in my pocket. I refused to even look at right now because I knew it was Harper. Looking at her right now would make me sick. I knew if I read whatever message she'd sent, it would cause me to look at her. All that shit she said she was feeling for me, might as well had been lies. It was like last weekend had been a dream. A high that I had no choice but to come down from.

I had only heard bits and pieces of what the promoters were talking about. Giving them my business card, I stood from the table to leave, because I couldn't stand being that close to Harper and ignoring her. They understood that I had to leave and had no qualms about it since the meeting was last minute anyway. When I turned to leave, I caught a glimpse of Harper and Zaire holding hands and my face twitched in anger. Before I could walk away, I heard, "Nice meeting you, Legend."

Everything in me wanted to fuck this dude up for hurting her, but at the same time, she was choosing to be hurt now. I looked their direction and my eyes met hers as I nodded, then walked out.

"Hey, Legend. How you doin', Daddy?"

"I'm good, lil mama."

The crawfish boil was crazy packed. Instead of having it at his house, Trey decided to use an open field on the main road. Women were everywhere and none of them seemed to be shy about speaking. I surely wasn't shy about speaking back. I felt a lot better today, and hopefully, I'd feel even better tonight. As I eased through the crowd toward some of my acquaintances, someone yelled my name. Turning around, I saw Shana trying to get to me. I took a deep breath. Harper was not going to be a topic of conversation today. When I got home last night, I'd deleted her text without reading it. I could see that the opening line was, I'm sorry. The apologies for shit she wanted to do was unnecessary and pointless. When Shana finally got to me, she hugged me tightly. "What's up?"

"Not too much. What'chu up too?"

"Ready to get into these mudbugs. I hadn't had any since last year."

"Me either."

She looked in my face, and I believed she could tell that I didn't want to talk about Harper. Nodding her head, she started to walk away from me. "See you later."

"Aight."

When I got to Red, I slapped his hand, along with a couple of other guys he was standing near. Before I could get involved in the conversation though, this fine ass female walked up to get crawfish. I think the conversation had ceased, 'cause everybody's eyes were on her. When she'd scooped enough out the cooler, she looked over at us, her eyes shifting from one person to the next until they landed on me.

I stared right back, then looked her from head to toe. "Hey, Legend Semien."

"What's up?"

"You."

I bit my bottom lip, then walked closer to her. "Oh yeah? I wouldn't mind being down."

She walked closer to me, holding her crawfish out to the side. "I'll dump this shit on the ground right now. Don't tempt me, legend in the making."

"Don't do that. Eat your crawfish. We got all night for you to back up that shit-talking."

"I don't shit-talk. Straight facts."

"We gon' see later. What's yo' name?"

"Amina."

"Okay, Amina. Holla at me before you leave."

She walked her fine ass away from me, and I couldn't help but lick my lips. She was thick in all the right places, and that ass was hanging out them shorts she had on. Just as I was about to go back to the fellas, I saw Shana staring at me. I didn't know what she was eyeballing me for. Legend Semien could do what the fuck he wanted. I raised my eyebrows at her, indicating that I was questioning why she was staring at me. She shook her head, then walked away.

I'd drunk a six pack of Dos Equis and had gone to Betty's Liquor across the railroad tracks to get some Hennessy. When I got back, I could see lil' mama looking for me. After giving up, she nearly ran right into me. "You was looking for me?"

"Yeah. I'm going to my girl's house to shower and change. She live right over there."

She pointed to one of the houses across the field, and I nodded. "I'll be over there in an hour."

"Okay."

I watched her sashay off with her friend as Red approached. "Back in the saddle."

"Shut up, Red."

"I'm just saying. My boy getting back to normal. I didn't know how to handle you earlier this week."

"Yep. Back to business as usual."

I got another round of crawfish and ate in peace with the dwindling crowd. Earlier, people were approaching me left and right, congratulating me on the livestock rodeo and asking if I was going to the Easter Rodeo. I was ready to get outta Texas for a minute. The Bill Pickett Rodeo was in Memphis and was in a little over two weeks, right after the Easter Rodeo. If I won the Bill Pickett, that would seal my invitation to the nationals in Vegas.

As I drove in the driveway across the way, lil mama came out of the house. Shit, I couldn't remember her name. Oh well. It didn't matter, really. She hopped in my truck with a smile on her pretty face. "We going to your house?"

"Naw. I'm going get a room."

"Oh."

She looked disappointed, but I didn't bring random women to my house. Actually, only one woman had been to my house. That was only because I didn't feel like leaving. She and I had been fucking around on and off for a while though. This chick, I didn't know her ass from Eve. Ain't no way I was taking her where I gotta lay my head. I always kept a change of clothes in my truck. That was just the life of a cowboy.

When we got to Best Western, I noticed she kinda turned her lip up a little. I started to act like I didn't see her, but the type of nigga I was wouldn't let that happen. "You gotta problem with Best Western?"

"No, I'm cool."

I jumped out the truck with my change of clothes and she did the same. After paying for the room and we'd gotten inside, I went to take a shower. Smelling like crawfish wasn't exactly sexy. While washing up, Harper flashed through my mind. Closing my eyes, I ran my hands down my face. She chose to go back. Why was I tripping?

When I got out, I peeked out at ol' girl and she was sitting on the bed waiting for me. My phone started ringing and I looked at it to see Red's number. I'd call him later. Not bothering to put on clothes, I walked out into the room, and her eyes widened. "Damn Legend. Let me find out if that shit a legend in the makin'."

She licked her lips as he hardened, then took off her clothes. Damn, she was fine as fuck. She walked over to me and tried to kiss me. That shit couldn't happen though. I forced her to her knees, and she grabbed my dick and stroked it a couple of times, then deep throated it. Allowing my head to drop back, I closed my eyes and bit my bottom lip, enjoying the feel of her warm mouth. I opened my eyes and looked down at her while she worked, jutting my hips forward.

As she continued to slob on me, I realized her dick sucking skills were trash. The longer she went, the worse it got. Almost to the point where I was starting to go down. I pulled my dick out of her mouth, then pulled her from the floor. Pushing her to the bed, I grabbed the condom I'd brought in from my truck. After I strapped up, she frowned at me. "You not gon' go down on me?"

"Naw. Ain't no protection for my mouth."

"But I went down on you."

"And? What the fuck that got to do with me?"

"Nigga..."

"You know what, let's just kill this all together."

"Yo' dick not even hard right now, anyway."

"That's cause yo' head game is wack. You ain't shit but a buckle bunny anyway."

I grabbed my clothes from the counter while she sat there stunned. We called hoes that chased us buckle bunnies. If you had a winning buckle, they was all on a nigga dick. Just like those damned groupies that followed other entertainers, like rappers and other professional athletes, them damned buckle bunnies did whatever it took to get them some rodeo dick. "Let's go, before I leave yo' ass."

I was so fucking frustrated, I should've just left her ass right there. Now, I was really thinking about Harper. I had to be honest with myself. I needed her.

arper

"You were acting like you were scared to look at him, Harper. Did something happen between you two?"

"No. He just likes me a lot, and I didn't want him to think I was into him."

There was no way I was going to reveal to Zaire that Legend and I had any type of connection. When I saw him at Pappadeaux's, I could have shit on myself. He looked so good, and I could tell by his eyes, that he still wanted me. He would have been able to tell that by my eyes if I would have kept looking at him. He never answered my text, so he probably just deleted it. I was trying to tell him why I was there with Zaire.

Zaire opted not to come in, and I couldn't be happier that he dropped me off and left. I took a shower and wished I was with

Legend, lying in his arms, feeling his tender kisses on my lips, neck, and shoulders. The way he made me feel was something I'd never forget. Was keeping my business worth me being miserable? Right now, it was, but I'd have to figure out something soon.

When I woke up, the first thing I thought about was the crawfish boil. I really wanted to go, but there was no way Legend would want to see me after last night. I grabbed my phone and called Shana. She and Red were getting along really well, and she was so happy. I was happy for her. This had been a long time coming. She'd never really had a boyfriend. Shana answered the phone on the first ring. "Hello?"

"Hey, girl."

"Hey, Harper. How are you?"

"I feel like I'm dying, Shana."

"I know. Why did you take him back, Harp? Truthfully."

"He threatened my business. I've had three cancellations already, and they were big orders."

"Oh, baby girl. I'm sorry."

"I can't lose my business. I'm losing people before I can even gain any. I need to build my clientele."

"Come to the Easter Rodeo. Bake something really good, cut it in squares or bites, put it in zip lock bags, and bring that shit to the rodeo and give it away with your business card."

"That's a good idea, Shana, but I can't."

"Why nooot?" Shana whined.

"Zaire met Legend last night."

"What?" she yelled.

"Zaire came over Thursday night, and he saw the flowers from Legend. So, when they met at the restaurant last night, they knew who each other was. Legend came right to our table and introduced himself to Zaire."

"Oh my God. Did you tell Zaire everything about Legend?"

"No. I just told him that Legend was one of your friends that liked me."

"Damn, Harp."

"I know. I miss Legend so much. Shana, I think about him all the time."

"Damn, girl."

The tears left my eyes. I did everything in my power not to let them fall last night. *God, this was so hard.* "So, I guess you aren't coming to the crawfish boil then."

"No."

"Damn. Who I'm supposed to kick it with? I'm gon' be bored as hell out there."

"Shana, how is he?"

"He's been miserable, girl. He don't know what to do with himself."

Damn. I sighed deeply. "Well, I gotta go. I have to go to the bakery for pick-ups."

"Your assistant couldn't be there today?"

"I had to let her go. I'm gonna be short $1,500 next week."

"Shit! Harper, why don't you talk to Legend about this?"

"I texted him last night, but he never responded. I was telling him what was going on."

"You want me to talk to him?"

"No."

"Okay. Well, I'll let you go. I love you, Harp."

"Love you too."

After ending the call, I got up and put clothes on to go to my bakery. I had baked and decorated all but one cake, and that was because they wanted fresh fruit in it. When I unlocked the door and went inside, someone came in behind me. I turned to see Zaire.

"You scared the hell outta me. I thought someone was about to rob me."

"I'm sorry. I needed to talk to you before I went into work."

"Okay. About what?"

I began getting fruit out of the fridge and everything I would need to decorate the strawberry cake. When I got back to the table, I looked up at him, waiting for him to spill whatever it was that he needed to speak to me about. It obviously couldn't wait. "I need you to bake a cake for a party my mom is having. I'm trying to get you more business, so you'll have to do it for free."

"I can't do that. I've had three cancellations for next weekend. I can't do any free cakes right now."

"It's for my mom, Harper."

"Your mother doesn't even like me, something I still hadn't figured out," I said as my phone rang.

"You're not gonna get that?"

I frowned. "Aren't we having a conversation? I'll check it once we're done."

"It may be that Legend guy."

"Come on, Zaire. You're the one that fucked up. Remember?"

"You will bake the cake for my mom's function, and I'll pay you."

"For what date, and how many people?"

"Tomorrow."

"Are you serious?"

"Yeah, and it's for fifty people. She wants a two-tier all white cake, inside and out, with intricate floral designs, and those diamond-looking, edible decorations."

"I can't do that on such short notice."

"You will do it, Harper. I begged her to let you do it."

"Zaire..."

"No more 'I can't'. I need to hear an 'I can', Harper."

I wanted to stab him with this knife. "Okay. Leave me alone so I can at least get the cake baked today. I'll have to go to Hobby Lobby to get some decorative, edible beading."

"I knew I could count on you."

He kissed my cheek, and I wanted to throw up. I usually didn't work on Sundays. Thursdays and Sundays were my days to rest. I finished decorating the cake I was working on because they were my first pick-up for the day. After getting it boxed, I heard the door close, so I went out front. "Hi, we're here to pick up a strawberry cake."

"For Melba?"

"Yes, ma'am. That's us."

One of them had on a cowboy hat, and it only made me think of Legend. I walked to the back to bring the cake out front, and I heard them say something about a crawfish boil. When I came back up front, I asked, "Is the crawfish boil in Nome?"

"Yes, ma'am. You coming out?"

"No, but my cousin is. We were just talking about it this morning. Her name is Shana."

Neither of them knew her. They were trying to figure out who she was though, so I said, "She's been talking to Red."

"Oh okay, yeah. I saw her out in Nome one day with him."

We made more small talk and they invited me to come out, then they left. If only I could. If I wouldn't be kissing Zaire's ass, I would be getting picked up at four for a crawfish boil that started at four.

After baking the cakes for Zaire's mother's shindig tomorrow, I locked up for the day. I'd come in tomorrow to decorate it. It was gonna take me a couple of hours to decorate that damned cake. I headed to Hobby Lobby to get the edibles, then went home to sulk.

Once I'd taken a shower and got in bed, my mind went to Legend. My mind stayed on Legend. I didn't know how I accomplished anything throughout my day. Constantly, I'd find myself in a daze, thinking about his touch or his rude remarks. Grabbing my phone, I looked through the pictures I'd taken at the livestock rodeo, wishing I could go back there. There, I didn't have a care in the world.

It was already ten and I wasn't tired, so I tried calling him, but he didn't answer. How was I gonna get him to talk to me if he wouldn't answer the phone or read my text messages? I sat my phone back on the nightstand, then rolled over to try to get some sleep. That didn't last long though. My phone was ringing. I hopped up, hoping it was Legend calling me back. Unfortunately, it wasn't. It was Phoenix. "Hello?"

"Hey, Harp. How are you?"

"I'm okay. You?"

"I'm good. I just wanted to check on you. I hadn't heard from you since you first got back home a week ago."

"I broke up with him, but that didn't last long."

"What?"

"We're still talking, Phoenix."

"Umm okay. So why go through investigating him if you weren't going to leave?"

"I just chose to forgive him."

"This doesn't sound like the Harper I know. You've always been a strong, no nonsense type of woman, especially when it comes to your personal life. I remember when you were dating poor Tyler in school. You found out he lied to you about something and you let his ass have it, then broke up with him. So, be straight with me."

I closed my eyes, then took a deep breath. Phoenix was my friend, but I didn't want him to try to get involved in this mess I was going through. He was already involved enough. I also knew he wasn't going to leave me alone about it until I told him the truth. Phoenix knew me as well as Shana did, and she'd known me my entire life.

"He's killing my business. Clients that I thought were loyal customers are canceling orders. I'm already at a loss for next week. I should have had a $2,000 profit."

"What?"

"Yeah. I've had three cancellations. I only have one order for next week. I've been holding my breath, hoping they don't cancel on me. It's a huge benefit at the hospital and this order has a $400 deposit. The total cost for their order is $1,200."

"Damn. So, you're staying with him to stay in business. Harper, I live alone. Don't let him muscle you into thinking you don't have options. You can always move in with me or Shana until you can get back on your feet. I know you don't like depending on anybody, but that's what we're here for."

"You're right, I don't like depending on anyone. Y'all have lives and livelihoods to concentrate on without worrying about my shit. I'll figure something out, Phoenix."

He exhaled loudly. There was no way I could live with Phoenix. Although we were friends, I wouldn't feel comfortable. "Promise me, Harper, that you won't let this go too far. Promise me that if you feel yourself drowning, you'll reach out for a lifeline."

"I promise."

"Okay. Well, I'll let you get some rest. I love you, Harp."

"Thanks, Phoenix. I love you too."

I ended the call and silently prayed for direction. My business depended on the elite and businesses that needed my services for meetings, banquets and what not. It wasn't like I could depend on the everyday, working customer. Those type of people only ordered from me for special occasions. I had a bank that ordered from me twice a month for their meetings and another company that ordered monthly for their safety meetings. Those were the kind of clients I needed.

I woke up at six, got dressed, and hauled my ass to the bakery to finish that damned cake. As soon as I walked in, Zaire was calling. "Hello?"

"Damn, Harper. Are you still sleeping?"

"No. I'm at the bakery."

"Okay, good. I'll be there at ten to pick it up."

"Alright."

I ended the call only for him to call right back. I rolled my eyes. He sucked the fucking energy out of me. "Yes?"

"I love you, Harper."

"Okay. Bye."

I couldn't fathom saying it back. While I still loved him, I couldn't verbalize that without the bile filling my throat. Uncovering the cake, I began visualizing how I would do this detail, then began making my icing.

When Zaire got here, I'd just put the finishing touches on it. He walked closer to it like he was inspecting my work. I literally wanted to push his face right in it. "She should love this. You did a good job, Harper."

My eyes narrowed as he kissed my forehead. I just wanted to go get back in bed. We boxed the cake and he left to deliver it. *Mama's boy.* After cleaning my mess, I went straight home. My bed was calling me. That all came to a screeching halt though when my phone rang and the caller ID said, Legend Semien. My heart was beating out of my chest and heat flushed my entire body.

"Hello?"

"Good morning, Harper."

"Good morning. I'm surprised you called me back."

"Well, you been blowing a nigga up, so I thought maybe you needed something."

I even missed his sarcasm. "I needed to explain."

"Harper, you don't have to explain anything to me. Okay?"

"But I feel like I need to, Legend."

"Listen. Will your explanation make you mine?"

I wanted to cry, but I refused. Tears wouldn't change the horrible truth. I was too proud to start my life over. "No. I'll stop bothering you, Legend."

"Harper..."

"God, I'm sorry I got you involved in all my shit. I'm just... never mind. Bye Legend."

I ended the call, then laid in my bed and stared at the ceiling for a while. Accepting my plight, I rolled over and pulled the covers over my head to go to sleep.

14

egend

"HERE COMES *the legend in the makin'! I hope y'all ready for a show! Leeegeeeend Semieeen!"*

I didn't know how I always got a bull that wanted to put on a good show, but I was grateful. I had to ride an additional second or two before I could dismount. The way he was spinning, made it difficult. When I made it off, the crowd was screaming their approval as I ran to the gate. ***"Another great ride for Legend Semien, with a score of 88.3!"***

I was happy with that. I needed to crack ninety. The Houston Livestock Rodeo was the closest I'd gotten. As I walked towards the chute, Red shook my hand. "That ought to seal the buckle for you."

"Yep. Now I gotta get ready for The Bill Pickett. If I win there, I think that'll guarantee my appearance at the nationals."

"I believe you right about that. Umm..."

He looked off like he was nervous about what he wanted to say. "What?"

"That chick you left with two weeks ago from the crawfish boil..."

"What about her?"

"Word around town is that she tested positive for HIV."

"Well, I guess it's a good thing I didn't fuck her."

He took a deep breath and blew out his relief. "Shit. Thank God. You gon' have to slow down on these fucking buckle bunnies, Legend."

"Yeah, I know. She sucked my dick for a couple of minutes though, so I'm still gon' get tested just to be safe."

"Please do. Why only a couple of minutes?"

"'Cause that shit was trash."

He chuckled. I walked off and got something to drink, and thanked God for altering my plans that night. The Easter rodeo had been in full swing. Everybody was putting on a show for these people today. There were three more riders after me, so I hung around to wait on the outcome. I'd come in here with blinders on today. Red didn't have to worry about these bunnies, no more. After that hoe tried to clown me, that was it.

It didn't help that I'd talked to Harper that next day. She got me all in my fucking feelings again. Knowing she was with that bitch-ass nigga didn't sit well with me. It felt like something shady was going on, but that wasn't my business. Harper had made her decision. I wanted to call her back after she'd hung up on me because my curiosity was getting the best of me about this explanation. What was there to explain? She'd chosen him. Period.

Heading to my truck after another first-place win, Shana caught up with me. "Hey, Legend. Congratulations."

"Thank you."

"Umm, I know you don't wanna talk about Harper, but I just want you to know that it's not what it seems."

"Then what is it?"

"I can't say. She would kill me if she knew I told you this much. So, try not to hold it against her. She misses you so much it's breaking *my* heart."

What the hell could it be, if it wasn't what it seemed? "I'll call or text her after the Bill Pickett. You riding out there with us?"

"Yep. I took vacation time to make sure I could go to Memphis to see you give that bull hell. Hopefully, next year Red will get invited."

"Aight then. If he keeps performing like he's been doing, he will."

She hugged me. "See you in a couple of days."

"Okay."

I got in my truck and just sat there for a minute. What was going on with Harper? My curiosity was piqued, but I couldn't call her right now. I needed my mind to stay calm for the next few days. Dealing with drama would have to wait until afterward. It was imperative that I did well, so I was shutting myself off from everyone but Red. He knew the drill. Last year was my first time to be invited, and I barely placed third. That wouldn't fly this year.

The more points I got, the better my chances were at making the nationals. So, anything less than first place for me was unacceptable. Bill Pickett and nationals weren't rodeos that you could just pay an entry fee to attend. The Bill Pickett was invitation only and for nationals, only the top scorers made it. Nothing was gonna get in the way of me turning the fuck outta the Bill Pickett.

❧

"You finally outta seclusion, huh?"

"Yep. I'm ready."

I got in Red's truck to see Shana in the backseat. She waved at me as she held the phone to her ear, so I gave her a head nod. We were about to take a nine-hour drive to Memphis. The past two days, I'd been practicing and meditating. I hadn't even talked to my parents until this morning. They wished me luck and my mama prayed for me. She even said the bull riders' theme in her prayer. *Ridin' on faith.* She was so nervous, and I could hear it in her voice. That was why I usually didn't talk to her before I rode, but I didn't know if I would have time tomorrow.

It would be late when we got to Memphis tonight, and the competition started tomorrow. I surely didn't want to talk to her tomorrow. She would be even more anxious than what she was this morning. Shana was in the backseat talking softly, so I knew she was talking to Harper. After Red checked his connections once again to the trailer, he got in. "Let's eat some road up."

When we got to Memphis and had gotten all checked in with the rodeo, I texted my parents to let them know we'd arrived safely. We stopped once for gas and to eat and that was it. I think we were all anxious to get here. Tomorrow was the big day and my nerves were starting to get the best of me. Red could definitely see my anxiety, so he reached in his pocket and handed me a blunt. I looked over at Shana. "Is this gon' bother you?"

"I'm around this rodeo shit all the time, so naw."

I chuckled a little bit, then decided to ask before I entered my cloud. "How's Harper?"

She took a deep breath, then looked up at the ceiling like she was trying to hold in her tears. "She's miserable, but she's so fucking hard-headed and independent."

"I'll call her tomorrow night."

I lit up and laid back on the sofa as she nodded and walked away. Inhaling, letting the herb touch my innermost parts, would have me sleeping like a baby tonight, and I couldn't wait. *Harper.* I couldn't think about Harper right now. *Harper.* She needed me though. I could feel it. *Harper.* It felt like she had a pull on my soul. She needed to let go right now though. At least until tomorrow night. *Harper.* I took another pull from the blunt and told my heart to shut the fuck up.

When I woke up, I took a shower, then got out the trailer to stretch and warm up. "You gon' need me today, Legend?"

I looked up to see Neffie's ass. She'd dick hopped her ass all the way to Memphis. She was on somebody's dick for her to even be here, 'cause I knew her ass wasn't invited. I guess she'd forgotten that good cussing she'd gotten at the livestock show. "Hell naw."

"Whatever."

She kept walking. Good for her ass. I wasn't trippin' when I said I was done with fuckin' around with these gold-diggin' skanks. I wanted Harper. *Shit!* I couldn't be thinking about her ass right now. As I stretched, I watched the women walk by, watching me. It was like Satan enacted a plan to immediately make me go against what I'd said. Women were a weakness of mine, especially at the rodeos, because they were always ready to give out some ass. There were always plenty of trailers around to fuck inside of.

Once I finished warming up, I went back inside to cook some breakfast. Bull-riding was always the last event, so I had time to rest, get my spirit right, and my mind focused on what I came to do. I scrambled some eggs, made toast, and cooked bacon. Before long, Shana and Red came out of their room, looking sexually satisfied and shit. "You made enough for us?"

"Yeah," I mumbled.

Neither of them responded to me, just kept staring at each other like they'd cut their session short or something. *Harper*. I took a deep breath, then went outside to eat. Just watching them was making my mind go places it shouldn't. I needed to stay clear and focused.

"The Lord is my light, and my salvation; whom shall I fear..."

Red was quoting my scriptures all the way to the chute. I'd smoked two blunts today and had a glass of Hennessey. I should be good to go. Most of my gear was on, except my helmet. "Put on the whole armour of God..."

I kissed my cross around my neck, then slid my helmet on. ***"This man has been convincing us all year that he's a legend in the makin'! Tonight, he'll be riding Jesse James, the rankest bull on the planet. He's gotten the bucking bull of the year for the past three years! So, I hope y'all ready to see heaven meet hell in this matchup! Legeeeend Semieeeen!***

I slid down the chute and onto the bull. That mutha-fucka was already bucking, ready to let me have it. He was gon' be in for a rude awakening though. I was ready like a mutha-fucka too. After getting a good grip on the rope, Red tightened it some more. "Ready?"

I nodded my head and threw up my left hand. Once that gate opened, he took off. He spun around, nearly pinning me between him and the gate. *Oh yeah, mutha-fucka?* I started spurring the fuck out of him as he bucked. I could feel the strain on my back, but I was hanging on 'til that fucking buzzer sounded. He took another turn, that almost caught me slipping, but somehow, I was able to keep my balance and hang on for dear life.

Just as the buzzer sounded, I was ready to dismount, but his ass took me on another spin. I hung on through it, riding for another couple of seconds, then dismounted. That was the most painful ride I'd ever taken. Before I could get on my feet, Jessie James decided he wasn't happy with me. He turned right toward me as the clowns ran in my direction. It was too late though, 'cause he kissed me right in the face.

15

I was tired of fighting to keep my sanity. This shit was so hard. That bitch told Zaire that my cake was dry and that she would never recommend me to anyone. He came to my apartment saying that I'd fucked the cake up on purpose. That bitch was lying. After I'd made my cuts, I tasted the cake my damned self, and it was perfect. I couldn't understand for the life of me what she had against me. I'd been respectful each time I was in her presence and dressed appropriately.

When I told him that she was lying, he yelled at me. Zaire never yelled. Lucky for me, since I knew she would probably do something like that, I saved pieces of what I'd trimmed off. When I shoved it in his mouth, he was about to curse at me but got sidetracked. Then he proceeded to say how good that was and how I should've baked his mother's order that way. I went the fuck off and screamed at him that he was eating his mother's order.

I'd only seen him twice since then and that was over two weeks ago. My business was dying, and I was so depressed about it, I couldn't focus on anything else. I only had ten grand saved up, and I had to use some of it to pay this month's rent at the bakery and at my apartment which had taken three grand. In the past three weeks, I'd only profited $900, and I'd used it to pay my car note and other bills.

I had to mentally prepare myself to accept the fact that I would have to live with Shana for a while. My mama lived in Lake Charles, but I wasn't trying to leave Texas. We weren't really all that close anyway. I'd lived with my daddy growing up until he died when I was fifteen of a brain aneurysm.

Just as I finished eating my homemade cheeseburger, and cleaned my mess, my phone rang. When I looked at it to see Shana's number, I figured she was calling to tell me about Legend's ride. I knew this rodeo was a big deal for him. It was an all-Black rodeo that traveled across the country. "Hello? How did Legend do?"

"Harper."

She was crying. My body stilled as I waited to hear what she would say. Shana wasn't a crier. "After Legend dismounted, the bull hit him in the face, head-on. The impact knocked off his helmet and he's unconscious."

"Nooo! Oh my God!" I screamed.

"They just put him on a stretcher and his body is so limp."

I couldn't stop the tears from falling from my eyes. Life was too short, and I was tired of wasting mine. Legend could die, and I'd missed the opportunity to know what it felt like to be his. My body felt like it wanted to crumble, but I needed to get to him, even if it was too late. "I'm about to get a flight. I'll call you when I know what time I'll arrive."

"Okay. I'm running to meet them. Pray Harper. This doesn't look good."

"I am."

I ended the call and quickly packed a bag. My savings be damned, I was going to Memphis to see about Legend. Just as I finished packing and was about to head out, there was a knock on the door. *Fuck!* I opened it to see Zaire standing there. He frowned, then asked, "Where are you going?"

I watched him look down at my luggage, then back to my tear-stained face. "Legend got hurt. They don't know how severe it is, but he was unconscious."

"What does that have to do with you?"

"I care about him. I lied to you about my history with him. We haven't had sex, but we've been intimate. I feel things for him that I never felt for you, and I'm tired of wasting my life away with you. My business is suffering anyway. I came to the conclusion that I will lose my business before I spend another minute of my time with you."

As I closed the door and locked it, he grabbed me by the arm. "You won't get rid of me this easy."

"Get yo' hands the fuck off me, Zaire."

He let me go, and I damn near ran to my car. I drove like a bat out of hell out of the parking lot. *Lord, please let him be okay. I need him to be okay. Don't die on me, Legend.* Those thoughts and prayers filled my heart and mind all the way to Houston to the airport. I prayed that there would be a flight leaving soon, and the Lord didn't disappoint me. There was a flight to Memphis leaving out in an hour. I purchased a one-way ticket because I could ride back with them.

I called Shana back. "Hello?"

"What are they saying, Shana?"

"Nothing yet, and it has me nervous as hell."

"The flight leaves out in an hour, so I should be in Memphis no later than ten."

"Okay. He won first place. His score was 91.2. He broke his personal best. I just pray he lives to see it."

"Legend's not gonna die! You hear me, Shana? Don't say that," I cried.

"Okay. I'll call you when I know something."

She was crying as much as I was. I was grateful that I'd eaten before she called because there was no way I could put food on top of these nerves now. *Legend, hang on. Please.*

When I landed in Memphis, I immediately called Shana. "Hello?"

"Shana, I'm in Memphis. Have they said anything?"

"He's conscious, but he's disoriented. He suffered a concussion."

"Thank God. Have y'all been able to see him yet?"

"We're waiting on the nurse to come get us."

"Okay. What hospital? I'm gonna call for an Uber, and I'll meet y'all there."

"Baptist Memorial."

"Okay."

When I ended the call, relief swept over me. I was so thankful that he was alive. *Thank you, Lord.* There was no way I was gonna risk not being in his life. Hopefully, he still wanted me there.

AFTER WALKING IN HIS ROOM, I nearly ran to him. No one else even mattered at that point. Getting to him was my main priority. He looked at me, but it was like he was trying to figure out what I was doing there. When I got close, I grabbed his hand. "Harper?"

It came out as a whisper. I was sure loud noises were bothering him as well as light since the lights were out in the room. "Yes," I said softly.

I leaned over and gently kissed his forehead as his hand went to my hip. I watched him close his eyes and tuck his bottom lip in his mouth. As I was about to walk away, he pulled me to him. "Stay right here, Harper."

He was in a lot of pain. I could see it all over his facial expressions. Doing as he asked, I stayed close to him and gently put my hand to his cheek as his eyes opened. "I was so scared, Legend."

"Shit, me too."

Red chuckled a little as the doctor came in. "I assume this is Harper?" The four of us looked at him with confusion written all over our faces. "The paramedic said when you came to, you kept asking for Harper."

Oh, that shit really had me in my feelings. The tears started to fall again. "Yes, I'm Harper."

He smiled, then looked at Legend. "How are you feeling, besides having a headache?"

"I'm okay. The light and loud noises make it worse."

"Good. We're gonna keep you overnight for observation and if all is well, you'll be discharged. Despite everything, congratulations on winning first place."

"Thank you."

He scooted over a little in the bed. "Get in, Harper."

I smiled softly at him, then took off my shoes. When I slid in, he wrapped his arm around me. His mouth was close to my ear as we laid there. "I can't let you go. Please put me outta my misery and tell me you won't let go of me either."

Facing him, I gently kissed his lips and put my hand to his cheek. "I'm here, Legend. I ain't going nowhere."

He smiled slightly, then laid his head against mine. "Congratulations on your ride."

"Thank you. I hit ninety."

I smiled as Red came to his bedside. "I told your parents that you would most likely get discharged tomorrow. So, they gon' wait until they hear from me before they come."

"Okay."

Legend pulled me closer to him, then kissed my lips again. Being in his arms felt amazing. I hated that he was in this predicament, but I was thankful that it brought me to him. "So, you gave that bull hell, huh?"

"Yeah. Pissed him off. He showed me who had the upper hand."

"Okay. Get some rest. We have forever to talk."

He smiled, then laid against me and went to sleep as Shana smiled at me. "Harp, y'all need each other. I'm so glad you're here."

"I made up my mind that I would swallow my pride and give in to what I was feeling for him."

I gently stroked his cheek as he took deep breaths with a slight smile on his face. Damn, I'd been dreaming about holding him like this for weeks. Red moved my suitcase to a corner, then stood next to me. "Looks like you gon' be staying here tonight, 'cause that nigga ain't letting you go no time soon."

"Shut up, Red," Legend whispered.

I thought he was asleep. Thankfully, he hadn't lost his sense of humor. Leaning to his ear, I said, "I'm never leaving you again."

"Good."

He softly kissed my neck, then drifted back off to sleep. I was curious to see if they recorded it, so I asked Shana in a soft voice, "Did you record it?"

"Yeah."

"Can I see it?"

"You may not be able to watch the end."

"Now that I know he's okay, I'll be fine to watch."

She lifted her eyebrows and shook her head slowly. "If you say so. I screamed when I saw it. So, try to contain your reaction."

When she started the video, Legend flinched in my arms. I had her mute the sound, even though the volume was low, to begin with. Legend was riding the hell out of that bull, but that damned bull looked like it was out for blood. No lie. I could see he was about to hop off but had to stay on a second longer. He looked to be in pain already when he hopped off. Then it happened. My hand went to my mouth as I watched him go limp. I would've had a heart attack had I been there. Jesus. The tears slid down my cheeks as I thanked God for that helmet he had on. Had it not been for that, he would've been dead.

With the strength of that bull and the force with which it hit Legend, it looked like his neck should've been broken. God. I didn't know if I'd ever be able to watch another competition. Although he would have to take a break for a while, I knew there was no way in hell he was gonna quit. Going to Vegas was his dream.

She watched me closely, then walked back to her seat. "I told you."

I kissed Legend's head softly, over and over again. God, I didn't know what I would have done if I would've lost him. "If being hurt gets me all this loving, I would have pretended to be hurt a long time ago."

I giggled softly. "Well, it's all yours now."

"All mine?"

"Yeah. You don't want it?"

"Oh, I want it, baby girl. I can't wait to show you how much I want it," he mumbled in my neck.

"Well, me and Shana goin' to the trailer. I ain't tryna see all that, Legend. You still in the hospital."

"Shut up, Red. You making my headache worse. Watch my playback. When you can take that shit, come talk to me."

Red rolled his eyes. "Stop talking, Legend. I don't want you to feel worse," I said as I gently rubbed his head. "Leave him alone, Red."

"Come on, Shana. I can see now, she gon' spoil his ass."

I kissed Legend's head and smiled at them. Red shook his head and came to the bed. "Seriously bruh, I'm glad you okay. I can't wait 'til you feel better, so we can celebrate that legendary ride."

Legend smiled as Shana kissed his cheek. When they left the room, Legend looked up at me. "Talk to me, Harper."

"About what?"

"What you wanted to explain to me."

"We'll talk about that later. Get some rest."

He laid on my chest, holding me tightly, then drifted off to sleep while my mind wondered what Zaire had in store for me when I got back.

16

egend

THIS RIDE WAS KILLING ME. All the bouncing from the road was killing my head. Louisiana needed to fix this shit immediately. The rodeo had been playing like a movie in my head. When I saw that bull coming straight to my face, I thought I was dead. The day before yesterday, I couldn't even remember what happened. I was still somewhat sensitive to loud noises and light, but that should get better as time goes on. What I hated the most was that I wouldn't be able to ride for a couple of months.

When I watched the video, I was proud as shit. That bull was all over the damned place, but I was giving him the business until he turned around and gave it to me. I cringed when I saw how my body fell like a sack of horse feed. Once I came to in the ambulance, they were all breathing sighs of relief. The paramedic said they couldn't wake me up, which was why I was already in the ambulance.

When Red told me my time, I wanted to jump off that gurney. I'd been dying to break ninety points, and I finally did it. Winning first place at the Bill Pickett was a big accomplishment, and I was glad I was able to hang on to win the title. Those points would look good added to my total. I just hoped I could get more points under my belt before nationals..

Things took a drastic turn for the better when Harper walked through that door. I was surprised to see she'd come all the way to Memphis to see about me. I thought she'd gotten back with her boyfriend. So, my first thought was how the hell did she come to Memphis without him? I wasn't in no shape to be trying to fight anybody. When she ran to my bed, it felt like God had sent me an angel, and I couldn't be more grateful. I hated that it took that incident to get her back to me, but hey, I wasn't complaining.

"Two more hours, and we'll be home," Red said.

Looking over at Harper, I could see the nervousness on her face. We still needed to talk about her fuck boy. I pulled her closer to me and took off my shades to look in her eyes. "What's up, Harper?"

"We need to talk."

"I know. When we get to town, we'll go to my house. Okay?"

"Okay."

"Don't worry. Everything's gonna be fine."

"How can you say that, when you don't know what all I have to say?"

"Because I got'chu. If need somewhere to stay, I got'chu. If you need some ends, I got'chu. I know you ain't one of them gold-diggin' skanks. If you need somebody to just hold you, I got'chu on that too. Whatever you need, Harper."

"You gon' make me cry."

She lowered her head and trained her gaze on her hands as she played with her nails. "Look at me, baby girl." I lifted her head by her chin. "This is normal. It shouldn't make you cry, you should expect it. If I'm supposed to be your man, why wouldn't I help you? I'm living the good life and my lady struggling? That shit don't even sound right. I'll tighten up that fuck boy too if I need to. Just not this week."

Harper giggled as I tickled her, then wrapped her arms around my neck. "Legend, you tryna make me fall for you, huh?"

"Hell yeah. No question about it."

I kissed her lips softly and allowed my tongue to explore her mouth. A slight moan left her lips, then Shana had to fuck our mood up. "Hell naw. Y'all ain't finna do that shit in here again. The last time y'all got hot and heavy back there, I saw way more than I wanted to see."

Harper ended our kiss with a smile on her lips, but neither of us said a word as Shana and Red cracked jokes about us.

We'd finally gotten back to Liberty. Before we got here, we stopped in Beaumont, so Harper could get her car. She and Shana followed us here. When Harper got out of her car, her mouth was open. I got that a lot when people saw my house. It was a traditional, two-story brick home. "Legend, this house is beautiful."

"Thank you. Come look inside."

I knew she would be impressed with the kitchen. It had two full-sized ovens and lots of countertop space in it. Since she was a baker, that alone would have her swooning. Grabbing her hand, I led her inside. She gasped the moment she walked in. Before I could show her around, she'd taken off without me as my parents walked through the door. "Legend, my baby. I'm so glad you okay."

"I'm aight, Ma. Stop that crying."

"We watched it on TV, and we both screamed. Legend, how you feeling?" my daddy asked as Harper came back in the room with us.

She had a smile on her face as I put my arm around her. "Ma, Daddy, this is Harper. Harper, these are my parents."

"Hi, Mr. and Mrs. Semien. It's nice to meet you."

My parents were grinning from ear to ear. I'd never introduced them to a woman. "It's nice to meet you too, sweetheart," my mama said. She continued, "You'd gone to Memphis with them?"

"No, ma'am. When my cousin called and told me about Legend getting hurt, I got a flight out to him."

"That was so sweet. Thank you for going to see about my baby."

Before I could even stop it, Mama had put her arm around Harper's arm and escorted her off. "This house is big enough to raise a family in."

That woman was something else. Daddy shook my hand and hugged me. I could feel a slight tremble in his embrace. He was scared. "I'd been trying to find footage online that maybe someone had posted. Before Red had even called, I saw it. Me and your mama were cheering you on. When that happened, we both screamed. I thought your mama was having a heart attack the way she clutched her chest. The way you fell out, sent a chill up my spine." He put his head down, then I saw a smile peeking out. "You got over ninety points, son. That ride was almost perfect. I'm so proud of you."

"Thanks, Daddy."

"So, she flew all the way to Memphis, huh? That's the same woman from the livestock show, isn't it?"

"Yes, sir."

"She's beautiful, and she seems really friendly. I hope it works out for y'all, so she can slow yo' ass down."

I shook my head slowly. My parents were something else. I looked around but didn't see Mama and Harper anywhere. Then I heard Harper and Shana laugh loudly. I could only imagine what my mama had said. They all walked back in the front room laughing as

Harper wrapped her arm around mine, similar to how my mama had done her. "What was so funny?"

"None of yo' damn business, Legend. That's between me, Shana, and my daughter-in-law."

Oh my God. They were so desperate. They were acting like I was damn near forty. Harper giggled as I rolled my eyes. "And she's a baker! I'm gonna have to hire her for 4th of July." She turned to Harper. "Harper, I'm usually up all night baking cakes the night before the fourth. We have a huge gathering for the fourth every year."

"Okay Rose, you ready? I think Legend is getting either antsy or embarrassed."

"I've been around y'all my entire life. If I'm still getting embarrassed at some of the mess that falls out y'all mouths, then I'm the one with the problem."

"Oh, so yo' slick ass tryna say we have problems?"

Harper covered her mouth, laughing at my mama. "Come on, Rose. We'll hem him up later."

Those two were something else. I pulled Harper in my arms. "You see what you have to look forward to?"

"I see. I love them already."

"Oh yeah?"

"Yes."

I started to go there, but I didn't wanna put her on the spot. I was about to ask, *What about their son?* "We're gonna go too, Legend. I'm tired as hell."

"Thanks, Red. Sorry I couldn't help you drive."

"It's cool, bruh. I'll check in on you tomorrow."

"Aight."

I hugged Shana and watched Harper do the same. Once everyone was gone, I grabbed Harper by the hand and led her to the family room. When I sat in my recliner, I pulled her down on my lap. "Now, we're all alone. I've been waiting for this moment since the other night."

"Have you?"

"Yep. So, tell me what's going on."

She took a deep breath and fidgeted. I put my hand atop hers, and she lifted her gaze to mine. "Zaire pretty much threatened to destroy my business."

I slowly shook my head as she continued. "Before I told him that we could work on us, I'd lost three clients, which cost me almost two grand. I don't want to lose my business, Legend."

"His picture gotta be next to the definition of fuck boy. So, he's the one that fucked up, but he's fucking wit' yo' business to keep you with him. If that's the case, why did you come to Memphis?"

"I'm tired of being miserable. I'd been thinking about it the whole day and mentally preparing myself to have to live with Shana when she called and told me about you. I figured that I would rather lose my business and be happy with you than to have it and be miserable."

"Damn. You willing to lose everything for me?"

"Yeah, but I won't be losing anything. I feel like if I have you, I'd be gaining the world."

"Shit, girl."

I pulled her to me and kissed her passionately, letting my hands slide down her back to her ass. Her words had me feeling like mush on the inside. I gently pulled away from her. "So, here's what we gon' do. Tomorrow, I'll call movers, and schedule to get your place packed up. You gon' move in with me and work on rebranding and marketing yourself. You don't need his help. If they canceling orders, then they ain't loyal customers. I don't care who introduced them to you. They weren't rocking with you anyway."

"I can't move in here, Legend."

"Why not, Harper?"

"I can't just live on you like that."

"Harper, what did we just talk about on the way here? You can't be stubborn about this. Let me help you. You were willing to stay in a fucked-up relationship to avoid losing his help. Give me that same courtesy. I'm gon' help you get out there. You hear me?"

"It's so sexy when you tell me what to do."

"Oh, it is, huh?"

"Yes."

"Well, I need you to straddle me right now."

She took off her shoes, then straddled me in my recliner. "Now what?"

"Put your lips on mine and kiss me with everything you got."

She did as I asked, and it felt like I got lost. Harper was everything I wanted and needed. I hoped she realized, that she was gon' be mine forever.

arper

It felt like Legend was my knight in shining armor. As much as I craved my independence, it felt overwhelming to have a man have my back like he did. Straddling him, giving him everything he'd asked for, I wanted more. I knew that he probably wouldn't be able to perform to the best of his abilities right now, though. Slowly pulling away from him, I held his face in my hands. His eyes were low, and I could see the desire in them. I could also feel his erection between my legs.

"Harper?"

"Yeah?"

"I want you, but I can't right now."

"Legend, I know. Just know that whenever you're ready, you don't need permission."

"Damn, girl. I'm gon' fuck you up. I hope you ready for all that."

"Beyond ready."

I stood from his lap, so I could get him to bed. We'd had a long day. Nine hours on the road was no joke. That shit could wear you out, so I could only imagine how he felt. Helping him keep his balance when he first stood, I held my hands at his waist. He looked in my eyes, silently saying all the things his lips weren't. I led him to his bedroom. His mama had shown me all around 'my' house. Shana and I hollered with laughter when she said, *Girl, this gon' be your house. Legend don't know what to do up in here. You gon' have to teach my baby what this love shit is all about.*

She was telling me that Legend loved me. Everyone close to him seemed to think so. They said Legend was different around me. "I need a shower, Harper."

Oh shit. How in the hell was I gon' wash him up with all that temptation staring me in the face? Instead of debating with him, I slowly took off his shirt. All that fine-ass, dark chocolate caused my breathing to go shallow. It wasn't my first time seeing him without a shirt, but fuck! I kissed his lips as I ran my hand down his stomach to his abs. This nigga was hiding a lot under those T-shirts and cowboy shirts. Stepping away from him, I went to the shower and got it started.

When I came back to him, he was standing in the same spot, but he looked somewhat disoriented. "Legend, you okay?"

"Yeah."

"You think maybe you should take a bath?"

"I'll sit on the bench in the shower."

"Okay."

I unbuttoned his pants and let them drop to the floor. The bulge in his underwear happily greeted me. I bit my bottom lip as he watched me closely. Sliding my hands in the waistband of his boxer briefs had me trembling and stretching them out to get them down over his erection had my ass sweating. *My God...* His shit was massive, and it felt like I was about to start drooling. Him placing his hand at the back of my neck brought me back to reality. "Come on."

Stepping out of his drawers, he followed me to the bathroom, then leaned against the vanity as I undressed. The way he looked over my body had me nervous as hell. He grabbed a couple of towels from the cabinet, then we got in the shower. *Jesus, this was hard.* And so was he. Standing under the shower head, he allowed the water to soak him, then he sat on the bench and pulled me between his legs. *God, he was beautiful.* I squirted some of his Old Spice shower gel into his towel, then began washing his upper torso.

The moan that escaped him as he rested his hands at my waist was one of satisfaction. As I washed his back, the gentle tug on my left nipple made me wanna sit on his dick with the quickness. This shit just wasn't fair! I felt like throwing a temper tantrum like a two-year-old. Looking at those full, tinted lips that were wrapped around my nipple had me wanting to cum everywhere. "Legend, you making me wanna ride your dick into the sunset."

He chuckled at my country innuendo, then grabbed my ass. I continued washing his back, then asked him to stand so I could wash his legs. His ass. His dick. Temptation was a mutha-fucka right now. I washed his muscled legs and feet as he rested his hand on my shoulder, helping him keep his balance. When I finished, he sat at the edge of the bench. I swear, he could probably wash his own dick. He just wanted to torture me.

I soaped it up, then began to stroke it with the soapy towel. Two could play that game. His eyes closed as I washed his genitalia. After rinsing him off, I grabbed his dick and began to stroke it. I yielded to temptation. "How does that feel, Legend?"

"Good as fuck, but you have to stop, baby."

"Aww, why?"

"The buildup is making my head hurt."

"Shit. Are you serious, Legend?" I whined.

"Unfortunately. I can do this, though."

He sat back down, then swiftly pushed his fingers inside of me. *Oh shit!* "Legend, oh shit."

I slowly grinded my hips on his fingers. That shit felt better than Zaire's dick. Legend was stroking the fuck out of my spot and I was already about to release. I wanted to sit on his dick so bad though. This would have to be my last time bathing him because a headache or not, his ass was gon' get it. Feeling the sensations that alerted me of my pending orgasm, I held his head against my chest. "Damn, girl. Let that shit go."

Even my fucking orgasm submitted to his power. It seemed like I came for minutes. My moans and lustful words seemed to be getting to him. When the wave subsided, I could see his dick was leaking. "Please? Just for a moment?"

He nodded as he sucked his fingers, so I stooped and took his dick into my mouth. The grip Legend had on my hair, was gon' give *me* a fucking headache. He must've realized how tight he'd grabbed it because he eased up and I sucked all that pre-cum out of him. "Okay, Harper. Fuck!"

He rubbed his hand over his face, and I could tell he wasn't feeling well. *Now I felt like shit.* I stood to my feet and gently rubbed his shoulders, trying to relax him. Once he loosened up a little, I helped him to his feet and out of the shower. After drying him off and getting his underwear on, we went to his bed and I draped the covers over him. "I'm sorry, Legend."

"It's okay. I want it too. Can you get me a pain pill? They're on the dresser. I have a mini-fridge over there with water."

I did as he asked, then kissed him good night. "You aren't leaving, right?"

"I'm not leaving you alone. I'm going back to wash up and put on PJ's."

"Okay."

Before I could step in the shower, my phone was going off like crazy. Zaire. He could kiss my ass. When the phone stopped ringing, I blocked his number. Tomorrow, I'd have to get Shana to bring me to the airport. My Camry was still there. I'd gotten Red to go to my apartment to get my Mustang, so I would have transportation until she could bring me. I wouldn't be surprised if Zaire had gone to my apartment and seen my Mustang was gone.

I got out of the shower and put on my PJ's. When I walked into the room, Legend looked to be asleep. I gathered my clothes and was about to go to the guestroom. Legend needed rest and I'd already made him feel worse by not being able to control my urges. "Harper?"

"Yes?"

"Where are you going?"

"I'm going to the guest room."

"Why?"

"So you can rest."

"C'mere Harper."

I sat my clothes on the floor and walked over to the bed. Stooping down, I stroked his cheek. "I'm here."

"No, I need you here," he said, patting the bed.

"But I've already caused you to hurt more."

"I caused myself to hurt more. I could have washed myself, Harper."

My mouth fell open as he chuckled. "I can't believe you. When you get better, you gon' pay for that shit."

He pulled me toward him, so I got in bed and let his embrace envelop me. I could still feel his erection on my ass. "You gon' get blue balls."

"I know, but I want you near me. I need to feel you next to me, so I know this is real."

I turned to him and kissed him softly on the lips. "It's so real, Legend. So real."

"So, you not just feeling sorry for me then, right?"

"Right."

"And when I introduce you to people, I can call you my lady, my girl, or my girlfriend. Am I right about that?"

"Well, you never really asked me to be your girlfriend."

"Lies. I asked if you were mine."

"What did I say?"

"You said, *I'm all yours, Legend. All yours,*" he said, trying to imitate my voice.

I laughed. "I am all yours. Are you all mine?"

"I wanted to be yours since before I made you cum on the dancefloor."

That night would forever be etched in memory. My inhibitions were non-existent. "Let's not talk about that night until you ready to give me what I can't get right now."

"What can't you get right now?"

"Quit playing, Legend."

"Say it."

"That monster dick. I see why you ain't scared to ride bulls."

"Yo' ass crazy."

"Yeah, but you like it."

"I do. I wanna love it."

He took my damn breath away, and I didn't know what to say in response. His facial expressions were so serious. The same way he looked when he was about to ride that bull, before getting his helmet all the way on. Lightly sweeping his thumb over my cheek, he licked his lips and asked, "You don't want me to love it? Love you?"

It felt like I'd melted in that damned bed from the fire between us. "Yes, I do. It just doesn't seem real. Legend, I just left a relationship, so I feel... I don't know."

"Rushed?"

"No. Gun shy? Scared maybe."

I put my head down, and he immediately lifted it. "I'm gon' prove to you that every nigga ain't like that mutha-fucka. I'm gonna make you fall in love with me, Harper. I ain't never been in love before, but I can feel that we're on our way there. I've never been so attracted to anyone like I am to you. I need you to trust me. Okay?"

"I trust you, Legend."

18

egend

MY HEAD WAS HURTING like somebody had fucked me up with a hammer in my sleep. I was still floating from those hospital meds yesterday. They'd damn near overdosed me since they knew I had a long ride home. Harper was still in my arms, her head on my shoulder. I shifted a little and she woke up. "Good morning, Legend."

I couldn't open my eyes just yet. The light shining through the blinds was bright. I'd forgotten to close them last night. When we got here, it was dark, so it slipped my mind. I could see how bright it was with my eyes closed. "Good morning, baby."

That came out as a whisper. She held my face in her hands and whispered back. "You feel okay?"

"No. My head is killing me."

"Okay. Should you eat before taking meds?"

"I don't know."

She eased out of the bed and went to the bathroom as I turned over. That shit hurt so bad, it felt like my brain shifted when I did. I had to grunt out the pain. When Harper walked out of the bathroom, she closed the blinds and the curtains. I opened my eyes slowly and stared at her. She came close to me. "Your eyes are puffy. I'm gonna get your medicine, then see what I can cook for breakfast."

"Call my mama. I don't have shit in here to cook. She'll bring some stuff over. Come lay with me."

"What's her phone number? I'll go out in the hallway and call her."

I gave her the number, and she went out to the hallway, closing the door behind her. When this headache passed, it would be on. I couldn't wait to enjoy my new relationship with Harper. She was everything I never even knew I wanted... needed. My life had been empty without her, and when I got a taste of what life was really about, I didn't want to let go. She came back in the room and gave me a pain pill and some water. "Your mom will be here in a little while. I hate that you're in so much pain."

"As long as you with me, I'm good, baby."

She eased in the bed as her phone rang. I squinted because that noise hurt like hell. "Shit. I'm sorry."

She quickly got out of the bed and silenced the call, then walked out of the room. I brought the covers over my head, and that was the last thing I remembered before falling asleep.

When I woke up, my head felt a lot better, and I could hear noise downstairs. Sitting up, I let my feet hang off the side of the bed. There was still a little discomfort, but it wasn't as bad as it was a couple of hours ago. My phone was buzzing on the nightstand. I'd put it on vibrate before we even left Memphis. There were a few text messages and five or six missed calls. Standing from the bed, I made sure I had my balance, then I went to the bathroom and handled my hygiene. As I bent over to spit out mouthwash, Harpers arms wrapped around my waist. I stood up straight to greet her. "You look so much better. How are you feeling?"

"I feel a lot better." I kissed her lips, then led her to the bedroom. "Did my mama show up?"

I slid some lounging shorts on, along with a T-shirt. "Yes. She's still downstairs with your dad, Shana, and Red. Umm... some chick named Neffie called for you."

I could tell she wanted to ask questions about her. Her possessiveness was coming through like light in a dark tunnel. "Who did she call? I never gave her my number."

"She called your phone, so she got your number from someone."

"So you know, I fucked around with her for a little while, but it was never anything serious. I barely remembered her name until recently. She ain't nothing but a buckle bunny. You have nothing to worry about. Okay?"

"Buckle bunny?"

"Yeah, she chase them winning buckles. Tryna make a come-up."

"Okay. I guess. A girl named Lacey also came over to check on you. She said she would come back later."

"Okay. I'm training her to barrel race. C'mere girl."

She slowly walked over to me. I could see a flicker of doubt in her eyes. She'd just gotten out of a relationship where she got cheated on, so I knew that had her on guard. "I've been single my whole adult life, but I know how to be faithful. I know it's still early in our relationship, but I will treat you with respect always. I'm yours. Nobody else's."

"Thank you, Legend. I'm trying to stay positive and keep my mind off my past experiences."

"It'll get better with time. I don't blame you, baby."

I hugged her tightly, then kissed her forehead. "Legend, please be patient with me. I want us to work, but thoughts are going to flood my mind sometimes. Normally, I wouldn't jump into another relationship this fast, but something about you makes me gravitate to you. I couldn't risk making you wait any longer and end up losing you."

"I understand, baby girl. You got me, and I'll be patient. Now let's go downstairs. I'm hungry as hell."

She giggled and led me downstairs as everyone stood to hug me. It was already almost noon, and mama had cooked lunch, or so I thought. "You wanna eat some smothered turkey wings?"

"Hell yeah."

"Well, you better thank God Harper likes to cook as much as she likes to bake. I'd planned to make sandwiches," my mama said.

"Damn, baby. Like that? A nigga get turkey wings during the week? That's a weekend kinda meal."

Everybody laughed as I pulled her in my arms. "You get whatever you want when you want it, Legend. Isn't that what you told me?"

"Mmm. You a good listener too. What'chu cooked with those wings?"

"Greens, black-eyed peas, and rice."

"Shiiid. Mama, you fired."

"Shut yo' ass up, Legend. When I saw she was cooking all that, I made my lil cornbread and fired my damn self."

I chuckled, then kissed Harper's neck and cheek. "I have a lot to learn about you, huh?"

"Not really. I'm not complicated."

"Me either, so we have that in common."

Mama sat that plate in front of me, and I took a deep breath. I was so ready to dig in, Harper stood from my lap with a smile on her face. "I better get up, before you throw me out'cho way."

Everyone laughed as I tore into the greens. After my first forkful, I looked up at her, eyes wide. As soon as I swallowed, I let her know what I thought about it. "Girl, you gon' be cooking a lot for me. This so damned good."

She blushed. "I'm glad you like it. I wouldn't let anyone eat until you tasted it."

"Damn, baby. Thank you."

She didn't know it yet, but she was gon' be my wife. Ain't no way in hell she was gon' get away from me. I watched her go to her phone and she seemed to lose all the color in her face when she looked at it. That was saying a lot since my baby's melanin was blinding folks. Shana noticed and walked over to her while I continued to eat. I kept glancing at them from the corner of my eye while I ate and while my mama talked shit. "Harper gon' have your ass spoiled."

"Like you didn't."

"I'm yo' mama. I'm supposed to have you spoiled."

"Whateva, Ma."

Harper made her way back to me. "I have to go to Beaumont to get more clothes."

I searched her face to see if there was something she wasn't telling me. After not finding the answer I wanted, I grabbed her hand. "You okay?"

"I'm okay."

"Red, you'll go with them to Beaumont?"

"Yeah, I gotchu."

Harper smiled at me. "Are you always gonna know what I need without me asking?"

"Yep, so you might as well tell me."

"Thank you, Legend."

She kissed my cheek, then went upstairs with Shana in tow. "Red?"

"Yeah?"

"I think that dude might be tryna get to her. Watch my baby. Okay?"

"Don't worry. I just hope I don't have to chin check his ass."

Red used to fight all the time. It didn't matter where he was. If you did or said something that offended him, he handled that shit right then. He was spiraling downward for a while until someone introduced him to steer wrestling about seven or eight years ago. He's been on the straight and narrow ever since, taking his anger out on them damned steers.

When the ladies came downstairs, I silently prayed that Zaire didn't feel like getting fucked up. If he showed up there, Red was gon' beat the fuck out of his ass.

arper

"Girl, you gon' have Red looking at my ass sideways. All that cooking you did for Legend."

I laughed. "Zaire always ate healthily, and I love cooking all types of meals. With Legend growing up the way he did, I knew he would appreciate a meal like that."

"Hell, Red appreciated that shit too. You know my cooking skills ain't on your level."

"I can teach you, Shana. It doesn't look like I'm gonna have much of a business to run."

I allowed the tear to trickle down my cheek. Another cancellation had come through. They'd text me while Legend was eating. Zaire was following through with his promise. He'd called me from an unknown number this morning, realizing I'd blocked his ass. His exact words were, *I guess I'm going to have to prove to you how much damage I can do.* I couldn't even go back in the room with Legend after that. It was the first time I took delight in knowing that he wasn't feeling well. He wouldn't remember to ask me about it.

"Everything's gonna work out, Harper. Just have faith. Have you talked to your mama?"

"No. I'll probably call her today."

"I know y'all aren't close, but she has influence in Lake Charles. Maybe she can get you some orders and loyal customers."

"Yeah. Lake Charles is only an hour away. Well, now two hours. Legend told me he was moving me in with him."

"What?"

"Yeah. I told him everything. Even when I said no, he said in so many words that it wasn't up for discussion and I would do what he said for me to do."

"Damn! I like that shit. Red is kinda the same way."

"I liked it too, surprisingly. He gon' get what he asking for as soon as he's feeling better."

She laughed. "Y'all feelings are strong for each other."

"Yeah. It's crazy."

"Well, come on, so we can get you back to your man. We'll go to Houston tomorrow to get your car. Or we can go later. I know the longer it sits there, the more you'll have to pay."

"Yeah. Can we do it today when we get back from Beaumont?"

"Yeah. I got'chu, girl. I meant to ask, have you heard from Journey's crazy ass?"

Journey was my sister that was involved in all kinds of shit. We weren't close at all, and we grew up differently. She lived with my mama and had a different father. My daddy had said he refused to let me grow up a spoiled ass kid that didn't know how to take care of herself. He was never married to my mama. He just told her that he wanted to raise me, and after a year of them going back and forth, she let me go. "Girl, no. I ain't talk to Journey since she had a whole fit about wanting me to make a cake for some party. When I told her I didn't have time to fill her last-minute request, she went off. That was almost a year ago."

"I remember that bullshit. I just thought that maybe she'd reached out to apologize or something."

"No. She represents everything my daddy didn't want me to become."

"I can't believe that as influential as Senator Thibodeaux is, that she's allowing it."

My mama's status had been the reason why she couldn't properly raise a child. She never took time with Journey, and she was a direct product of how that turned out for kids that just have money thrown at them all the time. She always sent money for me, but we never spent much time together when I was growing up. Maybe once every other month. She'd made the most out of our time when we were together, though. She was the person that taught me to cook and bake.

"I know. Let's go."

When we got back downstairs, Legend had finished his food and stood when I approached him. He hugged me tightly. "Harper, the food was delicious. Thank you so much."

He kissed my lips, and the heat between us felt like it was consuming me. *God, what is it about this man?* "Anything for you, Legend. I'm glad you enjoyed it. When we come back, Shana is going to bring me to Houston to get my other car."

"Aight, baby. Y'all be careful. You gon' come back in the house before y'all head to Houston, right?"

"Yes."

"Okay."

We stared at one another for a minute, neither of us being able to break our gaze until Red cleared his throat. "We are leaving sometime today, right?"

"Shut up, Red. Let me be in awe of my baby's presence."

"Nigga! Harper, you got this nigga all poetic and proper and shit. Let's go!"

Everyone laughed, but my breathing had taken a damned vacation. Legend had me falling and falling hard for his chocolate ass. He seemed so hard when we first met, but this nigga was like a damned pillow when it came to me, soft as hell. I loved that shit though. Shana grabbed my arm and pulled me away from him as his mama laughed. "Our grandbabies gon' be coming soon, Semien."

Legend licked his lips, clearly oblivious to what his mama had just said. Even walking away, I couldn't keep my eyes off him. "Bitch, you gon' run into something, then both y'all asses gon' have concussions. Let's go so we can get back!"

Legend finally released the hold he had on me, by laughing at Shana. I smiled at him and blew him a kiss.

Once we got to my apartment, I had to immediately roll my eyes when we reached the doorstep. There were flowers everywhere, and I wanted to call the police and file a harassment report. Zaire was irritating the fuck out of me. How could he think that he could threaten me one minute and send flowers the next? I slowly shook my head, then unlocked the door so we could get clothes and get the hell out of there.

I pulled out my luggage and duffle bags as my phone rang. It was Legend. "Hello?"

"Hey, baby girl. I scheduled your movers for this weekend. They are going to get your place packed up starting the day after tomorrow. So, we gon' go back out there tomorrow to see what will go to storage and what will come to Liberty. Okay?"

"Okay. Thank you, baby."

"I miss you already."

"I miss you too."

"Aww shit! Legend Semien! If y'all don't get off that phone. Harper can't function and do shit else when it comes to you."

We both laughed at Shana. "Legend, I'll call when we're on our way back, so I won't have to fight this girl."

"Aight."

I playfully rolled my eyes at Shana and continued to pack as much as possible. Since we were coming back tomorrow, I could get the rest of my clothes. Startling me from my thoughts, there was a knock at the door. My heart picked up speed. It had to be Zaire. No one else would show up unannounced. At that moment, I was glad Red had come with us.

When I walked up front, Red was standing at the door. As I peeked around him, I saw Zaire standing there with a smirk on his lips. "So, you have a bodyguard now, Harper?"

"No. Why are you here?"

"I'm here to claim what's mine."

"Zaire, do I look like a dumb bitch to you?"

"Oh, so you've gotten a little backing, now you're feisty again. You didn't ask that question two weeks ago."

"Yes, I have some backing. I should have never let you try to do that to me anyway. The whole time I felt sick to my stomach and miserable."

"Really? You didn't seem that way when you were moaning in my ear, Harper."

"I guess you don't know an act when you see it. Just like I didn't know our entire relationship was a Broadway production. Now please leave."

"You're going to regret this."

"Man shut the fuck and leave. She requested nicely, but my patience is running thin."

Red was literally turning red and looked like he wanted to knock the smirk off Zaire's face. Zaire gave him a head nod, then looked at me. "Talk to you soon, Harper."

"No, you won't. Just leave me alone."

He walked away, but what I saw in his eyes before he left had sent a chill through my body. I needed to get back to my baby. We hurriedly loaded Red's truck with most of my things, then headed back to Liberty. "Harper, you okay?" Shana asked.

"I just wanna get back to Legend."

She nodded, then I called him to let him know we were on our way. "Hey, baby girl."

"Hey. We're on our way back."

"Okay. What's wrong?"

"We'll talk when I get there."

"Okay."

I ended the call and silently prayed that Zaire didn't try to go after Legend about anything. He could get his mother to do almost anything for him. With her resources, she could have almost anything done. I was gonna have to call my mama, whether I wanted to or not. Shana glanced back at me. "Call your mama, Harp."

I guess she was reading my mind. Hesitantly, I dialed her number. I hadn't talked to her since before I found out about Zaire's cheating. But we always went a good month without talking to one another. "Hello?"

"Hey, Mama."

"Harper! Hey gorgeous. How are you?"

"I'm okay. I could be better."

"What's going on? I can hear it in your voice."

"Zaire and I broke up. I found out he's been cheating on me for our entire relationship."

"Oh, baby. I'm so sorry."

"Yeah. It gets worse."

"Oh, God."

"He's ruining my business. Customers have been canceling left and right. Last week alone, I lost nearly two grand. This week isn't shaping up to be any better."

"God. Let me send you some money Harper and we'll talk about building your clientele."

"Mama, I don't need you to send money, but I could use your help with building my clientele. I didn't know that most of my consistent customers were because of him." I took a deep breath as she listened. "I'm moving to Liberty."

"Liberty? Why?"

"I met someone else, and he's trying to help me."

"Harper, you don't think that's kind of fast? I mean, you just met him and you're moving in with him?"

"I trust him."

She sighed. "I never expected such a decision like that from you. Journey, yes. But whatever. I could have paid your rent."

"Mama, I didn't call for you to judge my decisions. You know what, don't worry about it. I'll figure something out on my own."

"Harper..."

I ended the call and rode the rest of the way to Liberty in silence.

 **egend**

"I LIKE THIS new Legend I'm seeing. If you ever let that girl go, I'm gon' beat yo' ass."

My mama had been running her mouth about Harper since they'd left. I told my daddy to watch out, 'cause mama may have lesbian tendencies. The laughter that escaped my daddy, had me cracking up. I'd taken another pain pill, just to stay ahead of the pain. The way Harper sounded on the phone had me on edge.

The minute they walked in, I could see the disgust on all their faces. What shit had popped off? Harper came straight to my arms as my parents got ready to leave. She laid her head on my chest, as Red and Shana went to the sofa. "What's wrong, baby?"

"I missed you."

"I missed you too."

I knew that wasn't what was wrong. She was waiting for my parents to leave. "We're gonna go, Legend. We'll be back later with dinner."

"Aight, Ma."

I released Harper long enough to kiss my mama and shake my daddy's hand, then instantly pulled her back in my arms. Not a second after they walked out, we went to the couch across from Red and Shana. "What's goin' on?"

"Zaire showed up at my apartment."

"He threatened her. I wanted to grab him by his fucking throat," Red interrupted.

"Threatened you how?"

I could feel my heart racing and my head pounding. This shit gotta get better soon because that fuck boy was begging for my fist to connect with his jaw. She fidgeted a bit, then averted her gaze. "He said I would regret this. It's not his words that got me a little shook. It was the way he looked at me when he said it. I could see the evilness in his eyes. I ain't never seen him look that way."

"Listen, as long as you wit' me, you ain't ever gotta feel shook. I don't give a damn if it's the devil himself. You hear that shit, baby girl? I ain't finna play wit' that mutha-fucka. I bet his ass ain't had shit to say to Red. Bitch-ass nigga. I got somethin' for his ass."

I had to stand from the sofa and pace. After a minute or two, Harper stood and got me to sit down. "I don't want you to get light-headed, Legend. Calm down some, okay? Please?"

She laid her hand on my chest and calmed the beast raging inside of me. It was like some *Legends of the Fall* shit. In the movie, the narrator said that there was a beast living inside of the main character, like the bear he fought twice. That damned bull seemed to be living inside of me, but Harper had the ability to calm him down from her touch, just like Isabella could calm down Tristan in the movie. I sat on the sofa and pulled her in my arms while Red looked on in disbelief. He knew how difficult it usually was to calm me down when I was pissed about something.

Harper rested her head on my arm, as I grabbed my pain pill bottle from the end table. Shana got up to get me some water, then I downed it. "Legend, you have an amazing career, and I would hate to see you lose it over this bullshit with Zaire. He wouldn't physically hurt me. I just don't see it in him."

"I don't put anything past him. Don't worry about my career, baby girl. I'm gon' take care of it. Y'all still going to Houston?"

"Yes. Shana, you'll help me with my things?"

"Yeah," she said standing from the sofa.

"Let me help y'all too," Red said.

As they all went outside, my phone vibrated. It was an unknown number. "Hello?"

"Legend?"

"Yeah. Who's this?"

"It's Neffie. I just wanted to check on you."

"I'm aight. Don't call my phone though. I don't want my girl doubting shit about me, and I already told her about our past. That's exactly where that shit gon' stay."

"Damn Legend. Why you always gotta be so fucking rude?"

"I wasn't being rude, but I don't need you checkin' on me. So, stop fucking calling my number, Neffie. I have a lady, and even before that, I didn't wanna talk to yo' ass. Now *that* shit was rude. Get the fuck off my line."

When I ended the call, I saw Harper staring at me. I took a deep breath. I never wanted her to hear me talking to a female like that, but Neffie rubbed my nerves raw by trying to make it seem like shit was more than what it was. She never meant shit to me. "I'm sorry you had to hear that, Harper. That bitch just get on my damned nerves."

I blocked the number she called from, then walked over to Harper. After pulling her in my arms, I kissed her forehead. "Don't worry, I would never speak to you that way."

She only nodded her head in response, then headed upstairs with her things. *Damn.* She was already feeling sensitive with the shit she had going on. That phone call didn't make her feel any better.

Once they'd finished, Shana and Harper were about to go to Houston. Harper looked so bothered. Pulling her in my arms, I hugged her tightly, trying to ease her mind. "Talk to me, Harper. Tell me what's up."

She shook her head no. "Shana, give us a minute, okay?"

"Okay."

I led Harper upstairs to my room... our room. "Okay, now tell me."

"I'm... I'm hoping that I'm not making a mistake by moving so fast. This shit is scaring the fuck out of me."

"I'm sorry. I know I didn't help ease your doubt. Harper, you're changing me, and I like it. When I'm near you, I feel emotions so strong... it scare the fuck outta me too. I just know that you 'posed to be with me. I'm gon' work on how I talk to other women. Okay? I'll do anything to make you feel at ease about this."

She nodded her head, then I lifted her chin and kissed her passionately. My hands slipped into the waistband of her tights and grabbed her ass. She didn't have on underwear. *Aww shit.* She was trying to get me caught up. I broke our kiss and pulled them down over her ass. "Legend... oh... we have to go."

I put my lips to her ear. "I know but give me a minute."

I sat on the bed and pulled her to me. Slowly laying back and licking my lips, I watched her eyes widen. "Bring that pussy up here, girl."

I felt her shiver. "No, Legend. We don't have time."

"Get'cho ass up here, Harper. This shit ain't gon' take but a minute. You doubting my abilities?"

She shook her head no, then crawled to my face. When she sat that shit on my face, her juices were already everywhere. I slurped that shit up, then assaulted her clit. Swirling my tongue around it as I sucked it, made her practically scream out in pleasure. Holding her ass in place, I started a rhythm on that pearl that had her riding my shit like she was on a dick. "Legend, oh God... shit!"

That creamy goodness that came out of her was gon' have my ass turned out, on some real shit. Her legs were clamped on my ears, and I could feel them tremble from her release. I needed her on my dick. I reached over my head and got a condom from the drawer, then unzipped and strapped up with the quickness. Her eyes were closed the whole time, still riding the wave. Sliding her from my face, I sat her on it, and her eyes popped open.

"Show me what you gon' do wit' it."

Her shit felt so good, I wanted my dick to live there forever. Harper was just staring at me as she sat there. "What's the matter? You don't want it?"

"I told you, whenever you were ready, I would be. I just... never mind."

She began her ride, and it felt like I'd died and gon' to heaven. I laid back and lifted my hips, meeting her every grind on my shit. The pressure in my head was building, but I would deal with that shit after I bust. "Fuck, Harper."

I opened my eyes and watched her work. It wasn't long before I needed to handle her ass though. Rolling her over, I pulled my pants to my knees and reentered her from the back. *That ass.* Her moans were gonna take me down faster than I wanted, but I'd be ready for her again when she got back. "Legend, fuck."

I watched her ass twerk on me for a few seconds, then I bust. I couldn't even hold that shit in. "Damn, Harper. Wait until you get back."

"How's your head?" she asked breathlessly.

"It feels fine, now. There was a little pain when it was building."

I stood from the bed, and helped her out, then led her to the bathroom. "I'm sorry. You probably didn't expect all that, but I couldn't resist any longer. I promise to take my time with you tonight. I know that's what you want. You forgive me?"

"Yeah. It was still amazing, Legend. Better than I imagined."

I pulled her in my arms and kissed her, gently pulling her bottom lip into my mouth. He was rising for more, but I knew they really needed to go, now. After getting washcloths, I gave her one, so she could get cleaned up. I noticed her Ivory and Olay soaps on the countertop. She cleaned herself quickly, just as Shana yelled. "Look, bitch, I ain't finna be leaving here at dark thirty!"

She giggled, then put her clothes on. "See you when I get back."

"Aight, baby girl."

She kissed my lips, then ran out to meet Shana. Her ass was gon' have me sprung. I hated that our first time was a quickie, but shit. All that ass in those tights was tempting as hell. Once I realized she wasn't wearing underwear, that was it.

I walked down the stairs to see Red in the kitchen eating again. "Nigga! You gon' eat us out of house and home."

"Aww shut up. You owe me this damn meal. Was that the first time?"

"What?"

"You know what I'm talking 'bout. We could hear y'all."

"That was the first time, but I can assure it won't be the last."

"Whatever. You don't have a romantic bone in your body, do you?"

"What'chu talkin' 'bout, now?"

"How you gon' make the first time a quickie?"

"Man, I wasn't thinking about that until after the fact. I just needed her right then."

"You gon' be aight 'til yo' parents get here?"

"Yeah, why?"

"I'm going to the store to buy flowers and shit fo' yo' country ass."

"Whatever."

I laughed, but I was glad he was saving the day. When Harper got back tonight, I'd have her a bubble bath ran, with some wine and music. That shit I did *was* kinda selfish. I went to the kitchen to see what I could snack on until Harper got back. When I opened the fridge, there was a huge cheesecake sitting there, with strawberries all over it. She was gon' make me fat as hell. Besides pussy, food was my weakness.

"Legend? You here by yourself?"

I looked up to see my parents walking to the kitchen. "Yeah, Red went to the store to get some flowers and stuff, so me and Harper can have a romantic evening."

"Aww. Legend I'm so happy for you."

"Thanks, Ma."

"That heifer can cook her ass off too. Where is my daughter-in-law?"

I slowly shook my head. "They went to the airport to get her car."

"Well, I brought some salmon. I'm gon' cook that with some garlic mashed potatoes and green beans. That okay with you?"

"Sounds good, Mama. Why y'all didn't tell me there was cheese-cake in here?"

"Harper said that was for dinner. I knew the only way to keep you out of it, was not to tell you."

"Ha. Ha. Ha," I said sarcastically.

I left the kitchen and sat on the sofa with Pops to wait on my baby to come back.

21

arper

"Girl, it was so good. I can't wait until I get back. He said he would take his time with me tonight."

"I can't believe y'all was up there gettin' it in while I was waiting on yo' ass."

"Whatever."

"You wasn't upset that the first time was a quickie?"

"Yeah, somewhat, but he promised to make it up to me. If it would have been horrible, then I would have been pissed."

Shana laughed as we traveled Highway 90, west to Houston. My car had been parked at Bush Airport for four days. I was extremely disappointed when Legend wanted to fuck. When I saw him reaching in the drawer for a condom, I was just thinking that this couldn't be happening this way. It made me wonder if he only wanted a live-in booty call. That thought quickly left me. The way he expressed himself to me, directly contradicted that thought. Maybe it had been a while for him, or maybe he just wasn't thinking.

I did know that the shit was amazing, regardless of how long it lasted. Getting back to Liberty was my number one priority. My body felt like it went up in flames. His dick game was something to brag about, but there was no way I would share details. Shana was my cousin, but when it came to my man, nobody needed to know those kinds of details but me.

When we got to the valet covered parking called The Parking Spot, I paid them the seventy dollars and was ready to haul ass until I got a text. When I looked at it, I could've thrown my fucking phone through the window. It was a picture from Zaire of him and my sister, Journey. How did he get in touch with her? They'd only met once. *What the fuck?* Had they been fucking around all this time behind my back?

The shit didn't matter. Journey and I didn't have the sister bond that we should have anyway. I surely couldn't give a fuck about Zaire's triflin' ass. I started my car and sped out of the garage. To say it didn't matter, I was still infuriated. I hit the beltway doing ninety miles per hour as my phone rang. "Hello?"

"Bitch, you wanna slow down?"

"Sorry."

I ended the call, then slowed my speed down to eighty, which was still speeding since the speed limit was sixty-five. Being away from Legend when I was feeling this emotional was detrimental to my sanity. He could make me feel better. Then I thought about my mama. Did she know this shit Journey was doing? The thought alone made me angrier by the minute. When I looked down at my speedometer, I was back up to ninety.

There was my phone again. "Hello?"

"Got damn it, bitch! Slow yo' ass down! Set yo' fucking cruise control."

I ended the call without responding to her, then slowed to seventy-five and set my cruise. Them fuckers weren't gonna steal my joy. I couldn't let them bastards be in control of my happiness. Taking several deep breaths, I could feel my body trying to relax. I turned up the radio as Michael Jackson's "P.Y.T." blared through the speakers. Before I knew it, I was grooving in my seat as I exited to Highway 90.

I'd be home in about thirty minutes. *Home.* I loved the sound of that. That's exactly what it felt like when I was with Legend. The radio was taking me through the '80s, for real. I was glad for the distraction, though. "All Night Long" by the Mary Jane Girls reiterated my exact feelings. I planned to give it Legend all night long. From what I saw earlier, he wasn't a one-hitta-quitter. His dick had risen to the occasion again before I even left the room.

When I finally got home, I could see his parents were there. Hopefully, no one would be there too long. As Shana got out her car, she was talking noise. I couldn't even hear what she was saying, but she was pissed. When she got close, she was about to let my ass have it. "If I would've gotten a ticket tryna keep up wit' yo' ass…"

Before she could finish, I put my phone in her face, showing her the picture of Zaire and Journey. "What the fuck?"

"My thoughts exactly."

"Are they fucking? Is that why he sent you that picture?"

"I don't know what the fuck the reason was, but while it did piss me off, their asses can have each other. If Journey and I were closer, then I would possibly give a fuck."

When we walked in the house, Red and Legend's parents were having a conversation quietly. *Was Legend okay?* He wasn't sitting there with him. I walked right over to them. "Is Legend not feeling well?"

"Naw. We about to go. He went to bed."

"Okay." Turning to Shana, I hugged her. "Thank you so much."

"Anytime, Harp. You know you my ride or die."

We both laughed. She always called me that, and I used to call her my boo thang when we were kids. People that didn't know we were cousins thought we were gay, and we wouldn't tell them anything different. I walked them all to the door and Legend's mama hugged me. "Take care of my baby."

"Yes ma'am, I will."

Once I locked the door, I ran up the stairs to check on him. When I got to the room, he wasn't in bed, but shortly after, I heard him coughing in the bathroom. I lightly knocked on the door. "Legend?"

"Come in, baby."

He didn't sound well. I opened the door and my hands went to cover my open mouth. He'd run me a bubble bath. Candles were lit, flower petals were everywhere, and there was a glass of wine and a slice of the cheesecake I'd made earlier sitting on the granite surrounding the tub. Summer Walker was playing through the speakers. "Legend... Wow."

He didn't say a word. He was shirtless with some white linen pants on. *Shit.* That white fabric against his dark skin was about to drive me wild. My eyes went from his tatted arms to his smooth chest to his amazing lips, then to his dark eyes. Walking toward me, he stretched out his arms, welcoming me back home. He hugged me. "I'm sorry for earlier. You deserve your heart's desires, and I plan to make sure you get whatever your heart wants."

He was making me weak with desire. Slowly, he lifted my shirt over my head, then unfastened my bra. His hands grazed my nipples and they got so hard, they were throbbing and sensitive to the touch.

Putting his hands in my tights, like he did earlier, he pulled them down and helped me out of them. As he stood, his fingers ran up my legs lightly, causing a slight tremble to take a course through my body. Grabbing my hand, he led me to the air tub and kissed my lips. "Get in, baby."

I got in the hot water, slowly sitting down, allowing my body to get acclimated to the temperature. This was perfect. As I laid back, I exhaled slowly, listening to Mint Condition sing "U Send Me Swingin". He picked the perfect songs to play. Was he trying to tell me something? Instead of thinking too much, I closed my eyes and enjoyed the hot water.

When I opened them, Legend was sitting on the floor watching me. He grabbed the plate of cheesecake and began feeding me. I savored every bite as he continued to stare at me. His treatment of me at this moment made me feel extremely sexy and horny. I took a sip of my wine and realized it was a Sangria. It was delicious. I was sure it was normally much sweeter being that I had been eating cheesecake, but it was still amazing.

When I'd finished the cheesecake, Legend stood to his feet and sat the plate on the vanity. "How's your water? Is it still hot?"

"Yes."

"Okay. Relax. I'll be back in a little bit to wash you up."

I smiled at him and laid back in the tub, then drank the rest of my Sangria. My baby was taking care of me. To say he took a horrible hit in the face four days ago, he seemed to be doing well. I hoped he wasn't feeling horrible but still trying to cater to me. Just as I was about to wash myself, he came back in the bathroom. "Harper, what are you doing?"

"Umm... I was about to wash myself. I don't want you catering to me if you aren't feeling your best, baby. I should be taking care of you."

"I feel fine."

"But..."

"Dead that shit you talkin'. I'm about to take care of you. I'm finna make you feel some shit you ain't never felt before. You tellin me you don't want that shit?"

I opened my mouth, then closed it. I couldn't say I didn't want that shit, 'cause my pussy was wetter than this water just thinking about it. "I didn't think you could say that shit."

He put some Olay soap on my loofah, as I sat up. After getting on his knees, Legend gently scrubbed my body. I moaned in satisfaction as his fingers grazed my skin. "Stand up, baby girl."

He grabbed my hand, helping me to my feet, then pulled one of my legs from the water, setting my foot on the edge of the tub. After washing that leg, he did the same with the other. Throwing my loofah in the water, he wet my towel and washed my face, slowly. *God, I wish he would hurry.* He rewet the towel, then looked at me. "Should I use the ivory soap for this?"

He was referring to washing my kitty cat. I nodded in the affirmative, then watched him soap the towel. When he came back to me, he slowly rubbed the towel over my mound, then eased it to the lips of my vagina, his eyes never leaving mine. *Shit!* This was torture. I moaned, then leaned in to try to kiss him, but he leaned back just enough for me to miss him.

"Legend..."

"Yeah, baby?"

"You teasing me."

"Uh huh."

He turned me around and washed my ass, then kissed my neck and shoulder. I turned back to face him as he let the water out, then turned on the sprayer. It was a light spray to get the soap off me. I allowed him to raise my arms to rinse me under there and help me spread my legs as he licked his lips. It was like I couldn't do a thing for myself because all I could think about was riding that chocolate in his pants. I could clearly see his erection and that he wasn't wearing underwear. Linen pants didn't hide shit.

Legend helped me from the tub, then pat me dry as I turned to him. He finally let me kiss those dark lips. Damn, they were soft. His fingers grazed my skin, setting it on fire everywhere he touched. He backed away from me, then led me to the bedroom. "Lay down, Harper."

I did as he commanded as I watched him grab a bottle of lotion that he'd obviously rummaged through my bag for. I could see it in disarray on the floor. Squirting some of it in his hand, he rubbed them together then massaged my legs. I closed my eyes and enjoyed every moment of it, thanking God for an amazing night, despite how it started.

After he'd finished my legs, I sat up to pull his pants off, but he pushed me back in the bed and rolled me over. He soon straddled me and began rubbing my back. I knew that he'd taken his pants off because I could feel his sack against my skin. Moaning softly only made him knead my shoulders and neck with more intensity and the right amount of pressure. He stopped momentarily, so I assumed he was getting more lotion.

When I felt his tongue in my ass, I flinched. That was unexpected. I was actually surprised that he'd ate me out earlier. He was so strong and hard, but the way he tenderly ate out my kitty cat had me wanting more. I tooted my ass up for him. "Legend, damn baby."

This was way more passion than I'd bargained for, and it felt like my emotions were about to spill. His tongue wandered to my pussy, and he began eating me out from the back. I wanted to pull all my fucking hair out. While squeezing my ass, he only went in deeper. This mutha-fucka was gon' make me fall in love real quick.

Zaire had never had my body begging him for his dick. Not like this.

Right now, I was on sensation overload, anticipating my orgasm. Legend was playing with me though. Judging by how quickly he made me cum earlier, he was doing just what he'd promised. Taking his time. He inserted his finger in my ass and made me squeal with excitement. "You like that shit, Harper?" he asked in a husky voice against my pussy.

"Yeees, Legend."

"Make that shit spit for me then, baby."

He sucked my clit and finger fucked my ass with so much passion, it felt like I nutted both ways. My body trembled so much, I thought I was having a fucking seizure. "Damn, your ass nutted for me too. I liked that shit, Harper."

What the fuck? I had an anal orgasm? He turned me over, then wiped his mouth and his beard. He grabbed a condom from the drawer as my body twitched in excitement. I sat up in bed and grabbed him by the dick. "Bring my shit here, Legend."

"Oh, this yo' shit?"

"Uh huh."

"Well, please suck the soul outta yo' shit."

I brought my mouth to it and did as he asked, first concentrating on the head, then deep throating his shit. He pulled my hair from my face and jutted his hips forward. "Fuck, Harper."

I had to give him my best, slobbing that dick like it was a damned Hennessey dipped popsicle. Massaging his sack with my hand and wrapping my other hand around the base of his dick, I began to stroke his shaft as he groaned deeply. Moving from his sack to his ass, I wanted to stimulate his prostate, but he wasn't having that shit. "Harper, stay in the front," he said roughly.

I almost laughed. I was just trying to give him a more powerful orgasm but to each his own. I continued sucking his soul from him until his knees buckled and almost dropped him to the floor. His nut coated the back of my throat, as his breathing became erratic. "Fuck!"

He eased his dick from my mouth and collapsed in the bed, and I laid next to him. He rolled to his side and kissed me gently on the lips. "Damn. I think you took my soul, for real."

I pulled his face to mine and kissed him passionately. He ended our kiss and began teasing my nipples with his tongue. "Legend, baby, yes."

My clit was so fucking sensitive, I could feel my orgasm building once again. Legend must have felt it too, because he inserted his finger and finger fucked my g-spot, making me cum all over the damned place. He left me for a moment, so he could strap up, then pushed inside of me. "Oh fuck!" I yelled.

Legend hovered over me and stared into my eyes as he stroked my pussy into submission, filling it to capacity. His strokes were intentional... filled with purpose... hell-bent on making me love him. Just as I was about to close my eyes, he said, "Naw. Open your eyes while you throw that pussy back at me."

I opened my eyes and stared into his as he made love to me. Wrapping my legs around his waist, caused him to increase in speed. He lowered his head and teased my nipples once again. I took that opportunity to close my eyes and fully concentrate on what I was feeling while squeezing his shoulders. He pulled one of my legs to my shoulder and thrust deeper. "Oh, Legend! Shit!"

He sucked my neck, then my earlobe and pulled my other leg up, both knees to my shoulder. That mutha-fucka wore my pussy out. I was screaming, begging for him to stop and keep going at the same damned time. "Rough ride your pussy, Legend!"

"Oh, this my pussy?"

"Yes. Shit!"

He kissed and sucked the back of my knees while I came all over his dick. The frown on his face was telling me that he was about to cum as well. He grunted and growled as the sweat dripped from him to my chest. His body stiffened as he growled out, "Fuuuck!"

He let my legs go and laid on top of me. This was by far the best sex I'd ever had, and the tears on my cheeks said so as well.

22

egend

I ALMOST TOLD Harper I loved her. We'd been fucking so much, it was unreal. All these years I thought I was enjoying sex. This shit with Harper was on a whole 'notha level. After our romantic evening the night she'd come back from Houston, we had sex all night, discovering each other's likes and dislikes. Falling more in tune with each other's bodies with each session. After a week, it felt like we'd been fucking for years.

We'd gotten Harper all moved in and her things organized. Then, we started outlining how we would remarket her business. We hired a publicist to get her some exposure and I had a spotlight for her added to my webpage. We'd even gotten her equipment moved from the bakery as well. Her lease would be up at the end of the month, and there was no point in renewing it right now.

Today, I'd worked with Lacey as Harper watched her practice. Her phone had been ringing and chiming non-stop today, and it seemed to be wearing on her. I made a mental note to talk to her about it, so we can kill that shit immediately. "Lacey, loosen up, lil mama. You too stiff. When you nervous, your horse can sense that."

"I know. It's just that this competition is coming up soon."

"Be confident in your abilities. You good. You have lots of potential, but fear will limit you."

"Okay. Thanks, Legend."

I helped her put her horse in my stable, then hugged her. She was so nervous. If she didn't get a handle on that, she wasn't gonna do well. Harper hugged her and told her how good she was, then she left.

After walking her to her truck, I went back to the barn and sat with Harper. "What's up, baby? I could hear your phone ringing non-stop."

"When Shana and I went to get my car, I got a picture message. Zaire is dating my sister."

"What the hell?"

"Yeah. Although Journey and I aren't close, I still feel like she stabbed me in the back. I was somewhat pissed about it, but of course, you made me forget all about it that night. Now, my sister is messaging me over and over with pictures of the two of them. My mama has been calling, but I haven't wanted to talk to her. She and I have never been close either because my daddy raised me until he died when I was fifteen. I haven't wanted to talk to her since the same night. She was criticizing me for moving so quickly with you."

"Does she know about your sister?"

"I don't know. I feel like she does, and that's why she's blowin' my damned phone up."

"What is he up to?"

"I don't know."

"I can't understand why he's going through so many lengths to piss you off or destroy you. I can't wait to get to his ass."

"Because he's a spoiled asshole that will go to any length to get what he wants. He wants to control me, and because he can't, he's throwing a tantrum." She took a deep breath and continued. "Well, in other news, I got an order. Someone saw my advertisement on your page. So, thank you, baby."

"You're welcome." I kissed her lips, then pulled her from her seat. "We gon' get to the bottom of this. Block your sister and call your mama back. She may want to apologize for what's going on."

"I doubt that. Senator Thibodeaux has never apologized to me for anything."

"Yo' mama a senator?" I asked, my eyes wide.

"Yeah, she just retired. That's where all her time went. At least I had my daddy and grandparents. Journey didn't have anyone. Her daddy went MIA after my mama got pregnant. Recently, Mama decided she was ready to get out. So, she didn't run again. She'd been a senator most of my life."

"Wow. She has so much influence. She could help your business."

"I know. That's what I'd called her for. Louisiana isn't that far, so I could make a killing out there if she would speak for me. However, I got irritated with her about me living with you."

"We did move fast Harper. However, had it not been for Zaire, you would still have your own place. I can't wait to fuck him up."

She wrapped her arms around my waist and kissed my lips. "Let's go inside. I'm hungry."

"Me too."

I kissed her neck, and she giggled as she tried to get away from me. "Legend! For food!"

I laughed with her, then followed her inside as her phone rang. When she looked at it, she rolled her eyes and answered on speaker. "Hello?"

"Oh God, Harper! I was praying nothing had happened to you. The last time we spoke, you told me you were moving in with someone that you barely had time to get to know. I was scared."

"Mama, you've been calling for a week. If you thought something had happened to me, wouldn't you have come to try to find me? You weren't afraid."

"Harper, I didn't call to argue with you. Why don't you come home?"

"Beaumont is home for me, not Lake Charles."

"Well, let me pay for your apartment. I'm not comfortable with you living with some man you just met."

"Well, Legend is no longer a stranger to me. I know him better than I know my back-stabbing, low down slut for a sister."

"Legend? Is that his name? I've only heard of one person named Legend, and he's a bull rider. I made an appearance at a rodeo here. Anyway, that's not important. I know it's not the same person."

I smiled slightly. I actually remembered who she was when she said that. We met and shook hands. "Why are you downing your sister?"

"She's dating Zaire."

"Oh, God. No."

I interrupted their conversation. "Hello, Senator Thibodeaux. I'm Legend Semien. We met at a rodeo in Lake Charles, before I won one of my first buckles. Harper is living with me, and I care for her a great deal."

She was completely quiet for a moment, while Harper laughed silently. "My daughter is dating a bull rider? I have to come to see this for myself. Harper!"

We both laughed, and she joined us. "Okay, look. I didn't know about Journey. I'm going to call her as soon as we hang up. Legend seems like a respectable young man. Do you really remember meeting me, Legend?"

"Yes, ma'am. You were extremely friendly, and I remember you congratulating me on the win."

"You were friendly as well. So, Harper, I guess it's okay that you live with him," she said under her breath.

I guess her somewhat knowing me, was good enough for her. Either that, or she didn't say what she really wanted to say because she knew I was listening. "Harper, my team and I are working on something that will help you. When I have more details about it, I will let you know. In the meantime, let me get in touch with your sister."

"Okay. Thanks, Mom."

She ended the call, and I gave her that 'I told you so' look. The smile that spread across her face made me smile though. "Thank you, Legend."

"For what?"

"For convincing me to talk to my mama."

"That's what I'm here for, baby girl. Now, come on, let's get cleaned up. I wanna take you to a nice restaurant for dinner. We'll cook tomorrow."

She kissed me gently on the lips, then stared into my eyes as a smile spread across her face. "Okay baby."

AFTER WE'D BEEN SEATED at Suga's Deep South Cuisine, we enjoyed the sounds of a live jazz band. "Thank you, Legend. This is great."

"Anytime Harper. I wanna talk to you about something. There are some things I feel I need to say to you."

She nodded in acceptance and looked quite nervous. Before I could say what was on my heart, I saw Zaire walking in with a woman. Harper noticed that something had caught my attention, so she turned in her seat to see what I was looking at. "Hell fucking no. Let's leave, Legend."

"We were here first, Harper."

"I don't care about that. I don't want to be in the same space as him and Journey."

I took a deep breath. "Aight. Let's go."

Before we could stand, her sister had come to our table. "Hey, Harper."

I grabbed Harper's hand and we were about to leave without her acknowledging them until that fuck boy grabbed her arm. "Harper, you aren't going to speak to your sister?"

That's when a side of me that Harper had never seen made an appearance. "Yo' best fucking bet is to not ever put your hands on what's mine."

"Legend, let's not go there. That's what he wants," Harper said quietly.

"Listen to my leftovers. That's all she is."

What the fuck he said that shit for? Before I could even think about where we were or anything else, I punched him in his slick-ass mouth. There was no way I was gonna let him disrespect Harper right in my face. What kinda nigga would I have been to ignore that shit, though? He fell to the floor and I could hear the yells of other patrons as Harper screamed, "Legend, no!"

That mutha-fucka was on the floor wiping the blood from his mouth with a smirk on his face. I wanted to kick him in his fucking mouth. "You got something else to say fuck boy?"

"Legend, let's go! This is so embarrassing."

I turned to Harper. She was embarrassed by me defending her honor? I frowned at her. "You embarrassed?"

"Yes! I'm sure the police have been called. The whole restaurant is watching us," she said as the manager walked up.

"Sir, we need you to leave, now."

As I began to walk out, Zaire said, "That's what happens when you let trashy people into a place of class."

I stopped walking, and Harper was begging me with her eyes to keep walking. She was shaking her head no, as I turned around and hit Zaire in his temple with so much force, he flew to a nearby table and was out cold."

Harper and her sister were both screaming. I didn't give a fuck at that moment. I could see the police lights outside, so I made my way to the door with my hands up as Harper ran behind me. "Why couldn't you just walk the fuck away, Legend?"

I reached in my pocket and handed her the keys to my truck. "Excuse me for defending the woman I love. For not letting another man openly disrespect her. I would have been less than a man to let him get away with that."

The police entered the building and immediately escorted me outside while Harper stood there with her mouth open. I was trying to tell her before her ex arrived, that I was in love with her. I couldn't fight it any longer. I'd fallen in love with her in just a short time and had fallen hard. After explaining what happened, they cuffed me, then one of the officers went inside and spoke to the manager and a now alert Zaire. I also saw one talking to Harper.

"Mr. Semien, we're gonna have to take you in. The gentleman you assaulted will be pressing charges."

"Of course, he is."

I got in the back of the police car as Harper walked out of the restaurant and just stared at me. Turning my head in the opposite direction, I couldn't help but hear in my ears that she said I embarrassed her. Once the officer got in the car, I turned to look out the window as Harper stood there staring at me with tears streaming down her face. "I would have knocked that smug-ass look off his face, too," the officer said.

He pulled away from the curb, then said, "Hopefully, this will only be a fine and a slap on the hand. You don't have a record. I'd hate to see this ruin your career."

My heart sank at the thought of that. When he disrespected Harper, my career or the thought of losing it, never entered my mind. Only defending my woman had. Now that she seemed to be mad at me for doing so, maybe I should've left well enough alone.

23

arper

I COULDN'T BELIEVE this shit. Legend had let Zaire drag him down to his level and I couldn't be more upset about it. However, what I couldn't stop thinking about was that he said I was the woman he loved. I had a feeling that was what he wanted to say to me before he saw Zaire. I stood in shock watching them drive away with Legend in the back seat as Zaire walked out of the door. "So, you picked this thug over me, huh?"

"Fuck you, Zaire. He's more man than you could ever be. Get the fuck outta my face before I end up in jail with him."

As if things couldn't get any worse, Journey brought her ass outside. "You always thought you were better than me."

I rubbed my temples with my fingertips, then prepared to walk to Legend's truck, but I had to respond to her ass. "You think I'm better than you. There's a difference. I'm living my life and conducting myself the way I was raised to do. So, if you think that makes me better than you, then so be it."

I walked away while she yelled obscenities. She was so disgusted with how her life turned out until she somehow tried to make that my fault. I didn't have time for the bullshit. My man was probably being booked right now, and I didn't have a clue what to do. After getting in his truck, I called Shana. "Hello?"

"Are you sleeping?"

"No, I just got off not too long ago."

"I need Red's phone number. Legend got arrested."

"What the fuck!"

"He got in a fight with Zaire at Suga's. I begged him to ignore Zaire, but after Zaire insulted me, it was like he was the damned bull that attacked him."

"Shit. I can't stand that mutha-fucka. I'll call Red and call you back."

"Okay."

I sat there nervously in his truck trying to figure out what to do next. Looking around the inside, I never realized how big this truck was. Now that I had to drive it, it seemed huge. Finally succumbing to my fears, I allowed my body to express the worry I felt inside in liquid form once again. Legend could lose his career, and this shit was all my fault. I started the engine as my phone rang. "Hello?"

"Hey Harper, it's Red. I'm on my way to the police station. Meet me there."

"Okay."

The police had gotten to Suga's so fast, because the station was only around the corner, not even a mile away. This felt like a horrible dream I couldn't wake up from. Shana was calling back. "Yeah?"

"Harper, don't worry. This isn't your fault. Zaire gon' get what's coming to him. God don't like ugly. Legend's career will be fine as well. I know how you think. If they don't let him out tonight, call me, and I'll meet you in Liberty. Okay?"

"Okay. Thank you, Shana."

As I parked, I allowed more tears to fall from my eyes. *Legend loved me.* That shit had my emotions going haywire. Killing the engine, I grabbed my purse and got out. I still only had five grand in my account, so hopefully, his bail wouldn't be more than that, if they let him go. Before I could walk in, I saw Red driving up, so I waited for him. When he got to me, he hugged me tightly. "If he can't see a judge today, he'll have to wait until the morning. Most likely, he'll be here overnight."

"Okay."

"Don't worry. Legend will be fine."

I nodded my head then walked inside with Red right behind me. He led me to the window to speak to the officer sitting there. She informed us that the last judge left at seven, so they would be keeping him overnight. We walked back out of the station, me with my head down.

"Hey, Mama."

"Hi, Harper. What's wrong? You sound disgusted."

"I am. Legend and I went out to dinner, and Zaire and Journey showed up."

"Shit. I can only imagine what happened after that."

"Legend got arrested. I was so embarrassed. The entire restaurant was watching us."

"Oh, my goodness. If he was defending your honor, why would you be embarrassed?"

"I don't know. I just wanted him to ignore Zaire. It was a huge scene."

"Can I tell you something without offending you?"

"Umm... sure."

I didn't know what she wanted to tell me, but it seemed like it was gonna be a lot. "Let that man be your man. And what I mean by that is let him protect you. Let him stand up for you, Harper. I know you are Miss Priss and somewhat bougie, but you have to be down for that man."

I sat in Legend's huge house, thinking about what Mama said, as the doorbell rang. "Mama, you tripping. I think I got that whole Miss Priss and bougie attitude while I was living with you."

"Girl, you don't even know. How do you think I met your daddy? I'm very well-rounded. I can be saddity just like the rest of these bougie politicians, but I can be ghetto too. You just have to know when to assert those qualities."

I laughed as I walked to the door to find Shana there waiting. "Hey girl, come in. Mama, Shana is here, so I'll call you back."

"Okay. Let me know if Legend has an attorney. I may be able to pull some strings."

"Thanks, Mama, I will."

I ended the call as Shana flopped down on the couch. "Hey. You okay?"

"I'm okay. Me and Red had a huge argument."

"Why?"

She and Red had seemed to be getting along well. I watched her fidget for a moment, then she exhaled loudly. "He wants more of a commitment from me. I'd rather not define what we have. I just wanna go with the flow."

"He calls you his woman all the time, so what's the real issue?"

"He does, but I never call him my man. When you called, we'd met up at Fuzzy's Tacos to get something to eat. One of my co-workers was there, and I introduced Red to him as my friend. He got really upset, but he didn't say anything while we were there. He followed me to my place and told me he wanted to be my man. He thinks I'm not ready to settle down."

"So, if you won't acknowledge him as your man, what is keeping you from doing so?"

"You know my past. I've never really had a steady boyfriend. While I do want him to be that, I don't want to be hurt either. Red has a lot of women that call his phone. He claims they are all friends or from the rodeo circuit. I want to believe him, but at the same time, I think that he's playing me."

"Have you talked to him about that? I think he might understand if you did."

"No, I haven't. Some things I just feel I shouldn't have to say. Why would he think any woman would be okay with a bunch of bitches calling her man? So, I haven't told any of the niggas calling me that I'm involved. If he hasn't done it to all the chicks calling him, why should I?"

"Y'all need to talk. He seems so good for you."

"I guess we will eventually, but he's mad at me right now. How was Legend?"

"I think he's a little irritated with me too. I told him I was embarrassed at the restaurant with how everything went down. He told me to excuse him for defending the woman he loved."

"Oh shit! He said he loved you?"

"Yeah. It made me feel like shit for being embarrassed. I wanted him to just walk away and not feed into Zaire's taunts. Legend punched him. If we would have left right then, he probably wouldn't be in jail. Then, Zaire had to say something else slick, and Legend literally knocked him out. After all that, and us somewhat arguing, the police had gotten there."

"Damn, Harp. Legend Semien is in love with you."

"Aww quit giving me those googly eyes."

She laughed. "What did you say in response?"

"Nothing. I was in shock."

"Do you love him, Harper?"

"I love him, but I don't know if I'm in love with him."

"The way you look at him says differently. The passion in your eyes is overwhelming, Harper."

"Well, both the men in our lives are mad at us. What are we gonna do about it?"

"Well, you just have to apologize. Red and I have a lot to talk about. I'm afraid that if we don't come to an agreement, we may be done."

"Don't say that, Shana."

"It's true. I can't handle a man that everyone has access to, even if it's innocent."

"I guess I can understand that."

We both sat back on the couch and stewed in our own thoughts until my phone rang. It was an unknown number, so I really didn't want to answer. Answering anyway, I said hesitantly, "Hello?"

"You have a collect call from... Legend. To accept the charges, press one..."

Before the automated system could finish, I pressed one. "Legend? Are you there?"

"Hey, Harper."

"Oh my God, I'm so sorry. I hate this situation that my past has gotten you in."

"It's okay. Don't worry about coming to get me tomorrow. Red will be here."

My heart sank to my feet. "What?"

"Well, I wouldn't want you to be embarrassed, Harper. So, don't worry about coming."

I could hear the hurt in his tone. At first, I thought he was being sarcastic, but he really took to heart what I'd said, and it only made me feel worse. "Legend, I'm so sorry. I want to be there for you like you've been there for me. Please let me."

"No. We'll talk when I get home. There's so much I need to say to you, but there's so much I need you to clarify too."

The tears fell from my eyes involuntarily. I couldn't believe he didn't want me there. "One minute..."

"Harper, I'll see you tomorrow when I get home."

"Legend, please let me be there. I'm begging you."

"Do what you want, Harper. I can't stop you from being there. I just prefer not to see you until we can speak privately."

"Legend..."

The call ended. I collapsed in Shana's arms and cried my eyes out. When I calmed down, I went upstairs and packed a bag, then came back down. "Let's go to your house."

These country-ass men had us all in our 'lil feelings.

24

 **egend**

"Bail will be granted and set at $5,000."

Red gave me a head nod as they led me back to the holding cell. This shit here was for the birds. That punk ass nigga needed to find himself a hobby. Why people had to be so damned evil? I was glad I told Harper not to come. My head was pounding. I wasn't in the best mood, and I was starting to regret telling her that I loved her. Telling her the way I did wasn't a part of the plan. When that fuck boy came in, he ruined it.

Harper had buried herself so deeply inside of me, I didn't know what to do at this point. She was asking me to do something I couldn't do. Although she'd apologized, I wondered just how long it would take her to stop letting Zaire have his way. Whenever he got under her skin, she took that shit out on me.

"Legend Semien... You're free to go, sir. You've made bail."

I stood from the bench in the holding cell, and the guard escorted me to the front where Red was waiting on me. After getting my belongings, we walked out to his truck. When I closed the door, I exhaled. "I called your representative at Budweiser. I told them about what happened, and they seemed to be okay with it. I didn't want them to find out on their own."

"That was good thinking Red, thanks."

Budweiser was my sponsor. They paid all my entry fees and traveling expenses for rodeos. In turn, I wore shirts with their logos on it when I was competing. It was like they were paying me to advertise for them. The more I won, the more they paid. So, if I made it to Vegas and won, that sponsorship would pay for even more.

My mind went back to Harper. I hoped we could have a calm conversation about what bothered me about this issue with Zaire. "Where's Shana?"

"We got into it before I found out you'd gotten arrested."

"What about?"

"She doesn't want to commit for some reason. Although she claims I'm the only guy she's seeing, she won't introduce me as her man. I'm always her friend. She doesn't seem to have an issue with me introducing her as my lady, so I don't understand it."

"We both going through with these women then."

"What you mean?"

"I told Harper that I loved her last night but not the way I wanted to tell her."

"Damn. Sound like we all fucked up."

He chuckled as we continued our ride to Liberty. Hopefully, we could get this situation understood and resolved.

When we got to Liberty, Harper's car wasn't there. She'd probably gone to Shana's. I didn't know why she would do that though since she knew I was coming home and that I needed to talk to her. Here we go with this bullshit again. I suppose I wouldn't hear from her again. The only difference this time is that it would hurt like hell.

Red used his key to let me inside. I'd given my keys to Harper last night. I went to the kitchen to fix me an egg sandwich. "You didn't call my parents, did you?"

"Naw. I didn't think you would want me to."

"Good. No, I don't want them to worry."

I fried a few eggs and Red and I sat at the bar to eat our egg sandwiches. "I'm going to Shana's house when I leave from here. You want me to tell Harper to call you?"

"No. She knew that I was getting out this morning. If she wants to talk to me, then she'll come home. I told her ass there was a lot I needed to talk to her about, and she still left because she was in her fucking feelings about me telling her not to come to the courthouse this morning."

It wasn't that I was tripping about spending a night in jail, it was just that she didn't seem to understand why I did what I did. "You sound like that nigga before Harper came along. I don't know which one I like better."

I slightly rolled my eyes. Harper had softened me up a little, but I see that was probably a mistake. After I finished eating my sandwich, I went up to my room to take a shower. My nerves were so damned shot; I just wanted to shower and go to sleep now. Before I could get in the shower, my phone was ringing. I thought it would have been Harper, but it wasn't. "Hello?"

"Hello, Mr. Semien?"

"Yes. Who's this?"

"This is Sidney Taylor. I'm a defense attorney in Beaumont,

Texas. Your friend, Craig Anderson called me to look over your case. Do you have time to talk?"

"Can I call you back after I shower? I just ate and was about to get this holding cell scent off me."

She giggled. "Sure. I'll be here for a few more hours."

"Thank you so much. I won't be long."

"No problem."

Red was on top of shit, and I was glad he was in my corner. I almost had to ask who she was talking about. I ain't called that nigga Craig in a hot minute. I was glad he'd thought about calling an attorney because the only thing on my mind was Harper. She needed to get off it, so I could handle my business though. I didn't seem to be on hers since she wasn't here. After washing up and drying off, I headed back downstairs to see Red was still here. "Thank you for calling an attorney for me."

"It's cool. I looked this chick up, and she don't play no games. She's never lost a case, and she's defended people you wouldn't believe. She's well connected."

"Well, that's cool. Hopefully, she can help me out."

"Yeah. Well, I'm about to head out. I'll talk to you later."

He shook my hand as I said, "Aight. Thanks, Red."

Once he left, I got comfortable on my couch and got situated. I took a pain pill from when I had my concussion, then called her back. "This is the office of Sidney Taylor. How may I help you?"

"May I speak to Sidney Taylor, please?"

"Sure. May I ask who's calling?"

"Legend Semien."

"Okay. Hold for a moment, Mr. Semien."

I listened to the music playing for a moment, then Mrs. Taylor came on the line. "Hello, Mr. Semien. That was quick."

"Yep. Call me Legend."

"Okay. So, tell me what happened exactly. Craig said that you got into an altercation at a restaurant, but he wasn't sure how it started."

Once I finished telling her what happened, along with background information about Zaire and Harper's relationship, she understood why I'd gotten so angry. "I'm willing to represent you, Mr. Semien if you would like to retain me as your attorney. You can read all about my credentials on my website, and the cases I've won. I don't like bullies, and I'm always willing to fight for the underdog."

"That sounds good to me, Mrs. Taylor. How much you charging me, though? That's gonna weigh in a lot on whether you represent me or not."

She laughed. "I understand, Legend. Don't worry, I'm not terribly expensive, especially for residents in the area. Now, high-profile clients, I compete with the best of them. I know you're famous in the rodeo arena, but again, you're homegrown."

I could tell she was a sista that time. Before, it was unclear. "Okay. I'm gon' check you out. For now, I'd like to retain you, though."

"Awesome! Would you be able to come to my office sometime this week?"

"I can come today or tomorrow if you want."

"Oh, that's great. Can you come before four today?"

"Yes, ma'am. Let me get a quick nap in, then I'll head your direction. Where are you located?"

"I'm on Highway 105, north of Major Drive. You can't miss it."

"Okay. Thank you. I'll call if I need further directions."

"Thank you. See you soon."

That bitch-ass nigga hadn't even filed charges yet, so at least she will be on standby just in case I need her. I set my alarm for ten, then took a nap.

THIS WOMAN WAS GORGEOUS. Her skin was dark, maybe a shade lighter than mine and was flawless. She looked to be about five-foot-ten or eleven. Her hair was down her back to her ass, and I could tell it was her hair, none added. I noticed a picture of her in a Longhorns basketball uniform on the wall, and a family portrait as well. She'd only asked for a $500 retainer, which was extremely cheap. "So, these are the contracts stating that you're hiring me to represent you and confidentiality agreements."

"Okay."

I signed the documents, then looked her over for a moment as she shuffled papers around. That was a habit that I needed to break. When she was done, she looked up at me and smiled. "So, what's it like being a bull rider? I looked you up, and you seem to be amazing at it."

I smiled at her and began explaining my career and passion while she listened intently. Just as I finished and was standing to leave, there was a knock on the door. "Come in."

"Hey, baby, you ready for lunch? Oh, I'm sorry. I didn't know you had a client."

"It's okay, Devin. We were just wrapping up. Devin, this is Legend Semien. Legend, this is my husband, Devin Taylor."

"Nice to meet you," he said with a smile.

"Likewise."

He walked to her and kissed her lips and that only made me miss Harper even more so. "If anything changes, please call me, no matter the time, Mr. Semien."

"I will. Thank you."

I left her office and was about to head back to my house, then decided I would get something to eat while I was here. I'd talked to my parents on my way to Beaumont and told them what was going on. It wasn't that I hadn't gotten into a fight before, but I'd never spent a night in jail. My mama went off on me, especially when I told her that he might be pressing charges on me.

I couldn't believe that Harper hadn't called me yet. It made me wonder what the fate of our relationship would be. However, when I got home, her Mustang was in the driveway. My heart rate picked up a bit. I'd gotten a footlong sub sandwich, and I'd had them cut it in half, so maybe she would eat the other half. I was no longer irritated with her. Just missing her presence was making me miserable.

When I got inside, I went to the kitchen to see she was taking a roast out of the oven. I set my keys on the countertop as she turned around and noticed me. Harper ran to me and fell against me. I instantly wrapped my arms around her. "Hey, baby."

"Hey, Legend. I'm sorry I wasn't here when you got here. I overslept. I'd gone to Shana's last night."

I nodded, then sat on a bar stool while she went back to the oven and took some yams out. My stomach was starting to growl as I looked at all the food she'd cooked. She probably saw me looking, because she said, "There's a banana pudding in the fridge."

I smiled slightly. My mama must have told her that I loved banana pudding. After she turned the fire off from the green beans and pinto beans, she sat next to me. Grabbing her hand, I looked in her beautiful eyes. "I'm sorry for embarrassing you, Harper."

Wait a got damned minute. That ain't what I was supposed to be saying. "I should be the one apologizing, Legend."

Damn right. "I was so worried about appearances, I missed the fact that a punk-ass man was disrespecting me in public. It was your job as my man to stand up for me. I'm sorry that I made it seem like you were overreacting." She took an unsteady breath. "Legend, you said you loved me. Did you mean that?"

I wiped my hand down my face. "Before I answer that, I need to say some other things. Whenever it comes to Zaire, you fold in front of him, but you take that shit out on me. I need to know why."

"What do you mean?"

"It's like you cower in his presence."

"It's because I'm embarrassed to have dated someone like him. When it's just me and him, I will curse him from here to hell and back. But in front of you, someone so genuine, I'm embarrassed."

Damn. My facial expressions softened, and I forgot about all the other shit I wanted to talk to her about. I pulled her in my arms and hugged her tightly. "You don't have a reason to be embarrassed, Harper." Lifting her chin, I kissed her beautiful lips. "I love you."

She kissed me again as she held me at the back of my head, not wanting my lips to leave hers. Scooping her in my arms, I went to the sofa and sat on it as we continued to kiss. She pulled away and straddled me, then pulled my shirt over my head. The way she kneaded my shoulders as she lowered her head to kiss me again, had my dick rock hard. I lifted her shirt and pulled it from her body, then unfastened her bra.

Damn, them nipples were erect for me, waiting on my tongue to tease them, willing me to do with them as I pleased. And I did. The way she grinded on my lap told me she was enjoying everything I was doing to her body. My hands slid down her back and gripped her ass as she held my head close to her. "Oh Legend."

Suddenly, my mind started working overtime. *She didn't respond to me saying I loved her.* "Harper?"

"Yes... Legend."

"Do you love me?"

She continued to grind on my lap as I slumped in the sofa, ignoring my question for now. I unzipped my pants and pulled out my dick as she lifted her skirt. *Shit.* I didn't have a condom near me.

Standing from the sofa, I picked her up and she wrapped her legs around my waist. She kept lowering her pussy on the head of my dick, and I could feel her juices leaking over it. "You better stop before I fuck the shit outta you against this wall without a condom."

"I'm on the pill, Legend."

"Well, you done fucked up now."

I literally slammed us against the wall at the top of the stairs and lowered her on my dick. She screamed out in passion as I pushed her legs to her shoulders and wore that pussy out. "Legend, fuck!"

I grunted as I pushed inside of her forcefully, causing her to scratch my back. "Fuck, Harper. Squeeze that dick, girl."

She did as I requested as I slowed my thrusts, being sure to go as deeply as possible. Feeling her end against the head of my dick did nothing to quench the sensations I felt. Before long, I felt her walls tighten around me and she screamed out in ecstasy. "Oh shit! I'm cumming, Legend!"

Stroking her more powerfully, I nibbled on her ear as she whimpered. Raising my head to stare at her, her sex faces brought me down. My final thrust, I grunted loudly, then allowed her legs to slide from my arms. I kissed her neck, then her cheek, and lips. "I love you, Harper."

She pulled my face in her hands and stared into my eyes. "I love you too, Legend."

25

arper

I SLID down to the floor with Legend as he stared at me. I'd said I loved him too. Avoiding the question earlier gave me time to think. Although, it was hard to think with dick running through me. "I hope you never miss a pill because now that I done felt you, that latex is on permanent vacation."

I laughed as we sat there on the floor. "Harper?"

"Yes?"

"You said you loved me."

"I know."

"Is that how you really feel or did you just say it back to say it back?"

"I love you, Legend. I don't know if I'm in love with you, though. I want to be."

"I understand that, baby girl."

"I've been a little hesitant about letting my guard down. Zaire really messed me up, and I'm sorry that it seems like you're the one suffering because of that. I'm really trying to be better for you."

"Don't worry. We're good."

He stood then helped me up from the floor and kissed me softly. After going to the bedroom, he started the shower, and I knew we would be going at it again within its confines. When he came back out, he pulled me close. He said in my ear, "Damn. I can't believe I'm in love."

I giggled a little as he grabbed my ass. He loved gripping it, and I loved for him to do so. Before we could get in the shower, his phone was ringing. As he went to it, I stood in the mirror, staring at the image staring back at me. The woman that looked at me was strong and beautiful. Daily, I had to remind myself of that fact, because Zaire had tried to tear me down.

I finally realized that Legend was trying to build me up and refused to let anyone try to bring me down. I was his queen, and no one would disrespect me, especially not in his presence. "Baby?"

"Yes?"

He walked in the bathroom. "So, it turns out that the attorney Red got for me, is the same attorney your mother wanted to get for me. You told her what was going on?"

"Yeah. I called her last night to tell her what Zaire and Journey had caused. She told me she would try to pull some strings."

"Thanks, baby. That was the attorney, Sidney Taylor, calling me to tell me that your mom had called her."

"Oh, well I'm glad she's doing what she said she would do."

"Yep, now let me finish doing what I need to do."

"Mmm, what's that, baby?"

"Fuck the shit outta you."

"Yes, please finish," I said as he led me to the shower.

I woke up with a smile on my face. Legend and I had made up all day yesterday, and I couldn't be happier. After our shower, we went downstairs to enjoy the food I'd cooked. That sub sandwich didn't stand a chance against that roast. Legend ate so much banana pudding, he nearly made himself sick. After turning over in the bed, I could hear Legend outside. Looking out the window, I saw him leaving. *Where was he going?*

Before I could leave the room, I saw a note on the dresser. He had a follow-up doctor's appointment. This visit would possibly determine whether he can start rodeoing again. I must admit, I've enjoyed the past couple of weeks with him. I grabbed my phone from the nightstand and called him. "Good morning, Harper."

"Good morning. Why didn't you wake me? I would have gone to the doctor with you."

"You were sleeping, snoring and slobbering all over the damn pillow. I didn't want to wake you up. You looked like you were getting the best sleep you've ever gotten."

I laughed. "I do not snore, and I surely wasn't slobbering."

"Aight. You might wanna check that pillow. It prolly smell like leftover morning breath."

"Legend!"

He laughed loudly. "I'm just playing, baby. You want me to bring you anything back?"

"Nope, just you."

"Yep. I got your cream-filled pastry right here ready for you when I get back."

"You so damn nasty. That's okay. I got some nasty shit waiting for you too."

"Oh yeah? Why don't you tell me?"

"Nope. Go to your doctor's appointment, and I'll see you later."

"Aight, baby girl. I'm gon' punish you when I get back."

"I'll gladly accept that punishment. Bye Legend."

"Bye Harper."

I laid back in the bed fully prepared to take a nap, when the doorbell rang. Frowning slightly, I put my robe on, then grabbed my phone and headed downstairs. Legend had told me that he rarely had pop-up visitors. Only Red and his parents did that and all of them had keys. Looking through the peephole, I saw that chick from the livestock show that was staring at him. *What the fuck did she want?* I hesitantly opened the door and her eyes widened slightly. We stared at each other for a moment. I was about to close the door on her ass since she had nothing to say. She finally stuttered, "Umm. Is Legend available?"

"No. He's not here."

I took my phone out and called him on speaker. He answered, "You still thinking about that cream-filled pastry?"

I laughed. "Always. I called because there's a woman here for you."

"Who?"

She looked like a White woman, but her hair texture let me know that she had to be bi-racial. I looked at her and held the phone out for her to say her name. She looked nervous as fuck. "Neffie."

"How the fuck you know where I live? And why the fuck are you there?"

"Legend, I just..."

"Nah. I told yo' ass when I got hurt to stop trying to contact me. You know I have a woman, but I told you I was done wit' yo' triflin' ass before then." He paused. "Harper, if you wanna beat her ass, you can. Or you can call the police because she's trespassing."

She walked off before he could finish talking. I'd heard him go off on her before, but I didn't realize who she was. Neffie. "She left Legend. You know I wasn't about to fight that woman."

"I'm gon' have to file a restraining order on her ass. I never gave her my phone number or told her where I live. She irritating as fuck."

"Well, that's what happens sometimes when you fuck random people. They don't understand that it was just a fuck. Her feelings have gotten involved."

"Naw. That shit ain't got nothing to do with her feelings. She wanna be associated with a winner. I told you that about her before I think."

"Yeah. You called her a buckle bunny."

"Shol' did. Aight, I gotta go. I'm at the doctor's office. If she comes back, call the police."

"Okay, Legend."

He ended the call as I walked back upstairs. This lil trick was gon' make me whoop her ass if she came back. I was trying to be nice and let him handle it. This was the third time I'd witnessed him rejecting her. She needed to get herself together before I had to help her on the path to self-betterment.

I had an order for tomorrow, so when Legend got back, I thought we'd do something fun by baking together. In the meantime, I laid back in the bed and snuggled under the covers. After all of this, I knew I probably wouldn't go to sleep, so I sent Shana a text to find out how things went with her and Red. She was probably at work, but I knew once she got the text, she'd call me.

~

"So, you want me to help you bake cupcakes? Have you met me?"

I laughed loudly. Legend was standing there in shock as I put an apron on him. "Baby, if you help me with these cupcakes, I'll let you teach me to ride a horse. So, what did the doctor say?"

"I'm clear. I'll be back on my grind next week. You already know how to ride a horse, Harper. The way you ride this stallion, you got to be a pro."

I giggled as I pulled his face to mine. "Damn, I love yo' nasty ass."

He lifted me and sat me on the island countertop, then stood between my legs. "I love yo' nasty ass too. Harper?"

"Yeah, baby?"

"I'm so glad we met. You exposed a side of me I didn't even know existed."

"Damn, baby."

I covered his lips with mine as his hands roamed to my ass and squeezed. Legend had awakened my inner freak, that was for sure. We were getting carried away though, so I pulled away. "Legend, I will give you all the shit you can handle *after* we finish these cupcakes."

"I'm gon' hold you to that," he said, backing away from me.

I hopped down from the countertop and gathered the ingredients I needed. Legend watched me move around until I summoned him. "I need you to measure the flour and drop it in this bowl."

He looked at the directions and got to work while I cracked eggs, added sugar and baking powder. When he finished with the flour, he added oil and water. After mixing, Legend ran his finger along the whisk and brought it to my lips. He rubbed batter along my bottom lip, then kissed me, sucking my lip into his mouth. I pulled away and he gently slid his finger into my mouth. I sucked that shit like it was his dick, causing him to yell, "Fuck! Let's get this shit in the oven, Harp."

I giggled, then filled the cups with batter. Not a minute after I slid them in the oven, he pulled me to him, letting his lips show my neck some attention until the doorbell rang. "What the fuck!"

"Don't answer it, Legend," I said while pulling my shirt over my head.

He groaned as he pulled my nipple in his mouth. The doorbell rang again. Them fuckers just wouldn't go away. I grabbed his hard dick through the pants. "Legend, I need you, shit."

"I need you too, but them bastards ain't goin' away. I'll be right back."

I pouted as he went to the door. After hearing some talking, the door slammed. I grabbed my shirt and slid it back on because I had a feeling our pending sex session was done. He walked back in the kitchen with a deep frown on his face and an envelope in his hand. "What's wrong?"

"I got served. Fuck-boy pressed charges. I have to appear in court in two weeks. Let me call Mrs. Taylor and we'll talk more in a minute."

My heart sank. This shit was starting to get to me and I needed to find out some negative information on Zaire's ass that would somehow help Legend. While in my thoughts, I was brought back to reality when I heard my name. "She's right here," Legend said.

"Hi, Ms. Richardson. My name is Sidney Taylor. Legend said that Zaire grabbed you. Would you be able to corroborate that story?"

"Yes, ma'am."

"Zaire totally understood that you wouldn't want him touching you, correct?"

"Yes, ma'am."

"Okay, that could be considered assault as well, no matter how minuscule it seems. It was very significant in how the situation escalated."

"So, you would be willing to testify, correct?"

"Anything I need to do for Legend, I'll do."

"Thank you, Ms. Richardson."

"Call me Harper."

The look he gave me after saying that I would do anything for him, caused my body to heat up with desire. I couldn't wait to see what would happen to me once these cupcakes were done. He licked his lips, then resumed his conversation with Mrs. Taylor. "I have no doubt in your abilities, and I'm aware that I will have to pay a fine or be on probation or something."

"Maybe but let me work. When I get through, he may drop the charges."

"That would be perfect. I'd pay you twice."

"Alright. Get yo' life together, 'cause I never disappoint." We all laughed, then she continued. "I'm just kidding. I have a feeling that I'm gonna find some interesting information on this spoiled jackass. Oh, and Harper, I love your mom, and she spoke so highly of you."

My eyebrows had risen. "Thank you."

"Okay. I'm going to get the footage from Suga's. This research shouldn't take me long. Maybe a couple of days. I'll be in touch."

"Thank you," we said in unison.

"You're welcome."

Legend ended the call, then turned his attention to me. "When those cupcakes get done, you next on the list."

I walked closer to him. "You promise?"

"Mmm hmm."

"Have you heard from Red? I texted Shana, but she's not gon' answer me until she gets off."

"Yeah. They aren't talking anymore."

"What?"

"I know."

"Shana is probably devastated. Did he say what happened?"

"He said she wanted him to stop talking to the women that call him."

"Okay. That's what respect is all about right?"

"Yeah, it is. He told her he would if she said that they were in a serious relationship."

"Let me guess, she said they weren't."

"I don't know what her exact words were, but it started a heated argument."

"Shit. I know where her mind is, Legend. She wants to see his effort before she admits that she wants the same thing he does. She's been hurt so much. There's a damned barb wired fence around her heart."

"I know. I'm gonna try to talk to him later."

I hoped Shana called me when she got off. I knew she was upset. When the last guy she talked to had said that she was just cool and a fuck buddy, it tore her to pieces. She'd asked him where their relationship was going. After that, she didn't talk to anyone seriously for two years. Red was the first guy I saw her have a genuine interest in since then. I hoped Legend and I could help them figure this out.

26

egend

"Okay, Lacey. One more round. You got this, so quit tripping. Pretend you right here on my property tomorrow, trying to show off. I'm telling you, you have it. Let's go."

"I got it. I'm ready. Tell me when to go."

"Aight. Whenever you ready, just take off and I'll start the timer."

We'd been practicing for the past hour and all week. Her competition was tomorrow in Jasper at the fairgrounds, and she was nervous as hell. I didn't know what else to say to her to calm her down. She was practically begging me to be there tomorrow. When I told her that I would come, she damn near tackled me to the ground.

When she took off, I started the timer. The horse was sliding and lunging around the barrels perfectly, and Lacey was doing exactly what she should do as well. Just as she crossed the line, I stopped the time. She was right at fourteen point two seconds. That was a great time for a teenager. "Lacey, damn!"

"Did I mess up?" she asked, spinning the horse around.

"Hell naw! You got fourteen point two!"

"That's my best time!"

"Congratulations!" Harper said from behind us.

I hadn't even heard her approach. My lips instinctively twisted to the side. She didn't know shit about barrel racing. She probably heard our exchange. I pulled her in my arms as she gave me the mail. "Thank you, Ms. Harper! Are you coming to the rodeo tomorrow?" Lacey asked.

"I suppose I can. If it's okay with Legend."

"Girl, why wouldn't it be okay with me?"

I pulled her in my arms and kissed her forehead as Lacey smiled. "Well, I'm gonna go, Legend. I'll see you in the morning."

"Okay, baby girl. Make sure you get a good dinner and breakfast."

"I will. Thanks!"

She led her horse to the trailer to load him, then waved at us again. We both waved back, then I pulled harper to me. "Why wouldn't I want you with me?"

"Well, I just know that's your thing, and you may be busy doing other things."

"I'm never too busy for you, but let's go inside and see how hard I have to work this summer to qualify for nationals."

"Okay. I thought you get invited."

"No. It's about how many points you have. That's all public record. I can see where I stand with the best of them."

"I guess. Whatever."

I hugged her and kissed her cheek. Tickling her caused her to erupt with laughter. "Legend!" she screamed.

I didn't realize how ticklish she was. Her screams had me laughing as well. When we got into the house, she immediately opened her laptop and gave it to me. Before going to the website, I sifted through the mail to see that my blood test was in. I'd done a blood test after I found out ol' girl had HIV, with her nasty ass. I'd have to open that later. Putting it to the side, I went to the website and when I saw my name in first place, I almost threw her computer to the floor. "Hell yeah!"

She practically hopped right out of her skin. "I take it that you're at good standings?"

"Yep. I'm in first place."

"That calls for a celebration."

I pulled her to my lap. "Shol' do. Come celebrate all over yo' shit."

"GOD, I feel so out of place, Legend."

"Don't worry, baby. You the most gorgeous woman out here."

We'd gotten to the rodeo ten minutes ago. Harper had worn some jeans, wedge heels, and a halter top. She looked good enough to eat. Most of the women out here had on cowboy boots, jeans, plain-looking shirts, and some had on cowboy hats. At smaller rodeos like this one, you rarely saw someone dressed like Harper.

As we took our seats, people were approaching to shake my hand left and right. Then I saw her ass. Neffie. If she brought her ass over here, she was gonna be sorry. Harper had noticed her too. "Your stalker is here."

I gave her the side-eye as she laughed like shit was funny. I continued to look around to see if Red was gonna show up. He usually didn't miss a rodeo. When I'd called to try to help him understand where Shana was coming from, he didn't want to hear it. Shana was so hurt. When she came over to the house to be with Harper the other day, I could see the depression all over her.

A few people stopped and spoke to me and introduced themselves to Harper. Whenever she tried to let me go, I held her tighter. "Legend, I'm okay. Go do you."

"I'm not leaving you until Lacey gets ready to race."

She smiled. When everything started, I could tell she was confused, so I took it upon myself to explain what everything was. After she realized that I was willing to explain everything, she started asking questions. Steer undecorating seemed to be the event she found the least entertaining. I laughed as she watched the horse run alongside the steer for the rider to pull the tape off the horn. She looked at me and asked, "That's it?"

"Yeah, baby. That's it."

"That looks simple. It's not all that entertaining either."

I chuckled as I held her hand. Bringing it to my lips, I kissed it. As I did, I could feel eyes on me. *Did I fuck her that good?* Neffie was all in my shit. I know I ain't put it to her ass like that for her to be all on my dick. "I'm about to go down to meet Lacey, okay?"

"Okay. I hope she does well."

"Me too. Pray she gets a time as good as yesterday. She'll probably win it all if she does."

Harper put her hands together like she was praying. I kissed her lips, then made my way down to the dirt. The moment I got down there, Lacey hugged me. She was pacing. "Hey. Calm down, lil mama. Close your eyes for a minute and take deep breaths."

As she did so, I looked in the crowd toward Harper and saw Neffie sitting beside her. *What the fuck!* Harper had a scowl on her face as Neffie was talking. I wanted to go up there and choke that bitch. I didn't know what she was saying, but Harper's scowl went to disgust. She looked like she wanted to throw up. I needed to get to her, but I couldn't leave Lacey hanging.

The announcer called Lacey's name, and she walked her horse closer to the starting line. Once she crossed it, the time would start. I looked up at Harper again to see her walking out the stands as Neffie sat with a satisfied smirk on her face. Giving my attention back to Lacey, I said, "You got this. Whenever you're ready."

She nodded, and seconds later, she took off. I watched as she did everything she did in practice yesterday. Again, her horse was sliding and lunging perfectly around the barrels, and Lacey was making good time. At thirteen seconds, she was already in the straight-a-way, heading home. When she crossed the line, her time stopped at 14.1. "You did it!" I yelled at her.

I could see her people jumping up and down in the stands as she took the lead. There were only two more racers after her. Harper still hadn't come back to her seat. I didn't feel like dealing with no bullshit today. Lacey jumped off her horse and ran to me and jumped in my arms. "You did so good!"

"Thanks, Legend. That was an amazing time!"

"Yes, it was."

We stood around watching the last two racers, and Lacey placed first by a half a second. I was so proud of her. She'd done exactly what I'd trained her to do. When she accepted her medal and jackpot, she brought me with her. The announcer then announced my name over the mic as her trainer. I knew that shit was gonna have my phone ringing off the hook. Immediately after we'd taken pictures, I went looking for Harper. Before I could get to her though, I ran right into Neffie's ass. "What the fuck was you doing?"

"Nothing. I don't know what you're talking about."

"You better be glad you're a woman, or I'd knock that damned smirk off yo' face."

"Aren't you already in trouble for that?"

I was steaming. Smoke felt like it was coming from my ears as I left her ass standing there. I'd looked everywhere except the women's bathroom for Harper and there was no sign of her. I knew she hadn't left, because I had the keys. After looking around the arena one more time and not finding her, I walked to my truck to find her sitting in the bed of it, crying. "Harper?"

"Don't talk to me right now. I need time to process some shit."

She hopped out as I unlocked the doors, then walked to the passenger side and hopped in. Fucking Neffie up was all that was on my mind right now. When I got in, she looked at me. She looked so angry, I was sure I was about to meet her fist. I ain't even done shit. Cautiously, I slid my hand to hers. She didn't move it, so that was a good sign. "Question number one. Have you fucked her since we met?"

"No. She sucked me off, but that was before my ride at the Houston Livestock Show. Nothing since then."

"She said she's pregnant and that you gave her HIV."

"What the fuck! That bitch done lost her fucking mind. I strapped up the last time we had sex, Harper. I promise you. And HIV? I know that bitch got a death wish."

"What am I supposed to think, Legend? You fucked her! Condom or not, she could be pregnant with your baby! What if there was a pinhole in it or some shit?"

"Harper, I swear that bitch lyin'. She's just jealous that I chose you."

"I saw that you got results in for some kind of blood test. What did it say?"

Damn. I thought I'd done a good job hiding that shit from her. "I'm clean, Harper. I don't have shit. That had nothing to do with her."

Fuck! What did I say that shit for? Harper frowned at me. "So, you just fucked around willy-nilly, huh? You mind telling me who in the fuck I got involved with that I let fuck me raw!"

"Harper, please." I inhaled deeply and exhaled. "I fucked around a lot, especially at rodeos. Before riding, sex always calmed me down. So, that's what I did. I fucked random women and smoked weed. I haven't had sex with anyone but you since we met in Houston. I swear. I'm sorry we in this predicament."

"I need time. Let's go. I'm going to Shana's tonight to clear my head. If she's pregnant with your baby, this won't be good, Legend."

I held my tongue as I started the truck. When I saw Neffie again, I hoped like hell that I wouldn't be alone. I didn't know if I would be able to keep myself from choking the shit out of her.

The whole drive home to Liberty was quiet as fuck. I was so mad, my fingers were cramping from holding the steering wheel so tight, and my head felt like it was about to explode. When I put the truck in park in the driveway, Harper jumped out. I jumped out right behind her. "Harper! Hol' up."

She stopped when she got to the back door, waiting for me to unlock it. "Look at me."

She turned her body, then shifted her weight and crossed her arms over her chest. "The man I've shown you is the man that I am. That lying-ass bitch ain't pregnant. Even if she is, it ain't for me. Please, don't leave."

"Open the door, Legend."

I stepped in front of her and unlocked the door, then disabled the alarm as she went up the stairs. I followed her, taking two steps at a time. When we got to the bedroom, she stopped and turned to me. "The HIV thing, I don't really believe her, but I still wanna see your test results. This pregnancy thing, though, I can't handle. Even though you say the shit happened before me, ain't no way I could deal with her ass. She claimed that's what she came to the house to talk to you about."

"Baby, please. I will go get her ass a pregnancy test, then we can get a DNA test as soon as she hits ten weeks. My boy told me about a place in Houston a few years back. I want you to be with me."

"Hell fucking no. I can't be around that bitch. I will fuck her up on the next sighting. Guaranteed."

I wiped my hand down my face as I watched her pack a bag. Red was gon' have to come with me to talk to Neffie's ass. There was no way I was going alone. I already had one assault charge I was trying to beat. If I went alone, I might get a murder charge. Harper had finished her bag and was about to walk past me. Grabbing her arm gently, I handed her the results from the dresser. "I'm clean, Harper."

She looked it over, then nodded. Putting her hand to my face, she kissed my lips softly. "I'm not leaving you, Legend, but I do need time to process this shit, so I don't snap on you. I'll be back tomorrow. I need to be with my girl anyway."

I let her arm go and allowed her to walk past me. She needed to stay here so we could work this out, but if she needed her space, I'd let her have it. I just wished she trusted me more.

arper

"THAT BITCH LYIN', Harper."

I'd just gotten to Shana's house, and she was waiting on the porch for me. She followed me to her spare bedroom. I flopped down on the bed. "I been going to rodeos and trail rides for a minute, and every time, I've seen that bitch with a different dude. Black, White, and Hispanic. The bitch don't care. Long as they have a winning record and a functional dick, she all on that shit."

"Shana, it still hurts. What if this is his baby?"

"That hoe probably not even pregnant, Harper. I'm not exaggerating about her. Everyone in this area knows she's a hoe and will do anything to make a come up."

"That still doesn't negate the fact that Legend slept with her. That bitch had the nerve to sit next to me and tell me that shit. I had to leave. I wanted to fuck her up. I sat in the back of Legend's pickup for an hour trying to cool off."

"Yeah, okay. He slept with her, but don't let that kill what y'all have. That was before you."

"I'm not. I told him that I just needed time to rationalize what was going on in my head. He said he's gonna buy a pregnancy test. If she's indeed pregnant, he's gonna get a DNA test at some place in Houston that does them while you're still pregnant. I done had it up to here with triflin' ass women," I said while motioning with my hand at my head.

"I feel you, girl. Triflin' ass men too."

My expression softened as I looked at her. She missed Red. "Have you talked to Red?"

"No."

"When you told him about all the women calling his phone, did you tell him that you wanted to be serious and that was what was holding you back?"

She looked at the floor and shook her head. "I asked him why he thought I would want a serious relationship with him with all those hoes calling him all the time."

"Oh shit, Shana. He's not going to stop talking to those other women if he doesn't at least know you want the same things he does."

"Well, it's too late for all that. We're done."

"It's not too late. It's only too late if he's married to someone else. You're miserable without him, and you know it. Quit being stubborn and pour your heart out to that man. At least you know that he wants only you."

"How do I know that? That's what his mouth says, but every time he entertains someone else, I doubt what he's saying."

"Shana, he's doing that so he won't go all in for something only he wants. He's trying to prevent being heartbroken just like you are. Please talk to him. I think y'all are more alike than you think."

She didn't respond to what I said, but when I saw those tears drop from her eyes, it broke my heart. I sat next to her and pulled her in my arms and allowed her to do something I'd never witnessed her doing. She broke down emotionally in my arms as I'd done on so many occasions in her arms. When she finally pulled herself together, she wiped her face and smiled at me. "I'm off tomorrow. Let's go get our men."

She stood from the bed and grabbed a duffle bag, then turned back to look at me sitting in the same spot. "Now."

My eyebrows lifted, then a smile spread across my face. I stood from the bed and hugged her tightly, then made my way to the front while she packed a bag. I silently prayed that Red would be willing to talk.

When we got to Liberty, Red's truck was in the driveway at Legend's house. I looked over at Shana and smiled. She smiled back and grabbed my hand. "We ain't letting their asses get away. They're both good men."

"I agree."

After getting our bags, we walked to the back door. Although I had a key, I decided to knock. Shana's hand trembled in mine, but her face maintained a confident expression. Not long after, Legend opened the door and immediately pulled me in his arms. "I'm so glad you came back. I'm sorry, Harper."

"No. I'm sorry, Legend. I can't be mad at something that happened before me. Yes, it's irritating, but so is my situation. I was wrong for leaving. I love you."

"Damn. I love you too, baby."

Shana slowly walked toward Red as he watched her. When she got close, he stood and pulled her in his embrace. That made me feel even better. He grabbed her hand, and they went outside to talk. Legend led me to the couch and pulled me down on his lap. "Hopefully, they leave soon. We need to apologize to each other properly."

I giggled. "Legend, is sex all you think about?"

"No. *You're* all I think about, and that eventually leads to thinking about sex with you."

"Shit. You flooded my panties just now."

"Mmm. I can't wait to slurp that shit up."

Good Lord, he knew how to turn me on. For a moment, his face became serious and he slid me from his lap. "I know I was asking for a lot when I asked for you to come with me to Neffie, but I wanted her to see that there was nothing she could do to break our bond."

"I'll go with you, Legend. I want her to see that shit too."

He slid his body over mine, causing me to lay back on the sofa. His lips grazed my neck as a slight moan left my lips. Damn, I loved the way he felt. Having him close to me, made me feel wanted, desired, and safe. I felt loved. Being near him healed my soul, and I could never stay angry with him. His lips made their way to mine, and he kissed me softly. Sitting up, he pulled me up as well. "I have a message for you."

"Oh yeah? What's that?"

He opened his messages on his phone, then handed it to me. I began reading and my eyebrows lifted more and more with every word.

Hello Legend. I recently found out that you're connected to Harper Richardson. I've heard so much about her business, Delectable Desserts. If at all possible, I'd like to get in touch with her about making treats for the rodeos put on in the area. Sort of like a vendor's booth. The difference is, we will pay her in advance and resell the items. Please have her contact me. This could lead to her also working the bigger rodeos as well.

"Legend! This is amazing!"

"I figured you would think so. Call him tomorrow."

"I will, first thing."

"Naw, first thing belongs to me."

"Oh, yes daddy."

"Say that shit again, Harper."

"Yeeesss daddy."

The fire danced in his eyes as he looked at me. I smiled at him, anticipating all the nasty shit we would do tonight. The back door opened, breaking the trance we were both in. "We gon' head out, Legend," Red said.

We turned to see them standing close, his arm draped around Shana's shoulders. I winked at her and she smiled brightly. My girl was happy again. "Aight man. Y'all be careful," Legend said, then stood to slap Red's hand.

I hugged Shana bye and told her I would talk to her later. Of course, I needed the details of the conversation. When they walked out of the door, Legend's cell phone rang. His face screwed up before he answered it on speakerphone. "What the fuck you want?"

"Legend, why you always so damned rude?"

"You know, I'm starting to think yo' ass is special as hell. You on medication?"

"I had to get your attention. You think you just gon' fuck me a couple of times and throw me away like I'm trash?"

"Bitch, you are trash!"

"You didn't think that when you was fucking me, Legend. I can't even get pregnant, because I had a hysterectomy. But you aren't going to just dismiss me like I don't matter."

I'd heard enough. Before he could respond, I snatched the phone from him. "Bitch, you listen, and yo' ass better listen well. I will fuck you up and think about the consequences later. I have connections and I will get off. You are harassing both of us. Carry yo' weak ass back to the gutter where you came from. However, you will take a pregnancy test, 'cause this shit ain't gon' pop up again. Tomorrow, you will take a pregnancy test."

"I'm not intimidated by you."

"Oh, you should be, bitch. Where are you? We coming tonight."

She ended the call as Legend stared at me in disbelief. "Where the hell this thug Harp come from?"

"Shut up, Legend. I want that bitch. I ain't had a fight in a long time, and I could work out on her bi-racial ass."

He laughed, then pulled me close. "Calm down, baby. I know where she is. You wanna run up on her tonight? We can."

"Hell yeah. I'm so mad right now."

My adrenaline was shooting through my veins like a saline flush. I went straight to the door as Legend grabbed his keys. He had a huge smile on his face. "What'chu smiling at Legend?"

"'Cause you a thug. I had no idea."

"Shana is my cousin, and Senator Thibodeaux is my mother. I got a lil hood in me. I never told you, but my daddy was kinda hood."

His brows lifted as he opened the door. "I done fell in love with a thug. I'm shocked as hell."

I slapped his arm as we walked to his truck. Once we got in, he turned in his seat. "We are not going there to beat her ass. If she don't open the door, then we won't bust it down. You got it, T.H.?"

I frowned. "T.H.?"

"Thug Harp. That's gon' be yo' nickname now that I done seen the hood come out ya."

"I'm gon' show yo' ass Thug Harp when we get back to the house, nigga."

"Oh, well I'm gon' make sure I make a playlist filled with Tank,

Trey Songz, Chris Brown, and any other nasty mutha-fucka I can find just to egg you on."

I slightly rolled my eyes with my lips twisted to the side. Watching where we were headed, my body didn't know whether it wanted to fight or get fucked. I was so fucking turned on, Legend might get it in this truck before we got back to the house. We crossed the bridge and it seemed we were leaving Liberty, heading west toward Dayton. "Where she live?"

"Right outside of Dayton. We'll be there in about fifteen minutes. You wanna go in CVS and get a test when we get to Dayton?"

"Yeah, I will."

Ten minutes later, we stopped at CVS. I couldn't wait to pop up on this bitch. She obviously didn't know that Legend knew where she lived. *How did he know where she lived?* Before I could dwell on that shit too long, coincidence fell right in my fucking hands. That bitch was at the damned register. I sent a text to Legend. *That bitch is at the register. If she get away from me, catch her ass outside.*

I walked to the register with the test and didn't bother to acknowledge her. It wasn't shit I could do in this store with cameras every damn where. I couldn't believe she didn't see me standing there right next to her. After I paid for my test, she was walking near the exit. Walking quickly, I caught up to her and grabbed her by the arm. When she noticed who I was, that bitch had the nerve to swing.

Oh, like hell. I leaned back right in the nick of time. Lord have mercy on her soul if she would have hit me. I popped her in the head. "Bitch, quit playin'. How you got here?"

"I drove!" she yelled as I looked around.

Legend walked up to us with a smirk on his face. "I told yo' ass I wasn't pregnant!" she yelled.

"Prove it. We gon' go to yo' hole in the wall and find out," Legend said with a frown on his face. "Get in with us, and we'll bring you back here after you take the test."

"I won't tell you where I live."

"Just like I didn't tell you where I live, but you somehow found out, I know where the fuck you live."

She jerked away from me and got in the truck. I got my ass in the backseat with her ass just in case she wanted to try something sneaky. She sat there with her arms folded the entire time.

When we got to her house, I saw why Legend called that shit a hole in the wall. It looked like a damned matchbox. All the dick she was supposed to be riding, she should have been living in a damned mansion. She got out of the truck and Legend and I followed her to the door. When she opened the door, it looked like some shit was gon' fall on me. Her house was filthy. I couldn't believe Legend fucked this bitch.

"I guess y'all gon' come in the bathroom with me too?"

"Legend won't, but I will. He don't need to have nightmares tonight."

"You a slick bitch, huh?"

"Watch who you calling a bitch," I said as I pushed her.

She talked a big game. This heifer could do whatever she wanted to me right now. I was in her house. The police would have barely questioned her. This was her sanctuary, no matter how small or raggedy it was. All bark and no bite. She walked into the bathroom and I remained in the doorway. I took the test from the CVS bag and handed it to her. She tore the box open and proceeded to handle her business. When she was done, she sat the stick on the vanity.

I stood there watching her, then finally asked, "You just fuck random men at rodeos? Legend said he didn't even know you like that and that he wasn't the only one. Maybe, one guy, I can understand, but this seems to be a lifestyle for you. Why?"

I thought she was gonna get hostile, but she did just the opposite. She lowered her head. "I've been on my own since I was fourteen. I don't know my daddy and my mama died. She told me she had family in San Antonio but came here with whoever the fuck my daddy was. We were always at a rodeo, so it's in me. I watched her talk to random men to help make ends meet. That's why I do it. I barrel race when I can afford the entry fee, but I'm not that good at it. If I don't fuck around, I don't eat."

I looked over at the stick on the vanity to only see one line. Thank God. I turned and walked out of her bathroom to find Legend standing in her front room. "The test was negative."

"Just as I thought. Let's get her back to CVS."

"I lied. I walked there, so I'm good."

I slowly shook my head. There were many options she could have taken beside what she was doing, but that shit had been engrained in her from a child. Legend grabbed my hand and led me out of that house. "I hope this is the end of you tryna start shit with me, Neffie."

"I'm sorry. I'm done."

Legend pulled me out the door, while I glanced back at her. When we got to his truck, I took a deep breath and exhaled loudly. "What?" he asked.

"I just... nothing."

Legend glanced at me, but he didn't push for me to say what the issue was. Something in me wanted to help her, but the logically thinking side of me said to leave her alone. Somebody else could help her, and maybe I would find that somebody to do so.

28

egend

THE TRAIL-RIDE this weekend would be the last event before I had to go to court behind this assault charge. I was ready too. Me and Harper could get fucked up, then come home and fuck. J Paul, Jr. and The Zydeco Nubreeds would be performing. I didn't know how Harper felt about Zydeco music, but I would find out. She'd had three orders this week that made her a quick grand. Work had been steadily coming in for her.

Today, we had to go meet with Mrs. Taylor to discuss how our day in court would go. I was a little nervous about it, but Harper kept telling me to relax, that everything would work out. When we got to her office in Beaumont, I slid from the seat and walked slowly to the entrance. The moment we walked in, we saw Mrs. Taylor standing at the front desk, talking to the lady sitting there. "Hi, Mr. Semien. Ms. Richardson! Y'all come on back."

We followed her to her office. She seemed happy, so I couldn't wait to see what she would say. We sat in the chairs in front of her desk as she smiled. "Mr. Semien..."

"Legend."

She smiled again. "Legend, you look uptight. I promise I have some good news."

She took a stack of papers from the counter space behind her. "Mr. Zaire Lewis has been extremely busy. He's filed assault charges on more people than the police department. Look at this."

She ran down a list of at least thirty people in various locations throughout East Texas. It seemed he got a kick out of provoking people. "What the hell?" Harper said.

"That was my exact thought, Ms. Richardson."

"Harper."

She smiled. "Okay, well y'all call me Sidney. I filed counter charges of assault as well. When we get to court, he's gonna... excuse how I'm going to say this, but... he's gon' shit on himself. I don't like bullies. I've probably said that before, but I'm about to shut him down. Monday can't get here fast enough. You ready to talk, Harper?"

"Yes, ma'am. I'm tired of his ass trying to control me. Although, he's been eerily quiet since the incident."

"Oh, he's around. He's been communicating with his lawyer and making trips to Louisiana."

Harper's eyebrows lifted slightly. She knew he was fucking her sister, I didn't know why she seemed surprised. What Sidney said next though, had my mouth open. "Although Senator Thibodeaux called me, I found out that she's been helping him too. Her daughter is dating him, but I'm sure you know that since she was there that evening. She's pregnant for Zaire."

"This shit just gets better and better."

"Don't worry, Harper. That has nothing to do with you. I think he's blackmailing your mom though. That's why she's helping him. I found evidence that looks fishy like she embezzled money back in 2013."

"Shit. I bet that was why she resigned."

"Possibly. I don't plan to bring that up unless I have to. All the assault and harassment cases should be enough proof that he's a jackass. And of course, we'll have your testimony and footage from Suga's showing that he grabbed you hard enough to stall your progress and make you take a step back. He still has time to drop the charges. He can actually do that in front of the judge. I'm almost sure, once he sees all this stuff I've researched, he'll see things our way."

"Damn. I'm glad this shit is almost over," I said, breaking my silence.

"Yes. So, do y'all have any questions for me?"

"How much do I owe you?"

"$500."

"So, $1,000 total. That's it?"

"I told you, I don't like bullies."

"That's why you're so blessed," Harper said.

Sidney smiled. "Okay, if that's it, I will see you guys on Monday morning. Meet me at the courthouse by 7:30 a.m., then we'll go to the courtroom together."

We all stood from our seats and Sidney escorted us to the front. I shook her hand and Harper did the same, then we exited the building to walk to the truck. "You okay, baby?"

"I'm okay. I just can't believe my mom is in trouble with his ass and didn't bother to say anything. I wonder how Zaire even knows what she did?"

"Rich people can be resourceful when they want to be. Let's not worry about that right now though. We gon' turn up this weekend. You ever been to a trail ride?"

"Nope. Are we gonna be on horses?"

"Yeah. You can ride with me. I know you probably won't be comfortable on your own horse yet... Shit!"

How did I let that shit slip? "Legend! You bought me a horse?"

"I didn't mean to tell you yet, but yeah."

She was giddy with excitement. "So, we're gonna be riding through trails?"

I laughed loudly while she frowned at me. She was killing me for real. "Naw. We gon' be on Highway 90, girl."

I couldn't stop laughing. She legit thought we were gonna be riding horses in the woods. I almost had to pull over, so I could laugh. "Legend! How was I supposed to know?"

"I'm sorry, baby, but that shit was funny. Back in the day, that's what they did, though. It has evolved now. It's gonna be a bunch of people on horses, four-wheelers, and whatever else they wanna ride. A long trail of folks riding. Trail ride."

"Oh."

"Then tomorrow night will be the party at Rivon's Arena in Raywood. Country folk turn up more than y'all city slickers. You about to see."

When we got back home and had eaten, I brought Harper to the shower. I loved making love to her in the shower. She was already sexy as fuck, but to see that body dripping wet did some wild things to me. That milk chocolate skin was my weakness. I backed her under the shower head, allowing the water to rain down on her from head to toe, then lowered my lips to hers. She moaned into my mouth as I gripped her thigh.

"Legend, please, make love to me now."

The foreplay was getting the best of her. Lifting her as her back rested against the wall, I lowered her on my dick. We both exhaled as I penetrated those hot, wet folds. Slowly, I made love to her. I wanted her to wanna climb these fucking walls. Lowering my head, I gently bit and teased her nipples. Her legs were draped over the crooks in my arms, so when I felt them begin to tremble, I went deeper. "Legend... shit, baby. I'm cumming. Fuck!"

Her nails dug into my back, causing me to bite my bottom lip. I maintained my slow pace, making love to her like she wanted. Giving her all of me was easy because she deserved it and more. All the passion I felt for her was in every stroke, the love I had for her was in every kiss, and the uninhibited desire I felt was in every groan and grunt that left my lips. "Harper," I said slightly above a whisper. "I love you."

"I love you too, Legend," she said into my ear, then gently bit it. "I'm in love with you."

I lifted my head and stared into her eyes. She was finally giving in to what she was feeling for me. That shit made me feel so complete. "Harper, I love you more than anything in this world. I'll give up everything for you. You make me so happy, baby. Nothing or no one is more important than you."

I watched the tears fall down her cheeks. That was some real shit. I'd give up rodeoing, never ride a bull or horse again if that meant she would be with me for life. She started throwing her hips back at me. That usually meant she wanted me to pick up the pace, but she was gon' have to tell me today. I kept my pace slow and deep, no matter how tortured I felt. That shit felt good at the same time. "Legend..."

"Yeah, baby?"

"You make me happy too. The happiest I've ever been."

It felt like my heart was about to explode while listening to her words amidst her moans. We had sexual chemistry that was out of this world, but the love between us was straight from heaven. It was so strong, it had the power to destroy me if I ever lost her. Before long I felt my nut rising, causing my extremities to tingle. "Legend! Shit, I'm cumming again! Oh my God!"

Her legs were trembling in my arms and her body looked to be drained of all it had. That pussy though, it was still wet as ever. The sloshing noises were what I loved about it. She got so damn wet for me. My pace quickened just a little as I licked her neck and played with her nipple. "Fuck, Harper."

"Cum for me, daddy."

"I'm about to. Shit!"

I almost dropped her ass, that shit felt so good. My knees had buckled. "Damn, Legend. I think it gets better every time."

I licked my lips as I caught my breath. "I think so too."

I kissed her softly, letting my tongue entangle with hers as I allowed her legs to slide from my arms. Her hands went to my face, pulling me even closer to her as if that was even possible. It seemed like our bodies were molded as one. My hands instinctively went to her ass and squeezed. I loved her ass. I loved everything about her. There was no denying it.

I grabbed her loofah and her Olay and lathered it good, then washed her body. Her eyes closed as I passed the loofah over her skin. Pulling her close to me, I washed her front. Her ass pressed against my dick was about to incite round two. I managed to control my desires though and continued to wash her. Once I was done, she washed me, paying extra attention to my hard dick.

After rinsing off, we left the shower. Before she could grab her towel to dry off, I'd bent her over the vanity and entered her in a hurry. She was about to get everything she didn't get in the shower. Grabbing her by the hair hanging down her back, I pulled her to me as I watched my dick slide in and out of her. Her juices coated me completely, making my assault even deadlier.

I released her hair, and she fell forward to the vanity. Gripping her jiggling ass, I dug that shit out as she screamed my name over and over again. Feeling her walls contract around me only fueled my drive. "That's it, Harper. Cum for me."

"Yes, Legend! Fuck me, baby."

My pace increased as I turned that pussy out. Killing it, reviving it, and killing it again. "Ahh, shit!" I yelled as my nut bolted from me.

I briefly rested my forehead on the back of her shoulder as my dick slid out of her. *My God.* She had to be made just for me because she satisfied me in ways unimaginable. After we cleaned up again, I moisturized her skin, then laid behind her in the bed to take a much-needed nap.

arper

I HAD NEVER SEEN so many drunk people in one spot. We'd gone on the trail ride this morning, and that was cool, I guess. We were just riding for miles. Cars on the highway blew at us as the Zydeco music blasted from someone's radio or from what Legend called the party wagon. I wasn't a fan of Zydeco, but I couldn't say that I hated it either. After the ride, we showered, ate lunch, then came back for the party. There was live music from a Zydeco band, and people were dancing and having a great time.

Shana and I sat toward the back as I watched people dance. Watching them dance to the music was extremely entertaining. I wished I knew how to dance to it. Shana was only taking a break sitting with me. She'd been keeping the floor hot. Legend was talking to a group of guys, but he'd occasionally look at me and wink or blow me a kiss. Red pulled Shana from her seat, and they made their way through the crowd to dance as I sipped my drink. "You wanna dance?"

I looked up to see a nice-looking man holding his hand out. Smiling, I responded, "No thank you. I'm enjoying watching everyone else."

"If you don't know how to Zydeco, I don't mind teaching you."

"Oh, no. Thank you."

"Beedie Bird, I know you ain't tryna flirt with my lady."

Legend had walked up as he offered to teach me to Zydeco. "I was! She's beautiful. I wouldn't leave her alone long if I were you."

They laughed, and he shook Legend's hand, then walked away. "Gotta watch that nigga. He'll have you swingin' all over the place. You enjoying yourself, baby?"

"Yeah, it's cool. It's not much different than a club, except we're listening to Zydeco music and we're outside. I'm glad I put my hair up."

"Yeah, it is kinda hot. Come on, I wanna introduce you to some people."

Legend helped me from my seat. I noticed a lot of people had on long-sleeved shirts. It was too hot for that shit. I realized that they were in trail riding clubs, though. There were different names on shirts. I didn't know this was that popular around here. Legend led me to a group of guys, and I felt like a lioness in the middle of a pack of hyenas. They all stared as he introduced me. Most of them were steer wrestlers and there were a couple of bull riders.

Each of them had grabbed my hand to shake, but the last one kissed my hand. Legend knocked his Stetson off his head, and they all laughed. Everything was light until another guy walked over. The woman on his arm caught my attention. She cleaned up good. Neffie. She looked nothing like she did the other day. Her face was made up, and her hair was straightened. She gave me a tight smile. I noticed everybody had gotten quiet. After shaking the guy's hand, Legend grabbed my hand. "Come on, baby."

"Who was that she was with? You didn't seem too friendly with him."

"My cousin, Randy. We never got along, and everybody knows it. That's why everybody got quiet."

"Oh. I thought it was because of Neffie."

"Naw. Everybody knows about her. She probably done slept with everybody that was standing there."

I shook my head as Legend led me to the dancefloor. "Legend, I don't know how to Zydeco or swing out."

"Who said we had to Zydeco or swing? We can do what we want."

"I don't know, Legend."

"Out of all the people here, who matters to you? Besides Shana, of course."

"Only you."

"Aight then. Fuck everybody else."

I smiled at him, then rested my arms on his shoulders as he put his hands at my waist and pulled me close. We were lost in each other, not caring what anyone thought about our love at that moment. His lips rested on mine and he kissed me like he wanted me right then. "I'm not wearing that sleazy shit I had on at the Sky Bar in Houston. Ain't gon' be no cummin' on the dancefloor."

He laughed. "Now that you're mine, you only gon' wear shit like that at home for me. And for the record, if I wanted to make you cum right here, I could."

Just his words excited me. He leaned to my ear and nibbled at it, making my clit pulsate with excitement. I could cum without him even touching my clit. That had happened before. Legend turned me on in ways I didn't think were possible. I heard giggling, and that's when I noticed Shana standing next to me. The band was taking a short recess. I grinned at her, then leaned into Legend once again. "Why don't y'all just go home?"

"Shut up, Shana."

The music cranked back up, and Legend and I got lost in one another once again.

"Your honor, I have evidence that proves Zaire Lewis is a bully that likes to provoke people to anger just so he can press charges. Not only that but no matter how minuscule it seems to him, he assaulted Ms. Richardson before Mr. Semien assaulted him."

Sidney was laying out all the stops for the judge at the proceedings. So far, I hadn't had to say a word. They were just presenting their opening arguments. I glanced over at Zaire, and his face was red. He leaned over to speak to his attorney. My mama and Journey were both here. Mama sat behind me and Journey sat behind Zaire. Her belly was noticeable now. It may have been noticeable then, but I didn't notice because I was trying to get away from them.

I still hadn't had the chance to talk to my mama about Zaire blackmailing her, but I would today, no matter how everything turned out. Once Sidney finished presenting her facts, the judge called for a brief recess. I stood from my seat and approached my mother. It was like she knew that I knew. She dropped her head and trained her gaze on the floor. "Mama, how did he find out?"

She looked up at me with tears in her eyes. "This is all my fault, Harper." I watched the tears leave her, and I knew this wasn't gonna be good. "His uncle used to be my financial advisor."

"God bless it, Mama. We'll talk once this is over."

"Okay."

I went back to Legend and sat next to him. Despite the reason we were here, he looked sexy as ever in his black suit, black shirt, tie, and hanky, looking like the business black panther. I grabbed his hand as Sidney turned to us. "I believe we're going to have good news. They never take a recess this soon."

She smiled just as the judge walked back in. We all stood, then sat after he did. "After a short deliberation, I was informed that Mr. Lewis would like to drop the charges. Is that correct counselor?"

"Yes, your honor."

"So, there is a countersuit. Is that still correct?"

Sidney turned to me and I shook my head. If he would drop the charges, so would I. I just wanted all of this to be over. "No, your honor. If Mr. Lewis is dropping the charges, so will Ms. Richardson. She just wants this whole fiasco to be over."

The judge nodded. This shit had been going on for too long and all because Zaire was in his feelings about me leaving him. This had gone too far, and I was sick of this shit. I just wanted to live in peace with Legend. I glanced over at Journey to find her looking at me. Slightly rolling my eyes, I turned back to Legend. She was a backstab-bing bitch. A whole traitor-ass bitch.

Once the judge dismissed us, I hurriedly left out with Legend, because I didn't want to talk to Journey, but of course, that didn't go as planned. "Harper, wait!"

Legend stopped me from walking because he was holding my hand when he stopped. I could feel my anger rising, and I just wanted to disappear. She caught up with me and reached for my hand as I jerked it away. I didn't know what gave her any clue that I would be okay with her touching me. "Harper, I'm sorry."

"No, you aren't, Journey. So, cut the bullshit."

"Harper, really I am. Fooling around with Zaire was wrong of me."

"So, you're leaving him?" She fidgeted and averted her gaze. "Just as I figured. Save your fucking fake-ass apology."

"Harper, I'm pregnant. I can't leave him."

"Whatever. I'm leaving. Enjoy the rest of your life."

"Harper, you aren't going to forgive me? Please. I need you to."

"Well, I need to stay as far away from you as possible. Some people never change, and you are one of those people. You're my sister, but you are worse than any enemy I could ever have. Just because we're blood, doesn't mean I have to fuck with you. Good riddance."

I practically ran toward Legend's truck. Standing there talking to her and looking at her swollen belly was making me nauseated. Six months ago, no one could have ever told me that I would be here. My life felt like it was in shambles. Legend had been my saving grace. I probably would have gone insane by now without him. He was still standing with my sister and mother. I didn't know what they were talking about, but just as I was about to go back over there, he walked away from them.

He unlocked the door, and I quickly hopped inside. I liked the fact that he didn't try to get involved in my family drama. He only stood there rubbing my back the whole time I talked to Journey. When he got in the truck, he started the engine, then grabbed my hand. "You okay?" he asked softly.

"Yeah. Thanks."

"Your mama said that you and her needed to talk. I told her that I would ask you if it was okay if she followed us home."

"Just her. Not Journey."

"I don't think Journey is crazy enough to follow us home after that tongue lashing you just gave her."

"Hmm. You don't know Journey."

"Well, let me make sure to relay that message. I'll be right back."

Legend kissed my lips, then left the truck to talk to my mother. He was far from the cocky bull rider I'd met in Houston. He was now my gentle stallion and I smiled at the thought.

When we got out to the house, Legend parked in the garage and I tried to mentally prepare for what my mama would say. My nerves were on edge, and it seemed that Jesus himself was gon' have to come down from heaven and calm me down. When I got out of the truck, Legend had walked around to my side. "I was about to open the door for you."

He circled his arms around my waist and pulled me close. "No matter what yo' mama has to say, remember one thing. I love you, and none of that shit is gonna change what happens with me and you. Everything she has to say is the past. Take a deep breath, relax, and think about the present with me and your future with your new business ventures."

"Thank you, Legend. I can feel my heart rate slowing as we speak."

He lightly rubbed my cheek and kissed my lips, then smiled at me. "Let's go inside."

When we walked out of the garage, my mama was standing there along with Legend's parents. "Where the hell you been all day, boy?" Mrs. Semien asked.

I giggled as Legend squeezed my hand. He would be explaining himself to his parents while I talked to my mama. She smiled at me, and I could see in her eyes, that she felt bad about whatever she was about to tell me. "Mama, this is Legend's parents, Mr. and Mrs. Semien. Mr. and Mrs. Semien, this is my mother, Charlotte Thibodeaux."

They greeted one another as Legend unlocked the door. "Boy,

you ain't answer me. Where yo' ass been to where you couldn't answer the damned phone?"

"Ma, come inside and I'll talk to y'all about that. Quit being loud and ghetto fo' my neighbors call the police."

She slapped him in the back of his head as he unsuccessfully ducked to try to miss the blow. I giggled as we all walked inside. Kissing Legend's lips, I grabbed Mama's hand. "Legend, we're going to go to your office, okay?"

"Okay, baby. I gotta corral Rose before she try to beat my ass."

"Watch yo' mouth, Legend," his mama yelled.

We laughed. I led my mama to Legend's study and closed the door behind us. Taking another calming, deep breath, I sat on the couch. She joined me and grabbed my hand. We sat there in silence for a couple of minutes before she began. "I need to start from the beginning, so you can understand how this all started."

I nodded my head, planning to listen with an open heart. I recalled Legend's words. *It's the past.* "When I met your dad, I'd just finished my degree in political science at Lamar. I was a legislative assistant for Senator Lampson for a few years as well. I'd been umm... stealing money from his campaign donations. Your dad, as you know, was a truck driver, but what you don't know is, he was also a damned private investigator. Since he owned his own truck, he often hired people to drive it for him."

That shit was news to me. *Daddy was a private investigator?* I wondered why he never told me that. "Someone had hired him to figure out what was going on. They realized that some funds were missing, but they didn't have a clear idea if they were actually missing or if they'd mistakenly accounted for funds they hadn't received. He found out the truth and approached me about it."

"He obviously didn't report his findings."

"No, he didn't. He asked me out. I was so grateful that he didn't turn me in. He made me promise to walk the straight and narrow, and I did. We became a couple and after a few months, I found out I was pregnant with you. Kenneth wanted to marry me, but I said no. He wouldn't fit into the career I wanted. Kenneth was hood, too hood to be in front of the camera."

I watched her shake her head. It was a decision she clearly regretted, even now. She swallowed hard. "After you were born, I moved back home to Lake Charles and began to pursue a future in politics. I hired a financial assistant when I began my campaign, by the name of Jeffrey King. He helped me market and strategize to get more donations. Your dad knew that I was probably doing something illegal because it was like I had an addiction. If I was around money, I was tempted like crazy.

He asked me to let you live with him. I didn't want to let you go, but at the same time, I knew he was right about being able to provide a better life for you. We went back and forth about it for almost a whole year before I agreed. I knew he could spend more time with you than I could. My career was everything to me, but that still didn't stop me from stealing money. Maybe after my fourth re-election, it was discovered that Jeffrey was misappropriating funds. What they didn't find out was that I was the one who had him doing it."

"He went to jail, didn't he?"

"Yes. He did a couple of years, but he refused to snitch on me. For that, I took care of him while he was locked up. Soon after he got out, they started investigating me, and I was given the option to resign. Since my term was almost up, I chose not to run for re-election. Somehow, Zaire found out about that. I think he may have searched the facts about his uncle's case or overheard something he shouldn't have. That's how I found out that Jeffrey was his mother's brother."

Oh shit! "That was probably why his mother couldn't stand me. Do you think he pursued me because of what he knew?"

"I don't know, baby. I didn't know he was related to Jeffrey until after you guys broke up, nor did I know that he knew about me being the reason his uncle got locked up."

"Damn, Mama. So, him going after Journey was because of what he knew about you or was it to get back at me for leaving him?"

"That was him trying to get back at you. Journey getting pregnant was her way of punishing him. He's going to have to take care of her now, voluntarily or involuntarily. She won't leave him, because she knows she'll get more out him right now by staying. His knowledge of our embezzlement was how he blackmailed me into helping him. Obviously, he didn't get my best."

"What if after this, he decides to report what he knows, Mama?"

"I'll handle it if it arises. I don't think he will though. After all the mess Sidney dug up on him, he might wanna stay out of court for a while."

I smiled at her. Saying that I was grateful this shit wasn't deeper than what was on the surface was more than a relief. It was like my nerves had immediately calmed. "Thanks, Mama. I know we didn't have the best relationship, but I hope that we can get closer now."

"I know. I'm sorry. Your dad did an amazing job raising you, though." She looked at the floor, then back at me. "I hope that you and Journey can mend your relationship."

"I don't think so, Mama. Journey and I have always been at odds because of her jealousy issues, but this was the icing on the cake. I can be cordial when I see her, but we will never have the relationship we should have had as sisters."

"I understand. I'm happy for you, Harper. Oh! I forgot to say that the current Senator and I talked, and he would like to discuss you providing delectable desserts for all of his catering needs, whether it's for his family or dinners at the state capitol."

"Are you serious?"

"Yes. I will send you his information by email."

I stood and hugged her tightly. It was the best thing she'd ever done for me that wasn't out of obligation, besides teaching me how to bake in the first place. What felt even greater, was that she hugged me as tightly as I hugged her. "Come on. Let's go enjoy Legend's family."

"Okay, Harper. I love you."

That caused the tears to spring from my eyes. It wasn't often that she expressed her love for me. Although I knew she did, it was still good to hear it. I hugged her again. "I love you too, Mom."

30

Legend

"NEXT TIME you don't answer that phone, I'm gon' beat yo' ass. I don't care how grown you think you are!"

"Oh, God. Okay, Ma. Damn. I heard you the first time."

"Legend..."

"Ma, I'm sorry. It won't happen again. I love you, okay?"

"See, now you patronizing me."

"Oh, my Lord. There's no pleasing you!"

My mama had been giving me grief the whole damn time Harper was in the room with her mama. I'd apologized a few times, promised it would never happen again, and told them everything that went on today. She still wasn't having it. "Okay, Rose. I think you've chewed his ass out enough."

"Thank you, Daddy."

Just as she was about to get cranked up again, Harper and her mama joined us in the front room. By the expression on her face, it seemed all had gone well. She sat next to me and softly kissed my cheek. My mama's facial expressions finally eased up. "Legend, Harper is the best thing that ever happened to you."

"You right, Mama. Even with all the championships I've won, nothing compares to the high I'm on right now."

"Good. So, when you gon' marry her, Legend?"

I put my hand over my face. This woman was too much. Harper's mother's eyebrows had risen drastically. Harper was used to her antics, though. She only laughed, but I could tell she was still a little embarrassed. Refusing to let her have the last word by not answering her question, I looked at Harper. Grabbing her hands, I looked in her eyes. Now she was nervous. I could feel her hands trembling. "When the time is right, I will."

Harper smiled brightly and took a deep breath. That answer would suffice for now. My mother had a huge smile on her face. "Now that you know I'm okay, get yo' messy ass out of here."

I laughed as my mama practically dove on me. We played like that all the time. Sometimes, it felt like we were brother and sister instead of mother and son. Daddy pulled her off me. "You and Legend done horse played enough. Let's go home."

"Okay, honey. Legend, don't forget what I told you. I can still whoop yo' big ass."

We laughed, and I hugged her tightly, lifting her from the ground as she yelled. "Put me down, boy!"

They both shook hands with Ms. Thibodeaux and exchanged pleasantries, then left.

Shortly after, Harper's mama left, and we made our way to the bedroom. "So, I take it the talk went well?"

"It did, baby. I feel a little lighter. It wasn't so bad to where I would have a difficult time getting over anything. There was nothing that made me angry or anything like that. She just enlightened me on the issues with Zaire."

"I'm glad. I would hate to see you hurt about something she did."

"Thank you, baby." She hesitated for a moment. "I know this should be over and done with, but I'm just curious. What happened between you and your cousin?"

I took a deep breath and rolled my eyes. Randy had always been a thorn in my flesh. Ever since we were kids, he wanted to be like me. So much so, until it got on my fucking nerves. If my daddy bought me a horse, he got his dad to buy him a horse. The same exact breed. If I got the latest pair of Jordan's, he got the latest pair. It all came to a head over a girl in middle school.

Eighth-grade prom was quickly approaching, and the girl he liked asked me to go with her. That nigga was so hot, he started spreading rumors around school that I was gay. We ended up fighting over that shit too. It was petty as fuck for us to still have beef, but his ass couldn't let that shit go.

Now even into adulthood, he copied my every move. He tried to bull ride, but that shit wasn't his calling. That was the only thing he couldn't copy. He had a house similar to mine in Raywood and a truck a year newer than mine. Randy always tried to be me. So, to say he annoyed me was an understatement. Instead of saying all that to Harper, I opted on the short version.

"He's always been jealous of the things my parents did for me. That ridiculous shit go all the way back into our childhood. He still tries to imitate or outdo every damn thing I do."

"It does sound extremely childish."

"That's cause that shit is," I said with a slight frown.

"So, I have a few orders this week. It won't keep me busy the whole week, but I won't be able to spend every waking moment with you."

She poked her lips out as if she was sad about that. I chuckled. "Well, my sponsor paid my entry fee for a rodeo in Vernon, Texas. It's a small rodeo, but I've been doing it for a few years. It's almost a seven-hour drive."

"Damn. When is it? You know I'm gonna want to go."

"It's in three weeks or so."

"Okay good. It's far enough away to where I won't take orders for that week. We would probably leave when?"

"That Wednesday, then head back that following Monday morning."

"Okay. I have a few orders for next week. Hopefully, I'll get more, so it will get booked tight. I have a couple for the week after that too."

"That's good, baby. While you're baking, I'll probably go kick it with Red and brush up on my skills. It's been almost a month since I've ridden."

"I know."

"I've enjoyed the time off though. Your riding skills are impeccable."

"Is that right?"

She grinned, then straddled my lap. "Uh huh. How about you get a ride in right now?"

"Right here?"

"Yep. Right here. There's no place off limits in this house when it comes to you. Now come settle him down, because he raging right now."

"I hope I don't get bucked off."

"Don't worry. I believe he knows you gon' ride him into submission."

"Mmm. The bull has to buck though. I need a full fifty points."

"A bull rarely gets fifty points."

"I beg to differ. My bull always gets fifty points. Sometimes I think he shatters fifty points because he's trying to get the full hundred himself."

"Is that right?"

"Yeah, baby. Now give me that legendary performance."

RED PUT his hand on his hip and watched as I got suited up for my practice ride. "Where my scriptures, Red?"

"I didn't think you needed me to say them since you were practicing."

"That's still a real bull, though."

"My bad, Legend. I got'chu. I got some new scriptures for you. Tell me what you think."

"Aight."

I closed my eyes and waited on him to begin. "But the Lord is faithful, and he will strengthen you and protect you from the evil one."

That was a good one. I continued suiting up. He continued as well. "Be strong and courageous. Do not be afraid or terrified because of them, for the Lord your God goes with you; he will never leave you nor forsake you."

I put on my boots and could feel my spirit calming. He'd learned some good ones. "So do not fear, for I am with you; do not be dismayed, for I am your God. I will strengthen you and help you; I will uphold you with my righteous hand."

As I put on my helmet, he said his last scripture. "May the Lord answer you when you are in distress; may the name of the God of Jacob protect you."

"Thank you, Red. Those were really good," I said, hearing the calmness in my voice.

I slid down the chute, and mounted the devil, ready to conquer. He wasn't as deadly as some of the ones I rode in the bigger rodeos, but he was good enough for practice. Red stood at the back of the chute, tightening my rope as he always did. "You ready?"

I nodded as one of Red's friends opened the gate. The bull began bucking, and I could feel the adrenaline pumping through me as he did. Everything went silent as I rode. The difference was, I could feel myself slipping a little. I hadn't missed eight seconds in a long time and ain't no way in hell I was gon' miss it today. Pulling myself up straight, I continued my ride until I heard the buzzer.

After dismounting, I clapped my hands together. I couldn't trip though. It was my first ride in a while. Red rested his hand on my shoulder. "That was good, Legend."

"Naw, that was horrible. I couldn't even spur him. I had to concentrate on making eight seconds. It'll get better though."

"You right, but it was a good ride to say you hadn't ridden in a while. I learned more scriptures that I'll try next time."

"Thanks, Red."

I walked to the side to watch others practice. I may get to ride again since there wasn't a lot of guys here. Closing my eyes, my mind dwelled on the scriptures Red was quoting until someone tapped my shoulder. I opened my eyes to see Randy. Slightly rolling my eyes, I shook his hand. "You good, cuz?"

"Yeah. What's up, Randy?"

"Not too much. Tryna see if I can get on."

I looked down to see his bull bag in his hand. This dude here. I never bothered to even acknowledge what he said. "Legend?"

"Yeah?"

"I wanted to talk to you."

Aww shit. I didn't have time for no bullshit, so I was hoping he wasn't about to come at me with it. Listening to him talk irritated me at times, especially when he talked about shit he was about to do that I had just done. He would talk about it like it was his idea to do it. I mean like, nigga be yo' own man. "What's up? What'chu wanna talk about?"

I put up a wall as big as that shit orange was trying to put at the border. "I know we haven't had the best relationship. It's mostly my fault. As an adult, I see you doing yo' thang. I'm proud of you, and I just look up to you."

I nodded my head. "You need to find yo' own lane though, Randy."

"You right. I just admire you and everything you do. Even as a kid, I looked up to you. Although we ain't but five months apart in age, you always seemed more mature and knew what you wanted out of life."

"Thanks."

I didn't know what else to say to that shit. A grown man was telling me I was his idol. "Legend!"

Thank God. Red had yelled at me, just the interruption I needed. "Yeah!"

"Come on. JB gon' let you go again before him."

"Aight." I turned back to Randy. "I'll talk to you later, man."

"Okay. Have a good ride."

"Thanks."

WHEN I GOT BACK to the house, Harper was in the kitchen decorating a cake. She was in deep thought and concentration because she never looked up as I approached her. Wrapping my arms around her slowly and inhaling the vanilla scent in the air and on her, caused her to flinch. "I hope I didn't mess you up, baby," I said softly in her ear.

"No, you didn't. I missed you."

"I missed you too. I'm going take a shower. I probably smell like cow shit."

"Well... you smell like outside for sure."

I chuckled. Only Black women said somebody smelled like outside. I kissed her cheek, then released her from my grasp. "I'll be right back."

"Okay. I should be done with this one by the time you come back."

"Aight."

I headed upstairs and thought about Randy. When I got done with my second ride, he'd approached me, asking for tips, like we were suddenly close. Just because he explained himself didn't mean I wanted him all in my space. Doing my best not to straight up ignore him and embarrass him in front of everyone, I told him that he needed to put more pressure on the bull at his knees and left it at that.

When I finished my shower, I went back downstairs to my baby. She was just closing the box on her cake. "I have to deliver this one. You wanna ride?"

"Of course. I haven't spent any time with you today. Where we going to deliver it?"

"Just to Dayton. You think maybe we can ride my horse when we get back?"

"Yeah, of course. I been waiting for you to ask. I'm gon' turn you into a cowgirl."

"Oh, you think?"

"Yep. I know."

"Okay then. I won't argue with you on that."

"You shouldn't. It would be a waste of time if you did."

She giggled, as we took the ten-minute drive to the destination she'd programmed in her navigation. When we'd gotten to the address, I carried the cake for her. "Legend, please don't drop it."

"Don't worry. I got it."

She rang the doorbell and shortly after, we heard someone unlocking the door. A guy about my height, six-foot-one, answered. Watching him give Harper a once over caused my heartbeat to slightly increase. "Hello. I'm Harper with Delectable Desserts. I have a delivery for Anya Stevens."

He licked his lips. "Let me get her for you."

"I can't come on deliveries no more, Harper. I'm gon' end up in jail for real."

She giggled again as he came back to the door. "She's coming. Did you wanna come in?"

"Thank you, but no. We'll wait outside for her."

He glanced at me and probably saw the frown on my face. "Okay."

He left the door slightly ajar, then walked away. When the door opened again, it was a young woman. "Oh my God! That's Legend Semien!"

Harper frowned slightly. Now she knew how I felt a minute ago. I chuckled as she stood there with her mouth agape. Harper cleared her throat. "Yes, he is."

"Is this your business, Mr. Semien?"

"No. This is my girlfriend, Harper's business. I'm just helping out."

"Oh. I'm sorry, Ms. Harper. I've just been watching Legend at rodeos for a couple of years."

"It's okay. He's a lot to take in."

The woman blushed, then took the cake from me. She went

inside and sat it on a table. We followed her in, so she could give her approval. When she opened the box, she gasped. "Ms. Harper, this is beautiful. My mama is gonna love this."

"I'm glad it meets your approval. I received your payment online, and I emailed your receipt. I also printed one if you would like it."

"Yes ma'am, please."

Harper handed her the receipt and we left. After getting on Highway 90, Harper said, "You're right. You can't come with me no more unless you stay in the car."

I laughed. "Uh huh. You didn't look too happy at first when she recognized me."

"Well, it wasn't that she recognized you. She was just kinda rude. I think she realized it, and that's why she apologized."

"Well, we agree on that then. I was about to tell ol' dude something. He was looking at you like you was a steak on a platter."

"I'm thinking about trading my Camry in for a mini-van. I need to be able to deliver larger cakes."

"We can do that. You still have your Mustang, so that would be perfect. Whenever you wanna go, let me know."

"I will, baby. I can't wait to ride Sophie."

She'd named her horse. It was a pretty Palomino horse. They were the horses with the golden colored coat and blonde to white mane. Sophie had a thin white slither in her face as well. She was a beautiful horse. "I can't wait to teach you. Starting from scratch is fun. By the time I go to Vegas, you gon' be a pro."

"You know for sure you're going?"

"Well, the last time I looked, I was ranked number one based on points. Second place was close, but I'm not tripping. Second place goes to Vegas too. If I can keep my number one spot, I'll be happy. I don't plan on slacking off. I'm just grateful the concussion wasn't as bad. Missing one rodeo was bad enough."

"I understand."

"My sponsor was more than happy that the charges were dropped as well. So, my record is still clean."

"That's good, baby."

I nodded as we drove into the driveway at the house. The minute we got out, Harper ran to the stables. That made me smile. She was taking a genuine interest in my world. Now I was gon' have to buy her some boots and a blinged out belt.

When I caught up with her, she was lightly rubbing Sophie's face. I could tell her horse loved her already. She'd dropped her head, so Harper could really baby her. She was so gentle. I'd purchased her from an old man that couldn't take care of her anymore. I'd always admired her from the road when she was on his property.

I saddled Sophie and put a bridle on her, then showed Harper how to get on. After watching me do it, she swung her leg perfectly and sat up there like she'd been doing it all her life. I smiled at her, then grabbed the bridle and walked her around until she got comfortable being up there.

After about thirty minutes of that, I pulled out my horse. I'd named him Midnight because he was an all-black Stallion. I paid a pretty penny for him. Once I had him saddled, I got on, then walked Harper through what to do. She didn't want to kick her horse. I had to assure her that she wasn't hurting her and that it was more of a nudge with her foot than an actual kick.

Once we got going, it was the most romantic shit I'd ever done. Horse-riding with Harper and teaching her at the same time had me all sensitive and shit. She was enjoying it more than I thought she would, and she was doing really good learning to ride. I was surprised that she was catching on so quickly. It helped that Sophie was so easy-going.

"Legend, this is amazing. I didn't realize how peaceful riding a horse could be. Tomorrow you'll have to show me how to saddle her myself."

I smiled big. "I will, Harper. It's pretty easy. I'm glad you're enjoying it."

"Me too. I feel even more connected to you."

"I feel that too, baby."

My heart had melted at her words and I was grateful that she was in my life.

31

arper

EVERYTHING HAD BEEN GOING WELL, and I couldn't wait to get on the road in a few hours. Legend and I had been riding horses every day, enjoying time with one another. In a little while, we'd be leaving out for Vernon, Texas. This would be my first time seeing him in action since the Houston Livestock show, and I was nervous as hell already. Legend was sleeping peacefully, but my eyes were fixed on the ceiling. My mind wouldn't stop thinking about the what if's.

I realized that he was one of the best, but just remembering what had happened the last time had me on edge. It didn't help that his mama was here earlier having a damned meltdown about him riding again so soon. Her antics had me wired up. Legend fucked me a couple of times after they left and made love to me. After all that, I'd dozed off and slept for a couple of hours, but that was it.

Since I couldn't sleep, I got up and took a shower. I'd already packed. Shana and Red were picking us up in like three hours. If Legend wasn't awake by six, I'd wake him. After washing up, I decided to wash my hair too. I had plenty of time to kill. By the time I finished blow drying and flat ironing my hair, Legend was walking in the bathroom. "Baby, you up early."

"Yeah, I couldn't sleep."

"Still worried about me?"

"Yeah."

"C'mere, Harper." He pulled me in his arms and held me close. "I'm glad Shana will be there."

"Me too. She'll do her best to keep me calm."

"That's funny that she calms you. Red calms me before I ride by reciting scriptures."

"Well, I remember you told me what else calms you before you ride. I'm glad I'll be there to help with that. Maybe it will calm me too."

"Shiiiid, yo' pussy damn near have a nigga wanting to go to sleep in the middle of the day. So, I know you gon' calm me all the way down."

I giggled. "Is Red competing?"

"Yeah, he is."

"Okay. Well, I'm gonna go cook breakfast before we go, so we don't have to stop too soon after we leave, while you take a shower."

"Okay, baby."

I made my way downstairs to the kitchen with my luggage in tow. After putting biscuits in the oven, I texted Shana. *I'm cooking breakfast, so y'all come in and eat.*

She responded immediately. *I love you.*

I giggled at her response. That girl loved food. She never passed up a free plate. I told her one day she gon' come across some shit that was gon' make her stomach turn inside out. When that happened, she would be turning down every damned thing. We'd laugh about that every time she accepted a plate from someone.

As I continued to cook, my phone chimed, alerting me of another text. *Hey, Harper. Is everything okay?*

It was Phoenix. I hadn't spoken to him since I told him I was staying in a relationship with Zaire. I responded. *I'm great! I have a new boyfriend, and all is well in my world. How are you?*

Phoenix: *I'm good. I have a new girlfriend also. I just wanted to check on you and make sure all was good wit'chu.*

Me: *Thank you, Phoenix. Talk to you later.*

As I scrambled eggs and took the bacon out of the microwave, Legend joined me downstairs, sitting his luggage next to mine. After I put eggs in the four plates on the countertop, he followed his nose back to the kitchen. "You know country niggas like me, love a woman that can cook."

"Is that why you fell in love with me Legend, because I can cook?"

"That was one of the reasons."

He laughed as I swung the oven mitt at him. After taking the biscuits from the oven, there was a knock at the door. Legend went to it, while I continued fixing our plates. Shana and Red walked in and came straight to the bar. I laughed at them both. Two peas in a pod. They'd been doing great since they'd gotten back together.

After we finished eating, we hit the road for Vernon. Legend and I sat in the backseat. Before we could even leave, Shana gave us the side-eye. I immediately knew what her mind went to. When I laughed loudly, Legend caught on. The moment he did, he unfastened my seatbelt and pulled me on his lap. "Don't start that shit! It's bad enough we all gon' be in that trailer for four days."

"Love you, Shana!"

She waved me off as I left Legend's lap and buckled up. Just that short while I was sitting on him, he'd gotten hard. This was gon' be a long ass ride.

~

"Harper, come sit on yo' dick, baby."

I obliged him as he laid in the bed. We'd been going at it for the past thirty minutes, and I couldn't wait to get him off. I loved watching his facial expressions when I rode. He grabbed his phone and found "So Gone" by Jill Scott, then sat it back on the stand. I slowly sat on his dick and started a nice lil rhythm to the beat of the song. I wound my hips in a circular motion as he rested his hands on my hips and bit his bottom lip.

Running my hands through my hair, I closed my eyes and vibed to the sound of his moans and Paul Wall's voice in the song. I planned to relax his ass so much, he was gon' almost need a nap when I finished. I knew he needed that shit before his ride. We'd gotten here the night before last, and Red had competed yesterday, winning first-place. Tonight, Legend would make his return to the dirt.

Legend began thrusting his hips upward, meeting my every downstroke. Feeling him hit my g-spot at the back of my pussy was bringing me closer to the edge. That shit was pulling me like a damned magnet pulled metal. "Ride the fuck out of yo' dick, Harper. Fuck!"

I moaned in response as I gave him my best work. Needing him to be relaxed was important. I couldn't have him getting hurt. As I got lost in my thoughts, he flipped me over and re-entered me from the back. The strokes were fast and deadly, killing my pussy with every stroke. "Legend! Fuck!"

"Throw that shit back at me."

I did as he requested. There was some pain, but damn, it was so pleasurable. He gripped my ass just like I liked and pounded my shit. He pulled out and shot cum all over my ass and back. I fell flat to the bed, practically hyperventilating. Apparently, Legend was just as spent as I was because he collapsed on top of me. We were gonna be so fucking sticky.

After laying that way for a few minutes, we went to the bathroom. I was about to start the shower, but Legend stopped me. "I can't wash off your scent. I can smell you on my lips. That shit gon' keep me calm, for real."

I giggled as he soaped a towel, then cleaned us both up. We got dressed, then he sat on the couch and lit a blunt. I'd never smoked before, but I was definitely getting a contact high. Before he finished, I was giggling more than normal and stroking his dick through his pants. "Baby, after this ride, I'm gon' give you just what you need. I can't do it right now, or I'm gon' be too fucking tired."

I giggled again, then kissed his cheek.

I sat in the stands with Shana. By the time it was go time, my high had worn off and I was a bundle of nerves. We'd watched six riders before Legend, and four of them didn't make it to eight seconds, and one guy had gotten stepped on by the bull. That didn't do anything but accelerate the butterflies flapping around in my stomach. I could see Legend standing there with his eyes closed and Red was talking to him. He must have been reciting his scriptures.

The announcer began, **"After that record-shattering ride almost two months ago, that had us at the edge of our seats, we didn't know if this fella would ever ride again. But he's proven that he's supposed to be doing this here** *thing for life. Are you ready to see a legend in the makin'?"*

The crowd screamed like crazy as I sat there biting my nails. "Harp, you gotta calm down. Take deep breaths like he's doing. Feel one with him right now if you can. Legend needs you to be calm."

Right after she said that he looked up at me. I gave him two thumbs up, as he put his helmet on and slid down onto the bull. Once the crowd's noise dwindled a little, the announcer yelled, *"Leg-eeeeend Semien!"*

I watched his body loosen. It was amazing. It almost looked like he was asleep as the bull raged. Then his head nodded, and the gate opened. My lips parted as my heart jumped in my throat. I clasped my hands together, intertwining my fingers as the seconds seemed to tick off slowly. Legends legs were moving, and just from my horse-riding lessons, I knew he was spurring the bull. The bull was bucking wildly as Legend hung on. It almost looked like the bull had done a three-sixty in the air as he bucked.

When the buzzer sounded and Legend had dismounted and ran to the gate, I screamed loudly. He was back, and the announcer said just that. He found me in the crowd and blew a kiss at me as I beamed with pride. That was my man, and he was the shit at every-thing he did. When the announcer started, he sounded solemn but that soon changed. *"Well, ladies and gentlemen, consider that record-breaking ride a thing of the past. Legend Semien has scored a 91.9!"*

Shana and I screamed in excitement as we watched Legend salute the crowd and jump down from the gate. Red hugged him tightly, then they walked out of the arena. There were five more riders after him. I quickly ran to the bottom to find him. Shana was right behind me. When I laid eyes on him, the smile spread across his face. I ran to him and jumped in his arms.

I kissed his lips and smiled. "You smell it?" he asked me, then bit his bottom lip.

"Yeah. I tasted it too."

"That shit had me calm as hell. I can't wait to make love to you tonight."

I smiled as he grabbed my hand, leading me back to the stands. "Congratulations, baby. I felt like I was holding my breath for your entire ride. I didn't breathe until you made it to that gate."

"Hell, me either. I was nervous as fuck."

"I'm so proud of you, baby."

Legend sat next to me as we watched the next riders. Two more got bucked off before their eight seconds and two others only scored in the eighties. The last rider was Legend's fiercest competition. I could feel him tense up as the guy got on the bull. "You got this baby. Relax."

He gave me a one-cheeked smile. Legend kissed my lips, then brought his attention back to the rider as they opened the gate. He rode, but in my opinion, not with the same passion Legend did. It seemed to me, that Legend just had a love for it that couldn't be fucked with. He stayed on the whole eight seconds, then ran to the gate to await his score.

I held Legend's hand tightly as I watched the sweat drip down the side of his face. I'd never seen him so nervous. You could hear a pin drop in the arena. Everyone was anticipating who the winner would be. The announcer started, ***"That was a fierce ride from Brody Harris! Will it be enough to beat Legend Semien's record?"***

Oh God, he was making it worse. It felt like I was starting to sweat. ***"It was a personal best for Brody Harris, but not*** *enough to take the lead! 91.5! I can't wait to see these two in Vegas this year! The competition is gonna be the closest I've ever seen! Congratulations to Legeeeend Semien!"*

I jumped from my seat and fell on top of Legend as he laughed. He hugged me tightly, then stood to his feet. He was still holding me in his arms as Red slapped his hand. Shana pushed me out of the way. "Let the man breathe, Harper. Shit."

She hugged him as she laughed at how excited I was. Legend grabbed my hand. "I want you to come with me to accept my buckle and check."

"Gladly, baby."

I kissed his cheek as he escorted me to the dirt. People kept stopping him to congratulate him. When we finally got to the bottom, his competition smiled at him. They shook hands and he congratulated Legend on his win and breaking his own record.

When it was time to present Legend, they gave him his buckle and a damn check for nearly ten grand. Eight seconds earned him ten grand. I slowly shook my head at the thought of it. The man with the microphone asked, "What were you thinking as you made this legendary ride?"

"Don't fall off."

Everyone laughed. "Who's this little lady next to you?"

"The love of my life, Harper Richardson. She makes amazing cakes and pastries. Check out her website, delectable desserts dot com. If you can't remember that, she has an advertisement on my page as well."

"Shameless plug, but I'm not mad at'chu."

We all laughed as Legend draped his arm around my shoulders. "This is going to be stiff competition in Vegas and I think everyone here, whether they will be there in person or not, can't wait to see how it will end for you and Brody Harris."

"I can't wait either. He's an excellent bull rider. Like me, he leaves it all on the dirt. So, we'll see who comes out on top."

"Yes, we will, Legend. Congratulations again."

He shook Legend's hand, then mine. Afterward, we posed for pictures. It seemed we'd been taking pictures for an hour before we finally made it back to the trailer. Red and Shana had even gotten in a couple of them. Legend and I went to the bedroom we were occupying and took a long shower, truly celebrating this victory.

"You know, I wouldn't have made it this far without you, Harper."

"How so?"

"I was so depressed without you. I don't know how I would have recovered without you. You played a significant role in my rapid healing. I was supposed to be out for two months before I could even practice. After one month, I was ready. That was because of you."

"Damn, Legend. You played a significant role in my healing too. My heart was broken behind what I thought was love. After falling so deeply for you, I realized that what I had with Zaire couldn't have been love at all. Congratulations, and I love you so much, Legend."

"I love you too, Harper. Now, come show me how proud of me you actually are. I need to feel that pride in every stroke."

"Oh, you gon' feel that and so much more."

EPILOGUE

*S*ix months later...

LEGEND

"LEGEND, this is my first time in Vegas."

"Really?"

"Yes."

"Well, I pray it's a trip neither of us will ever forget."

Harper smiled at me. "I'll never forget it simply because I'm here with you."

Harper and I had been together for ten months, and I couldn't be happier. I'd made it to Vegas, still the number one seed. My parents, Ms. Thibodeaux, Red, and Shana had all come for the showdown. Brody Harris was only fifty points behind me. Had I not missed that one rodeo, he would be further behind me. There was also another rodeo this past summer where I didn't get my eight seconds, but I'd handled it well.

Harper had been my everything. She calmed me significantly and my mama had noticed. Mama had been hounding me about marrying Harper, and I rolled my eyes every time she brought it up. Harper wasn't complaining about anything. Her business had flourished, and she was so busy, she'd hired an assistant.

We were also in the process of building her a small bakery on my property. Although I had two big ovens in my kitchen, it still wasn't enough. If she had more space, it wouldn't take her nearly as long to get orders completed. There were a few nights where she'd stayed up all night baking cake and making pastries.

She traded her Camry for a van as we'd talked about a few months ago. After that, she was able to do a few weddings. When I didn't have anything to prepare for or something else going on, I'd help her. Since Lacey won that rodeo, I had been training a few barrel racers.

We'd taken today to site-see after we landed and got checked in to our hotel. I also had to check in and fill out more registration papers. When we got back to the hotel room from dinner, I sat on the couch and tried to meditate. Harper wanted to give me some time alone, so she went to soak in the jacuzzi tub.

I was doing my best to calm my nerves. Besides my nerves about the rodeo, I was flying her sister in. She'd had a baby boy a month ago, and Zaire had eventually left her. We learned all that through their mother and were surprised they'd lasted as long as they did, especially since he was only with her to torture Harper. I knew Harper didn't have a relationship with her sister, but I could tell that it still hurt her to know that her sister had stabbed her in the back.

When she found out that Zaire had left her sister, I could see the empathy in her eyes. Even though her sister had done the worst, she still longed to restore that relationship. I could tell. Living with her and paying close attention to her had taught me a lot. It taught me to read the things and feelings that she would probably never talk about.

I was glad I'd reserved a smoking room. Pulling the blunt from my pocket, I fired up, letting the herb touch my insides.

WHEN WE WOKE up the next morning, I was so tired, I could have stayed asleep. Journey would be here in less than an hour, and I prayed Harper didn't flip out on me. We'd gone down for breakfast and had made our way back up to our room. She knew I wanted to relax today since I was riding my first bull tonight at the National Finals Rodeo.

The rodeo would last for ten days, so I would ride every night throughout the competition. Points would be added, and the rider with the most points would win the purse. That could get pretty high. The total purse for all the rodeo events would eventually increase to ten million by the end of 2024. This year, I could win a hundred grand or more if I placed first.

I lounged on the couch with Harper's legs draped over mine while she read a book. Just as I could feel my nerves ease, there was a knock at the door. Harper got up to answer it, but I quickly stood. "I got it, baby."

"I can get it, Legend. I know you wanted to relax."

"Can you promise me something?"

"What's that?"

"That you won't flip out when you see who's at the door."

She frowned, then walked to the door without answering me. We hadn't had a serious argument in a long time. So, I was hoping this wouldn't start one. She looked through the peephole. "Legend Semien, you gotta be shittin' me. You invited Journey?"

"Yeah. Babe, I can see that you hate the extreme distance between the two of you. Please, let her and your nephew in."

She cut her eyes at me, then flung the door open. I thought she was about to go off, and I believed she intended to until her eyes fell on that baby boy. Standing next to her, I rubbed her back. "Hi, Harper. Legend."

I nodded my head as Harper said, "Come in."

Journey walked through the door, holding her bundle of joy. He had a lot of hair for a one-month-old. She sat at the small table with the baby. Harper sat across from her, and I went to the sofa. "You look great as always, Harper."

"Thank you. What's his name?"

"Harley Ace."

"Can I hold him?"

"Of course."

Harper reached for the baby, and Journey gently laid him in her arms. The softened expression on her face was all I needed to see. "He's beautiful, Journey."

"Thank you. I'm sorry, Harper."

"No apologies needed. You've already done that. I just wasn't ready to accept it at the time. I am now." She kissed the top of the baby's head. "I'm an aunt. He's gonna be spoiled."

Journey smiled. I didn't know if they were ever going to talk again about what happened or if they would just move on. As Harper said, there had already been an apology and somewhat of an explanation. I was just glad that the baby was here. There was no telling how this would have gone otherwise.

Harper looked at me with a smile on her face. "Thank you, Legend."

"You're welcome, baby."

That baby looked good in her arms and one day, I would give her one to hold.

~

"THOUGH I WALK in the midst of trouble, you preserve my life. You stretch out your hand against the anger of my foes; with your right hand you save me."

We were walking to the arena, and Red was quoting my scriptures. My heart was running a race that my body was having a hard time keeping up with. I slipped on my boots. "Keep me safe, Lord, from the hands of the wicked; protect me from the violent, who devise ways to trip my feet."

I took deep breaths as I tried to focus on the scriptures Red was quoting. I grabbed my helmet and slid it on as he said, "Put on the whole armour of God, that ye may be able to stand against the wiles of the devil."

Help me, Lord. This is the big show and the final ride. Ease my nerves, relax my spirit, and help me to focus on the task at hand.

I could hear the announcer, but it was muffled. Slowly tuning everything out, I focused on doing my best. This was my last ride, and I was still in first place with Brody Harris and another young Brazilian rider right on my ass. This was my tenth ride. One slip up could cause me to lose the entire thing.

I slid down on the bull, Smooth Operator. He had a high buck-off percentage, so I needed the Lord like never before. This damned bull was about to tear the gate up. He wasn't happy, but I made sure that I didn't give a damn about his emotions. Getting situated, Red pulled my rope. "You ready?"

I took a deep, steady breath and put my arm in the air as I

nodded. The gate opened, and Smooth Operator got on his fucking job immediately. My leg hit the gate as he turned back inside. Oh, he was gon' pay for that shit. I started spurring the shit out of him as he took me on a ride I would never forget. My back felt like it was on fire, and I'd hit the back of my head on his backside. He spun around, then stutter-stepped, almost knocking me the fuck out.

I held it together, though and got my eight seconds. Just as I dismounted, he was about to spin back into me. Thank God for the rodeo clowns distracting him. I stood to my feet and ran to the gate as the crowd roared. Looking toward my baby, I blew her a kiss, then saluted to the crowd. That was a good ride. I could feel it. My parents and Harper's mama were all smiles as the announcer yelled in excitement, ***"92.8! Legend Semien! A living legend! He ain't in the making no more, ladies and gentlemen. Smooth Operator done met his match!"***

I was so damned excited, I couldn't focus. Red slapped my hand as I made my way out toward the common area. "That was a ride for their asses! I'm proud of you, Legend."

"Thanks man. Thank you for always being there for me. This will be your win too."

Being fifteen points ahead of the next rider, to begin with, all I really had to do was stay on the whole eight seconds. Instead, God decided to show out and let me set a new personal best and score one of the highest scores ever at the NFR. There was a perfect score once, but that was almost thirty years ago.

Harper met me and hugged me tightly, along with everyone else. Journey had stayed in the hotel room since the baby was so young. She didn't want to risk him getting sick by being around thousands of people. "Legend, you never cease to amaze me. How do you feel?" she asked.

"I feel great, baby. I'm still nervous to get in front of all those people."

"You were just in front of them, Legend."

"I was riding. Now, I'm gonna be talking. When I ride, I don't see or hear anybody. It was just me and Smooth Operator."

"Who names these bulls?"

I chuckled. "Most times the owner. There was one named Scene of the Crash a while back."

She laughed as her eyes widened. "Seriously?"

"Yep."

BRODY HARRIS TOOK his last ride, scoring a 91.3, officially ending the bull-riding competition. The crowd roared as he waved to them on his way out. When he got to me, he said, "You're a hell of a bull-rider, Legend. I wish you the best of luck in the coming year."

"Thanks, Brody. You gave me a run for my money. Best of luck to you as well."

We shook hands as the announcer yelled in the mic, **"Leg-eeeeend Semien!"**

Clutching Harper's hand, I walked out in front of the crowd, nerves on ten thousand. Someone must have told the family they could come out as well, because when I turned around, Shana, Red, my parents, and Harper's mom were all out there with me. They presented me with my first NFR buckle and I had to bite my lip to hold the emotions in.

My purse was $120 grand. Harper's eyes had widened significantly. She said in my ear, "Most people don't make that in a year, and you made that in a combined minute and twenty seconds."

I laughed at her, then pulled her in my arms for a picture. I kissed her lips, then pulled away from her and hugged Red. "We did it. This is as much your win as it is mine."

"Thanks man. So, you gon' split that check with me?"

I frowned, trying to fight the smile that broke out on my face anyway. "You gon' get a cut. I just hope you know it won't be split down the middle though."

He laughed, then moved to the side so my parents could congratulate me. "See what ridin' on faith get you, Ma?"

"I see, Legend. Although I hate that you put yourself in harm's way, I'm extremely proud of you."

"Thanks, Ma. That means a lot."

As I hugged her, then my dad, the correspondent came close. "Legend who are all the people here celebrating with you?"

"These are my parents, this is my right-hand man, Craig Anderson. Everyone calls him Red. Hopefully, he'll be here next year for steer wrestling. That's his girlfriend, Shana. This is my girlfriend's mother, Ms. Thibodeaux. Lastly, this is the love of my life, Ms. Harper Richardson, owner of Delectable Desserts."

"This has been a journey like none other for you. You haven't scored less than eighty-five points all year on a ride, except for the one you didn't make the time. Your picture should be next to the word consistent in the dictionary. What's your secret?"

"I pray. My family prays for me constantly. Red helps me practice. He tells me things that I miss and encourages me when I feel defeated. Him quoting scriptures the whole walk to the chute keeps me calm and in control."

"Well, we have definitely witnessed a legendary year for you. What's next?"

"Well, of course, I'm gonna keep riding with hopes of making it here again next year." I wiped the sweat from my brow, then reached in my pocket. I turned to look at Harper as she smiled and beamed with excitement. Grabbing her hand and facing her, I said, "I also plan to make some moves toward my future."

Taking off my cowboy hat, I went down on one knee in front of thousands of people. Amidst their screams and Harper's shock, I continued. "You have been a constant in my life for almost a year now. The moment I saw you, I knew you were the woman I wanted. I knew that if God allowed me to have you, I would never let go. You mean more to me than winning this title today. That says a lot. So, I wanted to solidify where we stood in our relationship. I love you, Harper. Will you marry me?"

I cracked open the box to reveal a three-karat, princess cut diamond on a platinum band as Harper's hands went to her mouth. She nodded quickly, then screamed. "Yes!"

I slid the ring on her finger, then stood and lifted her from her feet as the crowd roared. "So, how does it feel to know you're gonna marry a living legend one day?" the correspondent asked with a huge smile on his face.

"It feels like paradise."

The End

AFTERWORD

Whew! You're probably wondering where I got the idea to write about a bull rider. Well, my husband used to ride bulls. He never rode professionally, but he rode in a few local rodeo's years back. Thank God I never had to witness him riding. However, I've heard all the stories and even watched the NFR on TV with him. So, thank you, honey, for your expertise on the subject!

I truly hope you enjoyed reading this novel as much as I enjoyed writing it. There will be more drama-filled stories to read in the near future! There's also a great playlist on iTunes for this book under the same title. Please keep up with me on Facebook (@authormonicawalters), Instagram (@authormonicawalters), and Twitter (@monlwalters). You can also visit my Amazon author page at www.amazon.com/author/monica.walters to view my releases. For live discussions, giveaways, and inside information on upcoming releases join my Facebook group, Monica's Romantic Sweet Spot at https://bit.ly/2P2lo6X.

The Devil Goes to Church Too

The Book of Noah (A Crossover Novel with The Flow of Jah's Heart by
T Key)

The Revelations of Ryan, Jr. (A Crossover Novel with All That Jazz by
T Key)

ALSO BY B. LOVE PUBLICATIONS...

Just Love Me

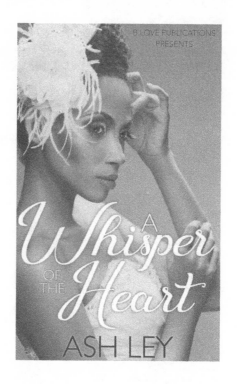

A Whisper of the Heart

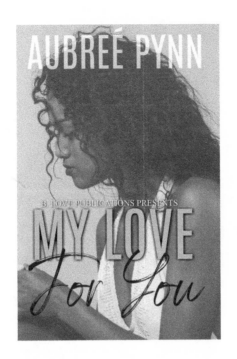

My Love for You

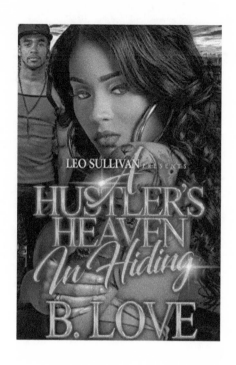

A Hustler's Heaven in Hiding

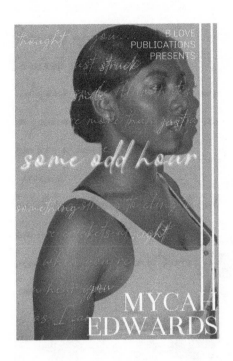

Some Odd Hour

Wordplay

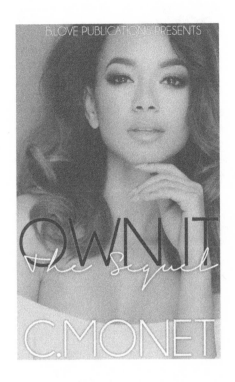

Own It: The Sequel

Coming soon...

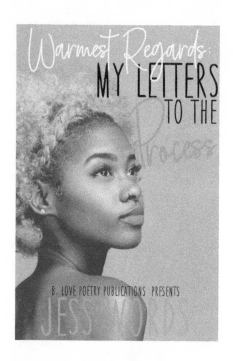

Warmest Regards

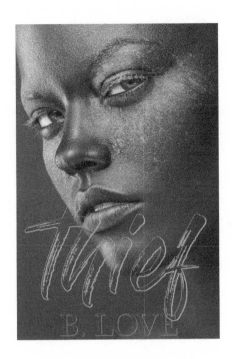

Thief

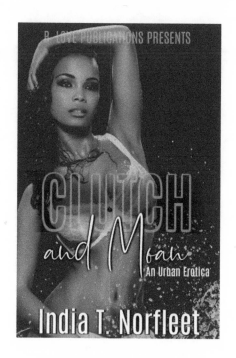

CLUTCH
and Moan
An Urban Erotica

India T. Norfleet

Clutch and Moan

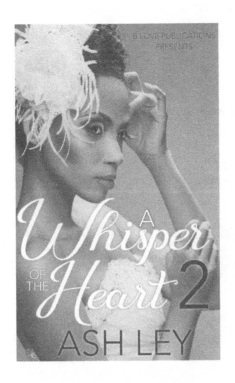

B. LOVE PUBLICATIONS
PRESENTS

A Whisper of the Heart II

Bonded by Fate

Visit bit.ly/BLovePub or click here to join our mailing list!

B. Love Publications - where Authors celebrate black men, black women, and black love.

To submit a manuscript for consideration, email your first three chapters to blovepublications@gmail.com with SUBMISSION as the subject.

Let's connect on social media!

Facebook - B. Love Publications

Twitter - @blovepub

Instagram - @blovepublications

CPSIA information can be obtained
at www.ICGtesting.com
Printed in the USA
LVHW092234011119
636084LV00002BA/344/P